Pride Publishing books by L.M. Brown:

To See the Sky
My Boyfriend's an Alien
One Perfect Wish

Merman and Magic
Forbidden Waters
Tempestuous Tides

Heavenly Sins
Between Heaven and Hell
Between Good and Evil
Between Life and Death

I0524360

Merman and Magic

TEMPESTUOUS TIDES

L.M. BROWN

Tempestuous Tides

ISBN # 978-1-78430-774-5

©Copyright L.M. Brown 2015

Cover Art by Posh Gosh ©Copyright September 2015

Interior text design by Claire Siemaszkiewicz

Pride Publishing

Published in 2015 by Pride Publishing, Newland House, The Point, Weaver Road, Lincoln, LN6 3QN, United Kingdom.

TEMPESTUOUS TIDES

Prologue

5 October 1989

Caspian, the Atlantean God of Justice, paced the sand dunes as he waited for his sister to appear. Cari had told him to meet her here, yet the area seemed completely deserted.

The sound made by the gentle lapping of the waves carried easily on the cool October night. Caspian shivered as a chilly wind swept across the beach. He suspected the Indian Summer they had been enjoying in September had finally given way to autumn.

"There you are." Cari appeared beside him and greeted him with a kiss on the cheek. Her Grecian style gown flowed down her lithe body and a beaded headdress adorned her hair. Even though he had never understood her reluctance to embrace the latest fashions of humans, he had to admit that she made a captivating sight.

"You told me a mermaid would be coming ashore tonight," Caspian reminded her. "I've shielded the area so no one will see her arrival or our presence here, just as you asked."

"Thank you," Cari replied. "She should be here soon. I checked on her just before you got here. She's about two miles from the shore, but it's been slow going. I've been protecting her on her journey here."

"Is she injured?"

"No, she's blind." Cari didn't meet his eyes as she spoke these words, and Caspian had a sinking feeling he knew what might be coming next.

"Please tell me she isn't what I think she is."

Cari sighed. "If you're thinking she's an Oracle, then yes, you're right."

"You know her powers won't work here on land, and that half the guards of Atlantis will be searching the ocean for her."

"Daphne experienced her final vision a short time ago. She knows her end is near. A new Oracle will be coming into her powers soon and will take her place in Atlantis."

Caspian didn't ask how Cari knew this. As the Goddess of Prophecy, she always saw these things, sometimes many years before they happened. "The mermaid heading this way is dying?" he asked. "I thought you said she wasn't injured?"

"She isn't, but the birth will be hard on her."

"She's pregnant? How the hell did that happen?"

Cari gave him a condescending smile. Even without the gift of prophecy, he could tell what was coming next and he raised his hand to stop her sarcastic rendition of the birds and the bees.

A small cry, clearly human, came from just off shore, and the two immortals hurried to meet the mermaid. It didn't take her long to reach the beach and she collapsed onto the sand, exhausted from her long journey.

"You're safe now," Cari assured her as she knelt at her side.

"That's debatable," Caspian muttered. The king of Atlantis could track the Oracle through any body of water in the world, and there was nothing to stop him sending a search party to land to track down the wayward mermaid.

Daphne gazed around, taking in her surroundings like a newborn child. Like all Oracles, her sight returned only when she took human form. Her wide-eyed wonder lasted only until the next contraction came. She gave a piercing scream that caused Caspian to cringe.

"Help me," she begged.

Cari took her hand and squeezed it gently. "That's what we're here for."

Caspian wasn't sure he would be much use. Despite his vast experience over thousands of years, he had managed to avoid getting into this particular situation. He knew nothing about childbirth.

Thankfully, Cari appeared to be better prepared, though he wasn't sure she had any more experience than he did. What she lacked in knowledge, though, she made up for with assertiveness, bossing him around like a sergeant major while reassuring the mermaid her child would be cared for.

The birth, as Cari had predicted, was long and painful. The sun had just appeared on the horizon when the tiny mer-baby made his entrance into the world.

"Protect him, Goddess," the mermaid begged before she closed her eyes for the last time.

Cari brushed Daphne's damp hair back from her face. "He'll have a good life," she promised, as she stepped back with the newborn boy in her arms.

"The nearest hospital is that way." Caspian pointed inland, at the main road leading out of the sleepy seaside hamlet and toward the nearest town.

Carrie shook her head. "The babe is healthy and well. I don't see the need to trouble the humans."

Caspian had a feeling Cari wasn't thinking along the same lines he was. "If we go to the hospital now, we can slip him into a crib and find parents to raise him. A bit of memory manipulation and the happy couple has unexpected twins. I'm sure we'll find someone suitable in no time at all."

"This child can't possibly be raised by humans," Cari pointed out in between cooing at the child. "What will happen when they try to bathe their new baby and he suddenly grows fins?"

"We could…" Caspian's voice trailed off. Altering the memory of the child's parents wouldn't be possible on a regular basis. They would need to watch over them every waking minute.

Cari cooed over the baby. "We'll just have to raise him ourselves. I think we should call him Justin."

"We?" Caspian shook his head and stepped back quickly. "Where are you getting this 'we' from? I don't know anything about babies."

"You'll learn. We both will." Cari walked across the sand toward the road, disappearing into thin air as she hummed a lullaby.

Caspian glanced down at the mermaid and sighed. It would be far too dangerous for humans to discover her. He bowed his head and recited the words the mer people spoke when bidding a final farewell to one of their own. Even though her body moved no more, he sensed her soul nearby and could tell she appreciated the gesture. Finally, with a wave of his hand, he removed all trace of her from the beach.

He lingered on the shore until the first humans arrived. They couldn't see him, yet for some reason animals could always sense his presence. When the first dog bounded in his direction, yapping excitedly, he headed home to Cari. He guessed after so many thousands of years, it was long past time he learnt about the joys of fatherhood.

Chapter One

Present day

Lucas lingered at the edge of the beach, partially hidden by the trees. He watched the nearby group of mermen as they sought out the mermaids who had come to the island before them.

The summer solstice was upon them and Lucas, just like the rest of the mermen and mermaids, had gone into heat with the desire to experience sexual fulfilment. Because the mer people could only have sex in their human forms, for two nights of the year it was far more likely to find a mermaid or merman on land than in the ocean. Just as most of his kind did, Lucas swam to land on the solstices with the sole purpose of finding release and breaking his mating fever. He just wished he could find pleasure with one of the pretty young mermaids, as the rest of his contemporaries did.

Across the sands, two mermen exchanged a knowing glance with each other. Lucas recognized one of them as a gatherer—mermen who ventured outside the boundaries of the sunken city to collect foods that could not grow within the city itself. He didn't recognize the other. It was common knowledge amongst the citizens of the sunken city that most of the homosexual mermen in the city worked as gatherers, one of the most menial of tasks. Not all of them—Lucas himself was an exception to the rule—but the majority.

Once he considered it safe to do so, Lucas slipped into the trees and found a place to wait out the night. With the mermen outnumbering the mermaids by such a large number, it wasn't unusual for him to be without a partner during the mating season. He didn't dwell on the fact that he didn't search too hard for one. In truth, no mermaid could give him what he needed.

Sitting beneath a large palm tree, Lucas closed his eyes and stroked his erection. The touch caused him to harden even more than he already had, yet no amount of stimulation would be enough to bring him off tonight.

As the night passed, most of the mer people returned to the sea, their fevers broken for the season. Past experience told Lucas some still lingered. The ones with the same preferences as him would remain until they found what they needed. Lucas stood and took a step back toward the beach. Staying here could be dangerous. If anyone should see him, he could find himself removed from his post. It was one thing for the gatherers to find pleasure with each other, but he wasn't one of their ilk. As a junior adviser to King Nereus, he couldn't risk being seen.

How many seasons had it been since he had been with another merman? Two? Three? Enough had passed to cause Lucas to be painfully desperate for release now. Could he *really* go another season without?

"I see you haven't swum back to the city yet."

Lucas jumped at the familiar voice. "Otus." He acknowledged the guard who had approached him with a stealth that would make a stingray envious. Otus was another exception to the rule. As a member of the guards, he wasn't as high ranking as Lucas, yet his position might be just as precarious if he should be discovered.

"It's been a few seasons since I've had you," Otus commented. "I had a feeling this time you'd be sticking around."

Lucas took another step toward the beach. "I'm just leaving."

"Don't be a fool." Otus stepped into his path. "We both know what you need tonight."

Otus ran his index finger down Lucas' chest before taking Lucas' hard cock in a firm grip.

Lucas whimpered as Otus grinned down at him. "Yes," he moaned.

"I missed you the last few seasons," Otus murmured into his ear. "Or at least I missed this hot, tight arse of yours. Are you going to give me what I need tonight?"

Lucas nodded and twisted round to face the tree. He didn't see the point in denying himself when Otus stood right in front of him, offering him what they both needed so desperately. He spread his legs and braced himself for Otus to take him. It would be rough and hard, even more so because of how many months had passed since he'd last been taken by another man.

Otus ran his hands over Lucas' buttocks and eased his cheeks apart. With nothing more than spit to ease his way, Otus took Lucas with one swift stroke. Lucas tensed under the invasion. He cursed whatever power had decided *this* was what he needed to break the mating fever each solstice. Why would anyone imagine this invasion of his body was something he would want if he had any other choice?

He buried his face in his arm and waited for Otus to finish. Lucas' relief would come when the heat of another man's seed filled his arse. Until then he could do nothing except ride out the fever as Otus took what he wanted.

It didn't take Otus long to come, and when the hot flood filled Lucas, his own orgasm crashed over him and he came hard, his semen staining the bark of the tree in front of him.

Otus pulled out of him as soon as he had finished. "You should stick around every mating season."

Lucas ignored his comment as he struggled to regain his breath.

"I know why you don't," Otus continued. "You're wasting your time trying to hide what you are. There's already talk about you."

"What?" Lucas paled, and when his heart rate quickened this time, it was for a totally different reason. "Who's talking about me?"

Otus smiled unpleasantly. "Everyone. Your fellow advisers already wonder how such a pretty little merman hasn't managed to find some fertile young mermaid to fuck each season."

"You're just trying to scare me."

"Why would I do that? From my point of view, I'd be happy for this to remain our little secret. After all, I wouldn't want any competition for your arse if everyone knew for sure that nothing brings off young Lucas like being taken roughly from behind."

Lucas cringed. "Roughness isn't my trigger, just so you know."

Otus didn't seem bothered. Lucas knew if they came together next mating season, Otus would treat him the same way he had tonight.

"No merman who likes the touch of his own gender has ever risen above junior adviser," Otus reminded him.

Lucas was well aware of the fact that the last homosexual merman who had taken a post within the palace had been banished. Of course, Kyle had been one of the personal bodyguards to the prince, and had been discovered to be in a relationship with his charge. That might have had some bearing on the decision to send him on his way. Lucas didn't know the exact truth of what had happened. Those who were aware of the circumstances weren't exactly talking. Everyone else happily speculated on just what the bodyguard and the prince had been doing when the king had caught them together.

The one thing everyone knew for sure was Kyle had been banished and within a year both the prince and his mother, the queen, had vanished from the sunken city as well.

Lucas didn't know anything of life outside the underwater city and the island the inhabitants visited during the mating season. He had no intention of risking banishment himself.

He glared at Otus. "If I find out you've been spreading rumors about me, I'll have you banished from the city."

Otus laughed. "Rumors are, by their nature, untrue. Anything I would have to say about you would be purely factual. You may think you hide your desires, but you're fooling no one."

Lucas shook his head in denial, but Otus had already begun to leave. Lucas followed after him. At least his fever had broken and he wouldn't have to suffer through the pain of riding it out this season. He hadn't yet reached the beach when he heard the sounds of other mermen nearby. Otus took no notice of his departure from the path to the beach. He had taken what he needed and had no further use for Lucas tonight.

Slipping through the trees, quietly and slowly, Lucas crept toward the noises. They didn't sound like the ones he and Otus had recently been making. They seemed softer somehow.

He couldn't see the two men, though he was certain they were male. One of them laughed quietly.

"Ticklish?" an unfamiliar voice asked.

"You know I am," the second man replied. "Now how about you stop teasing me and give me that gorgeous cock of yours?"

Even though Lucas could only see their silhouettes, he could make out their positions. One of the mermen lay on his back, his legs over the shoulders of the other, who was clearly doing as his lover requested. The one on his back groaned in obvious pleasure and Lucas' erection rose again at the sight and sounds before him.

When the two mermen strained toward each other, kissing deeply, Lucas had to bite back his own moan of desire.

The one being taken didn't seem to be in any pain or discomfort. Instead he seemed to be thoroughly enjoying the experience and was getting louder by the minute.

Lucas fisted his cock, relieved that now his mating fever had broken, he could find pleasure by his own hand. Shielded by the undergrowth, Lucas bit into his fingers to stifle any sound he might make as he watched the two mermen come together.

"I'm coming," the merman on his knees shouted as he pumped his hips.

"Me too," the second one gasped.

Their joint cries echoed through the trees and drowned out the small whimper of pleasure Lucas couldn't quite hide as he came for the second time, falling to his knees as his orgasm took him by surprise.

By the time he had recovered his senses, the two mermen had vanished from their place within the trees. Thankfully for Lucas, their route back to the beach didn't bring them past his hiding spot.

Hidden in the bushes, Lucas felt relaxed and heavy limbed. He wondered whether he might be able to find those mermen again next mating season, and whether they might be able to tell him what he was doing wrong. Even though he knew what triggered his release, he had never enjoyed sex the way they seemed to. The painful truth was even though he'd achieved an orgasm during the seasons when he had allowed Otus to take him, he had never actually found pleasure in what they did.

Lucas contemplated asking for advice all the way back to the beach. However, by the time he had transformed and swum to the sunken city, he had changed his mind completely. The fewer people who were aware of his desire for mermen, the better off he would be. Should the wrong person discover his secret, his chances of rising in the ranks to become a senior adviser to the king would vanish. He could not take such an unnecessary risk. He owed it to his father to follow in his footsteps, and he couldn't throw it all away because of his desires. He played a dangerous game by allowing Otus to take him. He would be better advised to return to the ocean at the first available opportunity each mating season, before anyone else discovered his secret desires.

His resolve set, Lucas hoped he could keep his promise, even though he knew the desire to be taken would grow stronger each mating season he denied himself. No merman could go for long without release, not unless they accepted the excruciating pain that came from denial. Lucas wondered how long he could keep this up, and whether it would be long enough to see his ambitions achieved.

Chapter Two

Two months later

King Nereus' meeting had already dragged on for twice as long as usual and yet no progress had been made. Lucas, who had never had a great deal of interest in the role his father was training him in, tried to hide his boredom.

When King Nereus finally drew the meeting to a close, the collective sigh of relief was loud enough to prompt a small smile from him as he shooed everyone from the room.

"Lucas, if you could remain behind please?" King Nereus called to him telepathically.

Lucas halted halfway toward the exit and swam back the way he had come.

His stomach did flips as he waited for the room to clear. He had heard rumors that the king could read the mind of anyone in the sunken city. Lucas hoped he couldn't, and that the reason he had been kept behind had nothing to do with his guilty secret.

Finally, he was alone with the king for the first time in his life.

"I have a job for you," the king stated without preamble.

"Yes, Your Majesty?"

"You will recall early on in the meeting there was some debate about whether I should take another mermaid as my queen."

"Yes."

"Ah, at least you were listening during some of the meeting."

Lucas tried to figure out whether the king was teasing him or not. King Nereus wasn't exactly known for having a sense of humor, yet since the abrupt departure of his queen, he had changed quite a lot. After several weeks of cursing and foul-tempered outbursts, he had suddenly taken a calmer approach to everything and had seemed to be almost a different person. Still, Lucas found it a little disconcerting to be teased by the merman.

"I have no intention of taking another mermaid as queen, not for the sole purpose of producing an heir."

"It's your decision to make," Lucas replied respectfully.

"I already have an heir and I'm entrusting you with the task of finding him."

"You mean Prince Finn?"

King Nereus shook his head. *"No, no. Finn has long gone from the city and, despite everything, I wish him well for his future. He was as much a victim of the queen as myself."*

Lucas didn't understand what the king was talking about, but it seemed he had no intention of elaborating any further.

"I want you to find my oldest son and bring him home to take his place here."

"You have another son?"

"Yes."

"Where is he? I mean, if I have to find him, I'll need to know where to search."

King Nereus shrugged. "I have no idea where he lives. I'm afraid I've never seen my son. His mother departed this place before his birth and did not return."

Lucas wondered how he would manage such a monumental task when the king spoke again.

"I give you permission to consult the Oracles for the purpose of questioning them about the location of my son."

"Um…"

"You have a question?" the king asked.

"If you haven't seen the child, how do you know you have a son? Wasn't there an equal chance the mer baby was born a girl?"

King Nereus chuckled. "Your father was right about you. You're smarter than you appear. Yes, there was an equal chance. However, I had it on the excellent authority of an Oracle the child would be a boy. The Oracles, as you will soon find out, are never wrong."

Lucas felt a little foolish for asking the question after hearing the answer. Of course the king would be able to ask the Oracles. They lived to serve the royal family and the sunken city.

"Is there anything else you can tell me?"

"There's little more to say. The mermaid who carried my child swam northeast of here. There are several land masses in that direction where she could have delivered the child. Knowing her as I did, I suspect she waited until the last minute before taking human form."

"How old would he be now?"

"He'll be twenty-five years this autumn."

"Um…"

"You have another question?"

Lucas could tell the king was getting impatient for Lucas to be on his way, but he couldn't seem to stop himself from asking one more question. In his mind, it might be the most important one. *"What if your son has forged a good life for himself away from here? What if he doesn't want to come with me?"*

King Nereus laughed. *"What could he possibly have in his life that would be better than being the heir to this wonderful city?"*

Lucas didn't give voice to his thoughts, but he couldn't help wondering, if life was so wonderful as the heir of the sunken city, why had Prince Finn left without so much as a backward glance?

King Nereus waved Lucas from the chamber. *"You may leave now."*

Lucas swam away once more, yet once again the king called him back. *"Oh, one more thing, Lucas."*

"Yes?"

"Tell no one except the Oracles of your mission. If anyone asks, I'm sending you north as an ambassador to Queen Coral's clan in an effort to establish communication with her."

"What if the Oracles say something?"

"They would have no reason to. Now, I would suggest you question them and leave within a day. I want my son brought here as soon as possible."

Lucas confirmed he understood the importance of his mission and swam from the room. He wondered why he, of all people, had been entrusted with such a job. Born and raised in the sunken city, Lucas had only ever left the city to go to the deserted island, first to learn how to walk, then later to partake of the pleasures to be had during the mating seasons. He had never seen a single human and yet now he would be traveling to the land they lived on. He wondered how much information the Oracles would be able to give him before he left.

* * * *

Lucas went directly to the temple straight from the palace. The ancient structure in which the Oracles made their home was second only to the palace itself in terms of luxuriousness. Their sponges were large and comfortable and the stone walls were completely clean of barnacles. Large bowls of sea fruits were laid out for their consumption, and the food appeared to be the pick of the crops. They seemed to want for nothing and each Oracle had a personal servant to tend to their every need.

Completely blind from the moment they came into their powers, the three Oracles could see only when they had a vision or took human form.

The servants of the Oracles left the main greeting chamber when he entered. It was forbidden for them to listen to anything the Oracles had to say when they used their gifts for another.

"Welcome, Lucas." Ula smiled in his direction. He didn't ask how she knew his name or where he hovered. As the Oracle with the gift to see into the future, she no doubt was aware of his visit to them before he had even spoken with the king.

"I have the permission of King Nereus to seek your advice," Lucas told them.

"Yes, we know," Ula replied. *"We will tell you what we know about the king's lost love and her son."*

"Thank you."

"Come take a seat." Ula waved at the spongy cushions on the ground and the three Oracles swam down toward them. Lucas followed and made himself comfortable.

Delwyn, the Oracle of the past and the youngest of the three, spoke first. *"Daphne, the king's lover, was a former Oracle of the future."*

It was the last thing Lucas had expected to hear. He tried to hide his shocked expression, even though no one could see him. He directed his next question to the current Oracle of the future. *"Are you sure?"*

Ula nodded. *"Very sure."*

"But it's forbidden for Oracles to leave the sunken city," Lucas pointed out. *"Not even during the mating season."*

Each Oracle simultaneously ducked their heads. *"Our guards weren't quite so strict then as they are now,"* Delwyn explained. *"And when the heir to the throne is the one taking the Oracle up to the island, what guard would dare to stand in his way?"*

"Why didn't the king tell me this when he asked me to search for his child?"

Kai gave a small snort of amusement. *"He probably thought we wouldn't tell you, but you need to have the full facts before you begin your journey."*

A hundred questions went through Lucas' mind. Where did he start? *"I don't want to tire you all out with my questions. I know how much the visions take out of you."*

"We don't need visions to tell you what happened," Delwyn explained. *"We can tell you from our memories."*

"Forgive me, but King Nereus told me his child would be nearly twenty-five years of age. I thought Oracles came into their powers shortly before their first mating season. You, er..."

Ula gave a light chuckle. *"Yes, we are all too young to have been Oracles when the heir was born. Kai was merely a babe himself, and Delwyn hadn't even been born. I was around five years old and living far away from here when one day my sight vanished. My parents brought me here. The search for the lost Oracle of the Future continued until our arrival. They understood nothing except the death of an Oracle could have caused me to come into my powers. Prince Nereus, as he was then, took the news badly, though he tried to hide his grief as best he could."*

"But you were so young." Lucas couldn't imagine what it must have been like for Ula.

"When an Oracle of the Future is due to pass from this world, they see their own death in a vision," Ula explained. *"They can also see when the other Oracles are nearing the end of their lives. As such, we each have enough time to prepare and search for one to take our place. Daphne, my predecessor, hoped to avoid her fate. She swam to the land where humans reside and planned to raise her child amongst them. But destiny cannot always be avoided, not even by those who can see it laid out before them. As her son took his first breaths, she took her last. We have no powers on land and so she could not choose her successor from the various candidates. At any given time, there are around half a dozen mer people who could potentially become Oracles. I was young, but apparently the one in closest proximity."*

Lucas understood what she told him, yet it still didn't explain how any of them could have known what had happened before. He repeated his question, hoping they could clear his confusion.

Delwyn was the one to explain. *"Each Oracle inherits the powers of their predecessor, and also their memories. We all have the memories of every Oracle who came before us from the moment they came into their powers until the time they passed from this world."*

"What? All of them?"

"Yes."

Lucas couldn't imagine having so much knowledge in his head. It had to be overwhelming. *"How do you cope with all of that?"*

"You get used to it. It's not quite as bad as it sounds. The memories are there if we need to see them, like now, but for the most part I don't tend to access them any more than I might try to remember what I ate for dinner on a particular date last year. The point is, we know what happened because

we have the memories of being here when the events took place."

The Oracles seemed to communicate amongst themselves for a few moments until Ula began the story. *"Daphne and Prince Nereus should never have been lovers. It was – and still is – strictly forbidden for any Oracle to have sexual relations. When Daphne discovered she was with child, the prince helped her escape from the city and she made her way northeast."*

"Did the prince go with her?"

"He escorted her for a few miles, until he had ensured she was safely away from the area. He could not make the full journey with her, lest he be missed. He also wanted to engineer the search efforts for the missing Oracle himself, making sure the guards concentrated their efforts in other directions, to give Daphne a good head start."

"How did she survive the journey?" Lucas asked. *"A blind mermaid would be nothing more than a target for the predators of the oceans."*

"Yes, she would," Ula agreed. *"Unless she knows exactly what is coming for her at any given time. Daphne had to use her powers repeatedly to stay safe on her journey. She arrived on land already exhausted both physically and psychically and her contractions began as soon as she took human form. Had she stayed here and given birth with the other mermaids who were expecting, she may have survived, but as I said, destiny and fate cannot be avoided."*

Lucas had to admire the determination of the mermaid. *"What happened to the child?"*

"We believe he has been raised on land," Kai told him, though he didn't sound entirely sure about his answer.

"Can't you see him to tell for sure?" Lucas questioned. Kai should be able to see anything happening in the present time, so surely he could see the lost heir wherever he might be.

Kai shook his head. *"We have each tried – many times over the years – to see the heir. We have all met with failure at every attempt. I cannot see him in the present, Delwyn cannot see his past and Ula cannot see his future. Without Ula's inherited memories of his birth, we wouldn't even know he survived."*

"I thought you could see everything?"

Kai snorted and shook his head. *"So did we. Yet we cannot see him. When the king asks us how his son is, we merely say he is well and hope we speak the truth."*

"Is there anyone else you can't see, or is it just him?"

"No one else that we know of is hidden to us," Ula confirmed. *"But that doesn't mean there aren't others."*

"How is that possible?" Lucas wondered how he was supposed to find the heir if even the Oracles couldn't locate him.

"We believe he is being protected by someone whose powers exceed our own," Kai explained.

"Then how am I expected to find him?"

"We can direct you to where he was born."

"That doesn't mean he'll be there now," Lucas pointed out.

"That's the best we can do." Kai sounded rather apologetic about the situation.

Ula gave him directions through the ocean, and Lucas tried his best to commit the information to memory. He could tell he had a long journey ahead of him.

Chapter Three

After leaving the Oracles, Lucas swam to find his brother, Halcyon. He found him in his rooms in the palace, playing with his eight-year-old son. His preferred mate during the mating seasons, Shayla, sat on her sponge sofa, watching them fondly. Like many mermaids, she hoped for more children, yet had been unsuccessful in becoming pregnant again. It had taken her several years to have Eirik and his parents doted on him. He was now at the age where he wanted to swim all over and needed constant supervision. Halcyon and Shayla took turns to watch over the youngster, though their parents and Lucas helped whenever they could.

Halcyon greeted Lucas with a wide grin as he swam into the room. *"What are you doing here at this time of day? Shouldn't you be with Father, learning the law?"*

"Not today," Lucas replied. *"I'm being sent on a mission for the king."*

Halcyon's jaw dropped in surprise. *"You?"*

Lucas bristled. *"There's no need to act so surprised."*

"But why you?" Halcyon pressed. *"You're still in training."*

"*Maybe that's why I've been chosen,*" Lucas suggested. "*He can't spare one of the senior advisers for longer than a few days.*"

Halcyon shot him a suspicious glance. "*What sort of mission is this? Are you leaving the city?*"

"*Yes.*"

"*Where are you going? How long for?*"

"*I'm being sent to Queen Coral's clan in the far north to see if we can establish communications with her.*" Halcyon swallowed the lie without question, and Lucas pushed aside his guilt at the deception.

Shayla appeared impressed. "*That's an important mission. Does your father know yet?*"

"*Not yet. I'll be going to tell him next. I didn't want to leave it too late to come here, though. I didn't want to risk waking Eirik, and I'll need to leave straight away, rather than wait until morning.*"

"*Shayla, can you take Eirik through to his chambers so I can have a few minutes alone with Lucas?*"

Lucas frowned. If Halcyon wanted to speak to him privately, all he had to do was send his thoughts to him and no one else. He sent a private thought to Halcyon, telling him as much.

"*I could,*" Halcyon agreed, "*but your thoughts are always written all over your face and you aren't going to be pleased by what I have to say.*"

Lucas didn't like the sound of this. "*Then why say it?*"

"*Because it needs saying,*" Halcyon told him. "*I should probably have said something a long time ago, but with things the way they are here… Well, I didn't see the point.*"

"*What are you talking about?*"

"*You, and the fact you desire mermen and not mermaids.*"

"*I don't know what you're talking about,*" Lucas quickly denied.

"*We both know exactly what I'm talking about,*" Halcyon replied. "*Did you think I hadn't noticed? I'm your older* brother. I've known since your first mating season. I watched over you that night to make sure you stayed safe."

"I didn't even have sex my first season," Lucas told him. "And for the record, having my brother watch me is kind of creepy."

Halcyon rolled his eyes. "I don't mean I followed you round the island all night. Like all of our people, I avoid being on the same part of the island as family members if I can help it. But I did make sure to see you safely ashore and I saw your face as you took in the sight of so many other naked male forms. You barely glanced at the mermaids waiting at the edge of the beach."

Lucas shook his head. "You don't know what you're talking about. I just watched the other mermen to see what was expected of me. It was all new to me."

"That first night I hoped that might be the case, though my suspicions were already raised. The next mating season, when I saw you again watching the mermen, I knew the truth for sure."

"It's not true," Lucas denied.

"Stop it," Halcyon snapped. "You don't need to lie to me. Do you think I care who you want to be with?"

"You know what you're saying is forbidden."

"Of course I know. But I also know none of us have any control over our mating season triggers, something the law doesn't take into account."

"The laws are in place for a reason." It was something the members of the Council said a great deal and for the most part, Lucas agreed with them.

"I know why the law against mating with our own genders was introduced," Halcyon said. "Just because I don't want to take Father's place as adviser doesn't mean I'm completely ignorant of the law. I just don't happen to agree with it, and if you were totally honest with yourself, you wouldn't either. It should be obvious after all these years, that forcing those who don't want it to engage in relations with the opposite gender isn't increasing our numbers. Even I can tell the number of births in the city is still falling."

"It's not my place to try to change the law," Lucas pointed out.

"Yet," Halcyon reminded him.

Lucas huffed and picked up one of his nephew's toys to play idly with. "So, is there any particular reason you're bringing this up now? Not that I'm admitting to anything, but it seems a bit random."

Halcyon nodded. "The law only applies to the mer people living here in the sunken city."

"I know that."

"You've never been outside the city, save for up to the island to mate. This could be a good opportunity for you."

"I know it's a good opportunity. It's a chance for me to do something important for our king. To prove I'm worthy of taking Father's place on the Council."

"It could also give you a chance to find happiness with someone suitable for you."

"I am coming back you know."

"I know, but all I'm saying is if you found someone, whoever that might be, you should consider making a life with them, even if doing so means being away from here."

"Do you think I could leave my entire family and let Father down by refusing to take his place on the Council?"

"There are others who would be able to advise the king on the law. It doesn't have to be you."

"The post has been held by our family for generations now."

"That doesn't mean you have to make yourself miserable by joining their number."

Lucas tossed the toy aside and watched it float across the room. It wasn't nearly as satisfying as throwing something above the waves.

"Can you at least just think about it?" Halcyon asked. "If you find someone?"

"Fine. I'll think about leaving here if I find a mermaid worth settling down with."

Halcyon gave him an annoyed glare. *"Or a merman?"*

Lucas started to deny his desires again, but Halcyon cut him off. *"Don't lie to me again. I'm not stupid and all I'm doing is trying to help you."*

Lucas, feeling thoroughly chastised, studied his fins, unable to meet his brother's steady gaze. Only when his brother wrapped his comforting arm around him did he feel the burden of his lies begin to ease. Yet he still couldn't bring himself to acknowledge the truth.

* * * *

Lucas went about his preparations for his journey, ensuring all his chores were completed before settling down to study the large maps of the world engraved on the floors of one of the larger rooms in the palace. The Atlanteans had carved the maps into the stone floor thousands of years ago, but they had done it with enough skill that even the erosion of the sea water had not destroyed them. Of course it probably helped that since Atlantis—as the humans had called it—had disappeared below the waves, the maps had not been walked on as much as they had above ground. The mermen who needed to use them merely swam above them, as Lucas did, to plan their journeys out into the vast ocean around them.

He studied the map, searching for the land the Oracles had told him of, finding it nearly as far to the north as the waters where Queen Coral's clan resided. It would take many weeks of swimming for him to reach the land the king's former lover had fled to.

Lucas sighed as he wondered again why he had been chosen for this mission. Considering the dangerous route he must take and his lack of skills in battling sharks and other sea creatures who preyed on mermen, he would be lucky to make it a mile past the city boundaries.

When he could put the inevitable off no longer, he swam home, bid his parents goodbye and set off for the northern boundaries of the city. He breathed a sigh of relief when he saw Otus wasn't one of the guards on duty. The last thing he needed was his snide comments to be the last words he heard before he set out on his own. Instead he found the leader of the guards, Calder, on duty along with a guard he didn't recognize. Alert in their duties, they made sure the sea dragons didn't attack any merman or mermaid who ventured too close to them. Dangerous and barely contained, only the most skillful of the guards could be trusted to watch over the creatures, and they never did so alone.

"It's not often we see you this far from the palace," Calder commented as Lucas swam close. "What brings you here?"

"I need to leave the city," Lucas explained.

Calder's eyes widened in surprise. "A trip to the island?"

"No, I'm swimming farther than that. I hope to be back by the next solstice, but I don't know for sure."

"You've never left the city before, have you?" Calder asked.

"No, why do you ask?"

"Because it's very dangerous out there," Calder explained. "You're not even carrying a spear."

"Will I need one?" Lucas asked.

"I hope not, but you should take one anyway. Here, have mine. I can get another from the barracks."

Lucas held the spear in a loose grip and poked at the tip. It was sharper than he expected.

"*That's the dangerous end,*" Calder teased. "*Be careful with it and try not to lose it. It's been blessed by Andaman, the Atlantean God of the Forge. It will never rust or break and it will always strike true.*"

"*Thank you.*"

"*You're welcome. So, where are you headed to?*"

"*I'm leaving on a mission for the king,*" Lucas explained.

Calder appeared as though he wanted to say something else, but he apparently thought better of it and stepped back. He waved to his fellow guard and gestured for him to keep the sea dragon back as Lucas passed.

Lucas swam forward, one eye on the dragon and the other on Calder. The huge beast snarled at him, his fangs flashing as he snapped his jaws. The guard urged the creature back, only narrowly escaping the dragon's sweeping tail as the animal thrashed from side to side. Lucas swam past as swiftly as he could and out of the boundaries of the city. He hoped the sea dragons really did live only in the sunken city.

With a last glance over his shoulder, he watched the magic of the sea dragons shield the city from his sight, then the dragon vanished too. To those who didn't know where to search, the land appeared identical to the rest of the barren seabed. As he swam away into the darkness ahead, Lucas wondered how long it would be before he saw his home again.

Chapter Four

Justin walked through the aquarium with a smile on his face. Although he had not expected to, he loved working here and was thrilled to answer questions about all the marine creatures the building housed.

The wide-eyed school party touring the place today was full of questions and eagerly peered into tanks in search of Nemo and Dory. Justin knew the most famous fish of all were found near the end of the tour and assured the kids they would get to see them before they left at the end of the day.

He waved them toward the next room, and they filed past him with *oohs* and *ahs* as they studied the contents of each glass-fronted tank lining the wall.

Again, Justin wondered at the irony of his loving working at the aquarium, when he hated everything else about the sea. He wandered over to one of the nearby tanks. Empty of any sea life, it instead contained an underwater scene that could be animated by anyone who put twenty pence into the machine. No one these days tended to bother with the animation, except for Justin. He took a coin from his pocket and put it into the slot. A moment later the chest of treasure opened and the diver began to move. His eyes remained on the large clam-like shell in the center and when it opened, the mermaid appeared. Justin had no idea what his mother had looked like, but sometimes he wondered if she was anything like the blonde toy in the tank. He suspected she probably wasn't. For one thing, the mermaid in the tank had the traditional green fins, yet his foster parents had told him his own golden fins had been inherited from his mother.

He rubbed his suddenly damp palm over the fabric of his jeans. It had been a long time since he'd seen his fins and he mostly tried to forget he had them. He never went swimming and if there was an option between a shower and a bath, he always took the former. He didn't want to see his fins, and he certainly had no intention of getting any closer to the sea than he was right now.

* * * *

Justin made sure to leave work on time, knowing his foster parents had made plans to take him out to celebrate his twenty-fifth birthday this evening. His mother had been as eager as a puppy for weeks.

He opened the door to his flat and found his father on the couch with a glass of whiskey in his hand and one of Justin's magazines in the other. Caspian didn't have a key to the flat, but little things like locked doors didn't stop him popping in whenever he liked.

"Hi, Dad." Justin smiled as he greeted the man who had raised him. "Have you been here long?"

"No, just half an hour or so," Caspian replied. "Cari will be meeting us at the restaurant."

Justin tossed his car keys into the dish on the side table. "Are you going to tell me where we're going yet?"

Caspian gave him a sly grin that told him clearly the answer to his question was no. "Just dress smart. If you're in jeans or leathers, you'll never get in."

"Damn, that means I have to mind my manners, right?"

Caspian chuckled. "We both need to be on our best behavior or Cari will have both our hides."

Justin went into the bedroom and rummaged through his wardrobe for something that might pass as smart without him having to run an iron over it. When his mother laid down the law, both Justin and Caspian jumped to attention. Being raised by two immortal beings with a wide array of powers meant Justin grew up as one of the most obedient children in England. Lying to his mother, the Atlantean Goddess of Prophecy, was as pointless as lying to himself. She knew what mischief he planned on cooking up before he had even begun. As an adult, he retained the same respect for his parents, though he found himself closer to his father, who had felt the sharp side of Cari's tongue even more than Justin. Of course, Caspian had many centuries head start on him in that regard.

"What are you doing in there?" Caspian called. "We're supposed to be at the restaurant by six."

"I'm just going to take a quick shower. I stink of fish."

Caspian laughed as Justin hurriedly undressed. "It'd be a little odd if you didn't," he pointed out. "In case you hadn't noticed, you *are* half fish, remember?"

"Like I can bloody well forget," Justin muttered as he turned on the shower and let the water heat up.

Thankfully Caspian didn't say anything more about fish or mermen and Justin soon joined him in the living room.

Caspian checked his watch. "We're going to be a bit late. It's nearly six already."

"Not the way you drive," Justin teased. "You can make it anywhere in town in five minutes."

"We're not eating in town." Caspian took hold of Justin's arm and immediately teleported them out of the flat.

"I really wish you wouldn't do that," Justin complained after his head had finished spinning. "Or at least give me some warning."

Caspian ignored him as Justin stared at his surroundings. "Where the hell are we?"

"Greece."

"Why?"

"You love Greek food and Cari thought it might be nice for you to eat some in the country it's made."

Justin should have guessed. His mother was always doing things like that. He just hoped they didn't disappear on him and leave him stranded in a foreign country without his passport, like they had a few years ago. The last thing he needed was a repeat of *that* disaster. His parents had been most apologetic, but they did tend to forget on occasion that he didn't have all the powers they did.

They walked the short distance to the restaurant and found Cari waiting at the entrance. Her long flowing gown was reminiscent of ancient Greece and Justin suspected she might have even worn it back then. He had never seen her in any modern clothes, which had made parents' evening at school an interesting experience, to say the least. His friends had thought his foster mother a little peculiar. Privately, Justin thought they had no idea just how strange she could be. Caspian, on the other hand, loved modern clothing and was—according to Justin's friends—the epitome of cool. Justin wasn't so sure about that, but of his two parents, only his father had taken to modern life.

"Happy birthday, darling." Cari tugged him down into a hug. Justin towered over her small frame, and he tried not to crush her as he squeezed her back.

"Sorry, we're late," Justin apologized. "I got delayed leaving work."

Cari gave him a knowing smile. "That's not the reason you're late, though, is it? You spent too long picking out a shirt, a task that wouldn't have taken so long if you did your ironing regularly."

There really was no getting anything past his mother. She could practically smell a lie on him, despite the annoying odor of fish that he could never completely shake.

"You caught me," Justin admitted. "So, am I presentable?"

Cari stepped back and studied him carefully. "I suppose so," she teased.

The restaurant was busy, which made sense since it was later than six p.m. in Greece. At least he didn't have to put up with long flights and the lack of leg room on planes when he wanted to visit other countries. Just call Mum or Dad and *voila*.

They took their seats and ordered their meals. Both Cari and Caspian were fluent in every human language known, and several dead languages. Justin had a little Greek, but not enough to follow Cari's entire conversation with the waiter.

"What was that all about?" Justin asked when the waiter walked away with a wink at his mother.

"You don't want to know," Caspian told him before turning to his sister. "Flirt."

Cari didn't seem bothered and made no secret of her appreciation of the waiter's arse. Justin didn't blame her. It was a fine specimen. He was pretty sure Caspian would agree with him.

Justin listened to the chatter of the other customers. No one around them appeared to be English. The place seemed to be away from the usual tourist destinations. It meant they could speak openly in English without worrying too much about anyone overhearing what could sometimes be rather odd conversations.

"What news of the family then?" Justin asked, as they waited for their food to arrive. When he referred to the family, they knew he was in fact making reference to the other immortals. Usually they gave him news and anecdotes about some of the more sociable beings, the ones who had stopped by on occasion to see the young merman they had chosen to raise.

This time, however, Cari and Caspian exchanged a look Justin couldn't quite interpret.

"What is it?" he asked.

"The sleeping ones are beginning to stir," Cari explained. "Medina, the Goddess of Love, has, in fact, woken up entirely."

Justin laughed. "Well, we could all do with some more love. Maybe she had something to do with our flirtatious waiter."

Cari chuckled. "I doubt it. You tend to know when she's involved. She's Goddess of Love, Lust and Carnal Desires."

"Busy lady."

Caspian laughed loudly, drawing the attention of the couple at the next table. "Medina's no lady. I never knew a goddess to get through so many men. She even tried it on with me once upon a time."

"More fool her then," Justin commented. His father, like himself, craved the hard body of a man in his bed and made no secret about the fact.

"She soon figured out who I preferred to have warming my bed." Caspian shot him a wicked grin.

Cari snorted in a most unladylike manner. "I still say you didn't have to bed quite so many of her priests. One or two would have been perfectly sufficient to make your point."

Justin goggled at Caspian. "Is that true?" He knew so little about his father that he savored every bit of information Cari let slip.

Caspian glared at his sister. "It was a *very* long time ago. And right now we have bigger problems to worry about than my sex life."

"We're waiting to see who wakes up next," Cari explained.

"What about your parents?" Justin asked. "Are they likely to rouse any time soon?"

Caspian gave a visible shiver. "I hope not. The last thing we need is my father popping round for tea."

"Is he that bad?" Justin didn't know much about Caspian's father, other than he was the God of War and Retribution. His parents rarely spoke of any of his grandparents.

"No, he isn't," Cari assured him. "He and Caspian just don't see eye-to-eye on certain things."

"Can we not talk about him?" Caspian asked. "I tend to lose my appetite when I'm reminded of him."

"What about your mother?" Justin asked.

Caspian glared at him. "How about we not talk about any of the other gods? They're nothing but trouble, and

I hope the lot of them stay asleep for another millennium at least."

"Okay." Justin raised his hands in surrender, wishing he hadn't brought up the subject of his grandparents.

"What about you?" Cari asked. "Are you seeing anyone?"

Justin groaned. They hadn't even got to the main course. Usually his mother at least waited until they were ordering dessert before bringing up relationships—or more specifically, his lack of commitment to one.

"Now, now, Cari," Caspian chided. "You know Justin isn't the type to settle down."

Cari gave her brother a sweet smile. "Neither was someone else I know, until the right man came along."

Justin scooted back from the table in case Caspian threw something, but he merely drew in a sharp breath and glared ominously. It seemed his father was in a good mood today. Normally, when Cari was foolish enough to bring up this particular subject, tempers flew, along with anything not nailed to the floor.

"Can we not talk about relationships at all?" Justin asked, before delivering the one line he knew Cari would accept. "It's my birthday, and I'd rather not be reminded I'm spending yet another one alone."

Cari gave him a sympathetic pat on the hand. "Oh, sweetie, you'll find someone soon. I *know* you will."

Justin didn't want to find someone, yet something in his mother's voice gave him the shivers. It wasn't so much the words, as the way she had said them. The inflection on the word know made him uncomfortable. Usually when the Goddess of Prophecy said something like that, it meant she'd had a vision. He wasn't sure he wanted to know what that vision was. He bit his tongue rather than ask the question, but Caspian was not so sensible.

"What vision have you seen?" Caspian questioned. "When was this, and why didn't you tell me?"

Justin rolled his eyes. Would the Fates spare him from overprotective parents?

Cari leaned forward eagerly. "It was this morning. I was watering the plants and all of a sudden, I saw our baby boy with a new man in his life."

"Many years down the line from now," Justin added.

"Or maybe a few weeks away." Cari gave him a small nudge and smiled. "You didn't appear any different in my vision than you do right now. And such a handsome young merman you're going to meet."

"What?" Justin gaped at the goddess. He had never in his entire life met another merman or mermaid. Not a single member of his family had bothered to come and find him since the day of his birth. The only family he had sat right here at the table with him. His mer heritage was something he tried not to think about. His mother—bless her soul—he had never had the opportunity to know, and his father clearly didn't care what had become of him. He didn't see any reason to start reaching out toward his birth family now.

"He's young, gorgeous and already heading this way," Cari continued. "I think he should be here fairly soon. Caspian will go and meet him, and pretty soon you'll be falling head over heels for our visitor."

Justin folded his arms across his chest. "I don't think so. I've got no intention of having anything to do with any merman who shows up here."

"Don't be silly, darling. You can't fight your destiny."

"I can give it a damn good try," Justin argued. "I don't need any more fish in my life and when this merman shows up here, I hope you'll send him back into the sea with orders not to bother coming back."

Caspian coughed uncomfortably. "You know I won't do that. I'm sworn to help any of the mer folk who come to land, and this includes the merman Cari has seen in her vision."

Justin didn't know the specifics about why Caspian had promised to help the mer people who chose to leave the sea. He did know he had been doing this longer than Justin had been alive, and it was because of this promise he had taken up the challenge of raising him from birth. Justin felt a small twinge of guilt that he had asked his father to refuse to help someone, even if that person was a grown merman, one more than capable of fending for himself.

"Fine. Help him if you like, but don't expect me to have anything to do with him."

"You won't be able to avoid him," Cari pointed out. "Destiny can't be thwarted by any amount of stubbornness."

"Maybe not, but I want the both of you to promise you won't try to set me up with this guy. I don't want to meet him and would much rather you encourage him to flipper back to whatever part of the ocean he swam from as soon as possible."

"He's from Atlantis," Cari informed him helpfully. "The same city your mother came from and where your father still resides."

"You two are my mother and father," Justin stated firmly. "I don't need to know the man who caused the death of my mother."

Cari patted Justin's hand. "I know you blame him for what happened, but you don't know the circumstances. Perhaps if you opened your mind to the possibility of him not being the monster you think him to be…"

"He sent my mother away when she was pregnant and if it weren't for the long journey she had to undertake, she might still be alive today. He then apparently forgets I exist for twenty-five years before..." Justin halted as he realized what words were tumbling from his lips.

"Before he sends someone to bring you home," Cari finished for him. "That *is* what you were about to say, isn't it?"

"I..." Justin shook his head to try to clear his thoughts. Knowing things without being told them was extremely disconcerting.

"You can't deny that part of your heritage either," Cari told him. "Your powers will increase over time, no matter how little you nurture them."

"I don't want these powers," Justin complained. "Do you have any idea how irritating it is to know things without being told?"

Cari smiled knowingly. "Of course I do. It's something you simply learn to live with. The gift you inherited from your mother is a precious one."

"It's a damn nuisance," Justin muttered. "Though at least the knowing things isn't quite as annoying as the actual visions. The last time one caught me by surprise, I nearly crashed the car."

Cari shook her head with obvious exasperation. "If you bothered to learn about your powers instead of rejecting them, you would start to recognize the signs of a vision coming and be able to take precautions to avoid such mishaps."

Justin fidgeted in his seat. His mother did have a point about that, though he was still reluctant to do anything to encourage his powers to manifest themselves.

Cari sighed. "I'll drop the subject for now, but I will tell you one last time that the call of Atlantis will not be denied. I have seen much of your future and no matter how much you resist, you cannot avoid your destiny. It's about to catch up with you, whether you want it to or not."

Justin nodded to acknowledge he had heard her warning, even if he had no intention of heeding it.

They ate a pleasant meal with chatter about Justin's work and his parents' latest news.

Toward the end of the meal, Justin felt the tingling at the backs of his eyes and swore under his breath. Too late to do anything about it, his vision clouded. The glass of wine fell from his hand and only Caspian's quick reflexes stopped it from shattering on the stone floor.

The vision was as all-encompassing as ever, blocking out all sights and sounds of the world around him. The single thing he was aware of in the real world was his mother's voice, soothing and calm. As the Goddess of Prophecy, she alone could connect to him when in the midst of a vision.

It took a moment for things to clear enough for him to see where he was, and when he did, a wave of panic crashed over him. He had been having visions since he'd hit his teens, yet none of them had been located under the water. He stared down at his body and saw his golden fins instead of the two legs he was used to.

He struggled against the water, trying to kick his legs, yet unable to do so. He spun head over tail as he tried to set himself to rights.

A hand appeared in his line of vision and he felt a strong grip on his arm. When he was right side up again, he opened his mouth to thank the merman who had come to his rescue, only to find he couldn't speak properly underwater.

Golden eyes watched him with amusement and for a moment, he thought he was gazing into a mirror.

Humans never had gold eyes and Justin generally wore contact lenses to make his own golden irises appear brown. The merman swimming in front of him shared his unusual eye color and when Justin glanced down, he saw he also shared the same golden fins. His hair, however, was completely different. Where Justin wore his blond hair long, this merman had short brown hair which, unlike Justin's, wasn't currently getting in the way.

Still, the similarities were enough to cause Justin to wonder if the merman might be a relative.

The stranger raised his hand toward Justin, brushing aside the wayward strands of hair, before leaning into him.

Not a relative then, Justin surmised when the stranger pressed his soft lips against Justin's.

Oh shit, he thought, as the underwater world vanished and the restaurant reappeared. Caspian and Cari watched him intently.

"What did you see?" Cari asked eagerly when it was clear Justin had returned to them.

"Nothing very interesting," Justin lied. He felt his face heat up as he recalled the kiss. Even though it had barely lasted more than a few seconds — or, more to the point, the vision had ended just when he was getting to the good part — he could still feel the lips against his.

"Let me be the judge of that," Cari insisted. "What did you see exactly?"

Justin shrugged. "I was underwater and couldn't control my movements properly. I was panicking in the water when another merman set me to rights. That was about it really."

Cari appeared skeptical, but Justin had no intention of elaborating.

The one thing all his visions had in common was they were things that would one day happen to him. He occasionally saw other people in his visions, but they were all connected to him in some way. Unlike his mother and the Oracles she had told him about, Justin only ever saw his own future. The fact that at some point in his future he would be under the water in what appeared to be a stone building terrified him. Even the thought of his rescuer's kiss didn't banish his fear.

Chapter Five

Lucas waited below the surface of the ocean for nearly an hour before going above again. When he had arrived at the place the Oracles had directed him to, there had been several groups of humans on the sandy beach. He had been too far out at sea for them to see him, and he had remained at a distance, waiting for them to depart. Unfortunately, it seemed that as soon as one group of humans left, another one arrived to take their place. The ones who had been preventing him going ashore the last time had been there with a strange creature he had never seen before. The beast ran on four legs, but was nothing like the animals he had occasionally seen on the island. Curious to know what it was, he had drifted closer to land. One of the younger humans had startled him by pointing out to sea, directly at him. Lucas had rushed below the waves and hoped the human child had simply been pointing to a bird or something else he had not noticed.

Deciding to err on the side of caution, Lucas had waited until the sky began to darken before surfacing again.

This time only one person stood on the beach. The chill in the evening air had probably sent the humans back to their homes. Lucas hoped the man pacing on the sand would leave soon.

Another hour passed and still it wasn't safe to go nearer. Lucas wondered what the man waited for. There was no one else in sight, and he didn't seem to be doing anything other than walking back and forth along the same stretch of sand.

Lucas ducked below the waves again as he contemplated finding somewhere comfortable to spend the night. The journey to land had taken nearly six weeks and he had missed his comfortable sponge every single night. He had hoped to be on land by now, preferably in one of the human buildings where he might find their equivalent of a nice soft sponge in which to curl up and sleep. Instead he found himself searching the seabed for a patch of ground without stones or human rubbish where he could rest.

* * * *

The next morning, when the sun had barely peeked over the horizon, Lucas hid his spear and swam back to the surface, where he discovered the beach had finally emptied. With firm and steady strokes, he swam for the shore as fast as he could.

The beach remained clear as he let the tide carry him in. He collapsed on the sand and waited for the few minutes it took for his fins to dry and his legs to appear. He cast several nervous glances over his shoulder as strange sounds caught his attention. He breathed a sigh of relief that no one had come across him before he got his legs.

"It's about time."

Lucas squeaked in surprise as a human appeared in front of him. It wouldn't have startled him so much if the man hadn't appeared right out of thin air. Lucas was the first to admit he didn't know a great deal about humans, but he was pretty sure they couldn't do what the man in front of him had just done.

"You do realize I have other things to do besides hang out at the beach all night?" the man complained. "You were off shore most of yesterday afternoon. I've been here since then, waiting for you to arrive. What the hell kept you?"

Lucas didn't know who this man thought he was, but he wasn't in any frame of mind to put up with his attitude. His back ached from another bad night and he was tired and cranky. He stood so he was eye-to-eye with the stranger. At least that had been his intention. The man still towered over him when Lucas was on his feet.

"The beach wasn't clear," he pointed out impatiently. "You were here."

"Waiting for you."

Lucas rolled his eyes. "And how was I supposed to know that? Our first rule when coming to land is not to let humans see what we are. Of course I waited until no one was about before I risked coming closer."

"I already know what you are."

"Again, how would I have known that last night?" A sudden thought occurred to Lucas, and he gasped in horror. The man in front of him appeared to be around twenty-five years of age, the same as the heir. "Oh no, you're not the one I'm searching for, are you? Are you the son of King Nereus and the Oracle Daphne?"

"Of course not. I'm not a merman. I'm Caspian."

"If you're not mer, how do you know about us?"

Caspian ignored his question as he looked him over. "We really don't have time for this. I have other things to do, and we need to get you sorted out if you're going to interact with the humans here in England."

"What do you mean by sorted out?" Lucas didn't like the sound of that and backed up a step or two.

"Or I could let you run around naked until you're arrested," Caspian suggested. "After keeping me waiting round here all night, I really couldn't care less either way."

Lucas recalled everyone he had seen on the beach the day before had been dressed in clothing. He had thought this had been because unlike the mer people they felt the cold more. He hadn't realized he would be expected to dress as humans did during his time away from the water. He looked Caspian up and down and cringed. The garments seemed awfully tight and restrictive.

"I don't have to wear anything like that, do I?" He gestured to Caspian's clothes.

Caspian glared at him and a moment later Lucas found himself wearing clothes. They were pink, frilly, itchy and annoying. On the plus side, they weren't anywhere near as tight as those Caspian wore.

"Do they come in other colors?" Lucas asked.

Caspian ignored the question and placed his hand on Lucas' arm. "This is something else you'll eventually need. While the one you're searching for speaks mer as fluently as English, most in this country speak the latter."

Lucas could tell Caspian had begun to speak another language. He was surprised to understand him perfectly and when he opened his mouth to say something in this new tongue, he found the words without even having to think about it.

"Do you know where the heir is?" Lucas asked, when he realized what Caspian had said.

Caspian gestured inland, away from the sea. "Do you see the car over there?"

Lucas nodded. "The thing humans travel in, right?"

"That one happens to be a taxi, with a driver waiting to take you to a place you can stay before you start your search. I've given you basic knowledge of this world and the people and things in it, which should be sufficient for your stay here."

"But you said you know the heir."

"I said no such thing," Caspian replied shortly. "I merely told you the heir speaks more than one language, as do you now. Go to the taxi and ask him to take you to this address. It isn't far. When you get there, ask for Jake. You'll need money as well. This should cover the fare."

Lucas took the pieces of paper Caspian handed to him and studied the strange markings on the top one. He could read the words without any difficulty, yet it didn't come quite as easily as speaking them. He supposed maybe that was because the mer people had no use for writing. There were inscriptions on the ancient Atlantean monuments and walls, but there was no one left who could read them. The other pieces of paper were all the same and he somehow knew this was money and how humans paid for goods and services.

"Do you understand what I'm saying to you?" Caspian asked.

"I'm not stupid," Lucas snapped.

"Then why are you standing here like an idiot?"

Lucas glared at the strange and powerful being. "There's no need to be so rude," he scolded. "I didn't ask you to interfere. I wasn't expecting your help, and I can probably do just as well without it."

Caspian folded his arms and shot him a dark glare of his own. "It would serve you right if I took back everything I just gave you, but despite your know-it-all attitude grating on my nerves, I'm actually in a good mood today, so I'll let you keep them. Now, I suggest you go to the taxi before he leaves. You'll find many humans are impatient and taxi drivers more so than most."

With that final piece of advice, Caspian vanished, leaving Lucas to hurry to the taxi.

When he approached the vehicle, the driver stared at him with obvious amusement. "Lose a bet?"

"What?"

"I asked if you lost a bet," the driver repeated as Lucas climbed into the back of the car.

"No. Can you take me to this address please?" he handed over the paper and the driver nodded.

"So, what are you running round in a tutu for?" he asked, as he steered the car out onto the road.

Lucas gripped the edge of the seat as the car sped up. Each bump caused his stomach to flip over and he hoped they arrived at their destination soon.

The driver soon seemed to realize Lucas wasn't going to answer his questions or engage in chatter, so the journey was made mostly in silence. Lucas gazed out of the window, taking in the sight of humans and the world they lived in.

The buildings were not completely dissimilar to those in the sunken city. Lucas wondered if the ones under the water might have once appeared like these human dwellings before time and the ocean took their toll.

When the car swung into a long driveway, Lucas guessed they were nearly at their destination. The road ended at a large house that seemed to be in the process of having some repairs done.

"Here you go." The driver held out his hand. "That'll be eight pounds."

Lucas counted out the money and passed it over. It didn't leave him much from what Caspian had given him and he hoped if he needed more, he would find a way to get some. He climbed out of the car and the driver hurried off without another word.

It was still early in the morning and there didn't appear to be anyone about. Lucas hoped he wasn't disturbing anybody when he banged on the door. He also sent up a quick prayer that this Jake was a bit more sociable than Caspian had been.

He was banging on the door for the third time when it finally opened. The human in front of him appeared to be half asleep.

"Can I help you?" he asked around a wide yawn.

"I'm looking for Jake," Lucas explained. "I was told to come here."

"I'm Jake. Who are you?"

"Lucas. I think you might be expecting me."

Jake shook his head. "Are you sure you've got the right Jake? I'm Jake Seabrook."

"I was just told to ask for Jake."

Jake, who seemed to be waking up a little, suddenly seemed to notice Lucas' clothing. "Did you lose a bet or something?"

Lucas frowned. "That's what the taxi driver asked."

"Well, did you?"

"No. Why do you ask?"

"Maybe because you're walking around in a pink tutu." Jake appeared to be having difficulty hiding his amusement at something, and Lucas suspected it was him.

"Is there something wrong with this? Caspian said I'd need clothes. Aren't they suitable?"

"Caspian?"

"You know him?"

"Sort of. You'd better come in. I'll see if I can find something more appropriate for you to wear."

"Um, thanks. So, who *is* Caspian?"

"He's an Atlantean god with a bit of a temper. I can't imagine what you might have said or done to piss him off enough that he'd dress you in *that*."

"He's a god? Are you sure?"

"Yeah, I'm sure."

"Are you a god, too?"

"No, though apparently I'm descended from one. It's a long story and it's too early in the morning to go into it."

"Okay."

"How come you didn't know the clothes he put you in were inappropriate?" Jake asked. "Where are you from?"

"A long way from here." Lucas wasn't sure how much he could say so he decided to keep his reply as vague as he could. Even though Caspian clearly knew him to be a merman, it didn't appear Jake did. Until he was more secure in this world, he thought it best to keep that information to himself.

"You didn't answer my question about the clothes," Jake pointed out.

Lucas didn't know what to say in response. He had the knowledge of human clothing and yet he couldn't quite figure out why Jake and the taxi driver said what he wore was wrong.

As they walked through the hallway, Lucas heard the sound of footsteps above them.

"Who was at the door?" a voice called from the floor above.

Lucas turned to see who had spoken. When he saw who it was, he dropped to his knees and bowed his head. "Your Highness," he said, as Prince Finn walked down the stairs.

Jake laughed. "I guess that answers *that* question, thankfully without my resorting to attempting to speak mer."

"What question?" the prince asked.

"Whether Lucas, our early morning visitor, is one of your people," Jake explained. "I did wonder when he mentioned Caspian, but it's not exactly something you can ask outright."

"Your Highness, forgive my intrusion in your home," Lucas said. "I'm here on a mission for your father and had no idea I would find you."

Finn gave a loud sigh. "I'm not a prince here, and there's no need to bow to me. Please get up from the floor. We're about to have breakfast and if you've just arrived, I'm guessing you're probably hungry."

"Starving," Lucas admitted as he rose.

"Just wait until you taste human food," Finn told him. "You'll never want to go home again."

"Did I hear food mentioned?" another man asked as he too came down the stairs. He stopped when he saw Lucas. "Oh shit!"

Lucas laughed at the newcomer's expression as he realized he was naked in the presence of company. His attempts to cover himself were futile.

"It's okay, Kyle," Finn explained. "Lucas is from the sunken city. He's quite familiar with naked men, or at least he should be."

Kyle relaxed and stopped covering his privates. "Why is he wearing a tutu?"

"Caspian dressed him," Jake explained.

"Wow, you must have *really* pissed him off," Kyle teased.

Finn openly studied Lucas as they followed Jake into the kitchen. "I know you, don't I?" he asked. "You worked for my father."

"I'm a junior adviser, training with my father," Lucas confirmed. "You might have seen me around the palace. I'm on a mission from King Nereus to bring his son home."

Finn stumbled. "I'm never going back to the sunken city. My home is here now."

"Um."

"If that's all you're here for, I would suggest you start your journey back home as soon as you've had breakfast and rested."

"I'm not here for you," Lucas assured him. "King Nereus has sent me for his other son."

"What are you talking about?" Finn asked.

Lucas sat at the table and explained his mission. Finn asked him a lot of questions, apparently not entirely convinced it wasn't a trick to get him to return to the city. Kyle asked a few more and Jake remained largely silent.

"Well, you can stay here until you find him," Finn finally agreed.

"Can you help me to track him down?" Lucas asked.

"I'm sorry, but I don't know where to start." Finn turned to Jake. "What about you? Any ideas?"

Jake shook his head. "If we had a name to go on, maybe, but without one I'm clueless."

Kyle chewed on his lower lip as they considered the problem. "It sounds like Caspian knows who he is. Maybe he'll point Lucas in the right direction."

"I don't think so," Lucas replied. "If he was going to do that, why didn't he just send me straight to him instead of sending me here?"

"Maybe Malcolm will know something?" Jake suggested. "He's lived here all his life. Perhaps he's heard something."

They chattered as they ate and Lucas noticed the way Finn and Kyle constantly touched each other. He smiled as he realized the rumors about the prince were true. He was a merman who desired others of the same gender, and it seemed he had found love with Kyle.

He pushed away a twinge of jealousy. The prince seemed happy with his life here and Lucas was relieved he hadn't been sent to bring him home, to a city where he would no doubt be separated from the man he loved and forced into a life of misery.

Chapter Six

When Lucas woke up later in the day, he wondered at first where he was. The bed was nothing like his sponge back in the sunken city or the rough patches of seabed he had rested on during his journey. When he remembered where he was, he smiled to himself and curled up into the warm blankets.

Rolling over in the bed, Lucas found his legs tangled up in the sheets and kicked them free. It was while he was wrestling his way out of the mess that he realized this was the first time he had ever woken up in human form. The fabric of the sheet brushed against his erection and he shivered. The sunken city was hundreds of miles away and no one here cared if he took another man into his bed. He thought back to his brother's advice about finding someone to be with who could give him what he needed. He didn't want to leave the city forever. It was his home, and his family were there, but maybe he should at least consider his options during his stay on land.

He pushed aside the sheets and let the cool air in the room wash over his heated skin. Although the next mating season wasn't until December, he felt slightly feverish as he pictured a handsome human male who might not be opposed to the idea of what Lucas had in mind to experience during his time here. Surely there must be someone out there who could make him feel the same way the other mermen felt when they came together?

The sound of the door opening yanked him from his thoughts and he climbed out of bed. Jake crept into the room, clearly trying to be quiet.

"Oh, you're awake. Sorry. Did I disturb you?"

Lucas shook his head. "No, I was already awake."

"Good. I just brought you some more suitable clothes."

The pink tutu, as Jake and the others had called it, was on a chair in the corner of the room. "Thanks. I think I'm going to need some help to get used to clothes."

Jake grinned. "Don't worry. If you're anything like Kyle and Finn, you'll just put up with them in public and spend the rest of the time wandering round naked. Just don't forget to put something on when you do go out. I've also brought you a pair of sunglasses."

"What are they?"

Jake held up the strange item and put them onto his face. "They protect our eyes from the bright sun, and in your case, they'll hide those pretty golden eyes."

"Is there something wrong with my eyes?"

"No, of course not, but human eyes don't come in as many colors as the mer people's do. They are mostly blue, brown or green. Golden might draw attention you don't want." Jake took the glasses off and placed them on top of the pile of clothing.

"Oh." Lucas took the bundle of clothes from Jake. The material didn't feel as scratchy as the tutu, but he was still reluctant to put any of them on just yet. Everything was still so new and unfamiliar. He placed the clothes on the bed.

"Thanks. Um…"

"What is it?" Jake asked.

"I know it's not your problem, but have you had any ideas how I can go about finding the lost heir?"

Jake shook his head. "I'm sorry. I wish I knew where to start. We asked Malcolm and Coral and neither of them know anything about where he might be. Coral only arrived in Atlantis after the mermaid carrying the child had left."

"They don't know of any other mer here?"

"Unfortunately not. The thing is, most humans don't believe you exist."

"Me?"

"Mer people," Jake clarified. "I know why you keep your fins secret, and I don't blame you in the slightest, but when you're all hiding what you are, it makes it pretty much impossible to find one of you amongst so many humans that live on land. I could know a dozen mermen and mermaids without even knowing it."

"How am I ever going to find him?" Lucas didn't want to sound this disheartened so soon in his mission, but he truly had no idea where to start his search.

"I think Caspian is our best option," Jake said after a few moments thought. "From what he told you, he clearly knows who he is, even if he wasn't willing to tell you anything else. We need to find a way to get that information out of him, though I really don't know how we're going to manage it."

"Do you know where he lives?" Lucas asked. "I clearly did something to offend him when I arrived. Maybe if I go and apologize, he'll be more helpful."

Jake laughed and shook his head. "I have no idea. He's a god. For all I know, he could live in another dimension or something. Finding him could take as long as finding the heir, if not even longer. He just shows up when it suits him, which isn't very often."

Lucas sat on the edge of the bed and gave another loud sigh. "I don't think I had any idea how difficult this was going to be when I agreed to come here. I hadn't a clue just how many humans there are."

"And you've only seen a few of us locals. We don't even know if the heir stayed here in this area after his mother came to land. He could have moved to another town or even another country."

Lucas swallowed hard. He felt the enormity of the task ahead of him weighing down on his shoulders. How was he ever going to find one single merman in a whole world of humans? Especially if the merman in question didn't want to be found.

Jake didn't seem to have any suggestions and so left him to think things over while settling in.

Lucas took some time to explore the bedroom and the furniture it contained. Everything appeared so clean and well kept. The wooden chest of drawers wasn't decayed and rotting like the wood he had seen under the ocean. He ran his hand over the polished surface as he stared into the mirror above it. He had never seen his reflection so clearly before. There were no mirrors in the sunken city. If there had ever been any, they were long since broken and the mer people had no knowledge of how to make new ones.

He took a few minutes to study himself. His golden eyes were bright and he picked up the sunglasses. He tried them on and grimaced at how dark everything became. He removed them and decided he would only wear them if he had to leave the house. After living most of his life under the ocean, at depths where the rays of the sun never reached, he was eager to see the world above. Although he could see perfectly well under the ocean, everything there was dim and murky. Even the island was shrouded in darkness since he mostly went there at night. Now he saw the world in a completely different light, literally.

He ran his hands through his hair and tried to straighten it out a little. He didn't recall it getting quite so messy under the ocean, or maybe it had and he simply hadn't noticed due to the lack of a reflection.

His stomach growled and he decided to go in search of something to eat. Jake had told him to make himself at home, and they had made sure he knew what and where the fridge was. He hoped one day he could repay the kindness they had shown him.

Wandering down the stairs, Lucas took in everything around him. The carpet on the floor beneath his bare feet, the way the light shone through the windows, making rainbows appear on the walls. The faint smell of paint as well as the strong smell of flowers from the vase on the table at the foot of the stairs.

From the back of the house came the sound of water splashing and he remembered being shown the large swimming pool earlier in the day. All thoughts of food vanished from his mind at the idea of going for a swim. He had never had his legs for such a lengthy period of time before. He hoped a swim in his other form might give him some clarity and maybe an idea for what his next move might be.

He walked toward the entrance to the pool, eager to regain his fins for a little while. He was about to dive into the water when he noticed what he had walked in on. Deciding not to disturb Kyle and Finn at such an intimate moment, Lucas chose instead to get dressed and head for the beach.

There was a chill to the air and a light rain fell as he hurried down the driveway and back to the beach and the sanctuary of the ocean.

By the time he reached the beach, the rain was falling heavily and the wind howled. Lucas found a secluded spot, ducked behind some nearby rocks and stripped out of his clothes, hiding them safely away until he came back to land. Even if he decided to give up so soon in his quest, he would want to return the items to their owner before he left. He ran into the waves and dove beneath them, relief flooding through him as his fins appeared and he felt the comforting waters surround his body. He sank to the bottom of the seabed and stretched out on his back. Above him, he could see the occasional lightning strike in the dark sky. The wind was strong, and he had a feeling the storm would pass quickly.

Sure enough, an hour later the sky lightened and the rain stopped. He decided to go ashore quickly, before he found himself trapped in the water again when the humans came to the beach once more.

He wrung out the wet shorts as best he could and tugged them on. He was just doing the same with the shirt when he realized he wasn't alone. A beautiful woman stood before him. Her dark hair flowed over her shoulders in waves. It was obvious that unlike him, she had not been caught in the rain. Her clothes were strange, not like those the other human women wore. They seemed old-fashioned and reminded him of the clothing he had seen the Atlanteans of centuries ago wearing in the wall murals in the city.

"You're one of the gods, aren't you?" he asked.

"Yes. I'm Cari."

Lucas frowned as the goddess continued to watch him with a small smile playing on her lips. "I don't want to be rude, but what do you want with me?"

Cari smiled. "Just a little conversation. I was curious about who had come here seeking my Justin."

"Justin?" Lucas gasped. "Do you mean the heir?"

"Yes. I wanted to make sure you didn't give up on your search for him just yet."

"I nearly did," Lucas admitted.

"I know."

"How?"

Cari simply gazed back at him and with a wave of her hand his clothes dried.

"Thanks," he said as he fumbled with the buttons of his borrowed shirt. "So, where is this Justin?"

"I can't tell you. He's not quite ready to meet you yet."

"He knows I'm here to find him?"

"I don't think he knows you've arrived, but he's known for a while you're coming here."

Cari didn't elaborate, but Lucas guessed either she or Caspian had warned Justin of him. Suddenly, he remembered how Cari had referred to the heir as 'my Justin'. He wondered if they were lovers and how that worked. Justin, as far as he knew, was merely a merman, while Cari was clearly a goddess. The thought had barely entered his mind when Cari gave a soft chuckle and shook her head. "No, my young merman, Justin isn't my lover. I have raised him as my son, and, I assure you, I'm not his type."

"You can read my mind?"

"All gods have the power to read the minds of mortals, though most rarely bother to do so, as they don't interact with them much."

"Are you saying Caspian could read my mind too?"

"Yes, though since you weren't very good at keeping your opinions to yourself, it made little difference that he could. Anyway, like I said, I'm not Justin's type. Though the same can't be said for you."

Lucas scrambled for the word humans used to describe lovers of other men. "Justin's gay?"

"Very much so. If you want to learn about the pleasures to be found between two men, my Justin is rather well versed in such matters."

"I don't know what you mean," Lucas lied.

"Do you truly believe you can lie to a goddess?" Cari chuckled and patted his arm. "I know what is in your mind and I can see what future lies ahead of you, if you continue on the path you have chosen."

Lucas shivered even though he didn't feel the cold.

"I'm the Goddess of Prophecy," Cari explained. "It is through me the Oracles receive their gifts, and they see only a small portion of what I do. I can see the future of every mortal who walks this Earth."

"Are you saying you know whether or not I'll find Justin?"

Cari smiled again and hooked her arm through his as she guided him back up the sand. "I'm sure you will find him."

"If I'm going to find him anyway, why can't you just tell me where he is and get it over with?"

"I already told you, Justin isn't quite ready to meet you yet. He needs a little more time."

"How much time? Can you tell me what day to go find him?"

"I'm afraid not. Your future is not set in stone."

"But you said I would find him and that you could see my future."

"You will and I can, but your future can always be changed if you find yourself on a path that isn't the one for you. Then my vision of your life will change with it. Predicting the future isn't an exact science."

"So if I just swam off right now, whatever you saw of my future would be wrong?"

"But you're not going to swim back home, are you?" Since she was steering him away from the water, he didn't have much of a choice.

"That's not the point. Either you can see the future or you can't. You can tell me now that I'm definitely going to find the heir, but I might do something to change that at any minute and so what you've told me is totally useless."

"That's right."

"Then what's the point of seeing the future if it changes all the time?"

"Because those who have the gift to see what is to come can alter their own destinies."

Lucas sighed. "You're not going to tell me where Justin is, are you?"

"No, but if you stay on your current course, it won't be long before you find him. Convincing him to travel to Atlantis with you might take considerably longer."

Lucas stopped walking and faced the goddess. "He doesn't want to meet his father?"

"As far as Justin is concerned, Caspian and I are his parents. We raised him together and he has known no other family."

"But surely he knows you can't be his biological parents. He's a merman!"

Cari shook her head and gave him a pained look. "Of course he knows he isn't our natural child, but we're still his family. We watch out for each other, all three of us."

"I'm surprised you're even telling me this much if he doesn't want to be found."

Cari took hold of his arm and held it tight. "Close your eyes."

"Why?"

"Okay, don't," Cari replied as a flash of white light temporarily blinded him.

When his vision returned, he realized he was back on the front step of Jake's house. He rubbed his eyes and waited for the spots to disappear.

"If you'd taken my advice, you'd be able to see perfectly well right now," Cari commented. "Perhaps you might like to consider my other piece of advice. Give Justin time before you track him down."

Lucas huffed. "It's not like I have any choice, is it? I have no idea where to find him."

Cari's chuckle lingered in the air after she had vanished.

"Where have you been?" Jake asked as Lucas opened the door. "I see you found somewhere to shelter from the storm."

"Not exactly," Lucas mumbled.

"Hey, Lucas." Jake stopped him from walking away. "Has something happened?"

"I just had a visit from the heir's mother."

Jake stared at him in obvious surprise. "I thought his mother had died?"

"Not his real mother, the woman—or should I say goddess?—who raised him with Caspian."

"So that's how Caspian knows about him?"

"Yes. His name is Justin and according to his mother, I *will* find him. I just have to be patient because apparently he isn't ready for all this yet."

"Well, that's good, isn't it?"

"Yes, except it means I'll have to impose on you all for even longer."

"It's no imposition. This place is huge, and as you can see, we're in the middle of fixing it up. An extra pair of hands when we're doing the heavy lifting would be more than adequate payment for your room and board."

Lucas stuck out his hand for Jake to shake. "Deal."

Chapter Seven

Justin found Caspian waiting for him at home for the first time since his birthday.

"You're late home tonight," Caspian commented.

"We all went for drinks to celebrate Jodie's engagement. She's actually found someone crazy enough to marry her." Justin grinned at his father to show he was teasing. Caspian had met Jodie on several occasions and thought her to be a charming young lady. "Have you been waiting here long?"

"Just an hour or so."

"Why didn't you ask Mum where I was?" Justin asked. "Surely the all-seeing goddess would have known where to find me."

"I'm sure she would, but she's been a little busy."

"Yeah?"

Caspian nodded. "Our powers are being boosted all the time and for Cari, that means more visions than usual. She was in the middle of her third for the day when I dropped in to see her this afternoon."

Justin didn't like the sound of that. "My visions aren't going to get more frequent, are they?"

"Probably. Your visions are inherited from your birth mother and her gift is traced back to Cari. As the other gods awaken, all our powers will increase and those who have received gifts from the gods will find their talents expanding."

Justin sighed. He had hoped for a different answer to his question. "Is that why you're here? To warn me about the visions increasing?"

"No, I thought you might enjoy hearing about the latest merman to visit our fair shores."

"Why would I? I've no interest in him, any more than I cared about the others to come here. Let them go on their way and stay out of mine."

"Lucas doesn't want to stay out of your way," Caspian told him. "He's here to find you."

"Well, he can carry on searching. Eventually he'll get bored and swim back to where he came from."

"He's quite a determined young man," Caspian replied. "I suspect he'll stay here in England indefinitely until he tracks you down."

"You haven't told him where I am, have you?" Justin glared at his father, who wasn't phased in the slightest.

"Not yet."

"Dad, you can't do this to me!"

Caspian laughed. "I'm not doing anything to you. Lucas has swum six weeks straight to get here. He wants to see you and bring you home to Atlantis. Maybe you could at least hear him out?"

"England is my home," Justin reminded him. "Atlantis is just some city that sank below the ocean so long ago no one even believes it existed anymore."

"Oh there are plenty of people who believe in Atlantis, most of those being the mer people who live there. They call it the sunken city and it has been their home since it sank."

"You're missing my point. Why would I want to leave England? I've lived here all my life. I've got my home, my job, my friends and my family. I don't need some merman showing up here and turning my life upside down."

"Maybe your life could do with shaking up a little," Caspian suggested. "You've been stuck in a rut the last couple of years."

"I'm perfectly happy with my life just as it is. What you call a rut, I call content."

Caspian shook his head in obvious frustration. "Your mother asked me to give you a message."

"What's that?"

"She told me to tell you, you shouldn't be afraid of your future, but of the life not lived."

Justin rolled his eyes. "Who said I'm afraid? Just because I'm not falling all over myself to go find this merman."

"Cari was right about him being your type," Caspian commented. "He looks similar to most of the men you go for, except for his eyes, which are the same as your own."

That caught Justin's attention. "He has golden eyes?"

"And fins," Caspian confirmed.

"Obviously," Justin muttered. According to his parents, all mer people's eye color matched their fins. It was all well and good for those who lived under the water—or who had green or blue fins—but the more unusual colorings made life a little difficult for those who needed to pass for human.

"So, how about you come round for dinner this weekend, and we invite Lucas—to see how he's getting on?" Caspian suggested.

"How about we don't?" Justin countered. "I don't need you or Mum trying to set me up."

"Set you up?"

Justin jumped at the disembodied female voice that didn't belong to his mother. "Who's that?"

A flash of red in front of him caused spots to appear in front of his eyes. When the spots had receded a beautiful woman stood before him.

"Who the hell are you?" he asked.

"I'm Medina, Goddess of Love." The stranger greeted him with a bright smile.

"Haven't you ever heard of knocking before barging into someone's home?" Justin snapped. "Not to mention it's rude to eavesdrop on private conversations."

"Oh, don't be like that." Medina's voice positively cooed. "The Goddess of Love hears everything when it comes to matters of the heart. You might call it an occupational hazard."

Justin snorted. "I still call it eavesdropping or sticking your nose into someone else's business."

Medina didn't seem to appreciate his comments. Instead of leaving, she settled down on the sofa, spreading her long gauzy robes out around her. Justin supposed at least she wasn't out in public in clothing that was not only centuries out of fashion, but also borderline indecent.

Caspian gave a nervous-sounding cough. "Medina, perhaps this isn't the best time for a visit."

"Why ever not? We're talking matters of the heart here, after all."

Justin glared at her. "No we're not. We're talking about matters which don't concern you."

Medina waved him away and focused her attention on Caspian. "How about I help your boy here win the man of his dreams?"

"Justin is perfectly capable of finding men all on his own. He doesn't need magical interference."

"You're not still sore about what happened all those years ago, are you?"

Justin's ears perked up as his father's expression became cold as ice. Something told him the history between Caspian and Medina was far more complex than him spurning her affections. He wondered what had transpired between them, yet didn't dare ask. If there was one thing Justin had learned in the last twenty-five years, it was never to ask Caspian about his past. Or if you did, then not to expect an answer.

"Why don't you just fuck off and leave us alone?" Justin snapped at the goddess. "You weren't invited here, and we don't need your so-called help."

Medina shot him an ugly glare. "What did you just say to me?"

"Now, now, Medina," Caspian interrupted. "Justin didn't mean any insult. It's just modern terminology."

Medina shook off Caspian's soothing hand. "I came here today with nothing except good intentions. I thought I could mend some bridges and make a few new friends in this strange world I find myself in. Most people are grateful to receive a gift of love from me. They don't throw it back in my face."

"Most people don't believe in you anymore," Justin snarled.

Medina clutched a hand to her breast as though wounded. "Now that was just cruel."

"Justin didn't mean it." Caspian tried to appease her. "Perhaps an apology might help."

"It might," Justin agreed. "If she apologies for coming in here unannounced and interfering, I might refrain from physically throwing her out."

"Justin!" Caspian snapped. "I meant you apologize to Medina for being so rude to her."

"*Me* being rude?" Justin shouted. "I can't believe you're taking her side in this."

"I'm not taking any side."

Medina stood and walked over to Justin. "You need to learn a lesson."

Caspian continued to try to smooth things over, but Medina wasn't listening to him at all.

"You believe you can refuse my gift so rudely? Think again, mortal. I give you the gift of love anyway. You will find love very soon, and it will be the greatest love of your life. Your soulmate is close and I will ensure you find each other, regardless of how hard you try to avoid your fate."

"Great, thanks. Is that all?" Justin asked. "Can we get back to the conversation we were having before you showed up now?"

"I haven't finished," Medina replied. "Love you will find, but only for a short time. As soon as that love is consummated, the clock will begin ticking."

"What do you mean?"

"The love you find will be taken from you, never to be found again."

"No!" Caspian grabbed Medina's arm. "Don't do this. Justin, apologize to Medina, now."

"It's too late," Medina declared. "It's done. Since Justin scorns love, it won't matter to him if he loses it. Will it?"

She reached out her hand and placed it on Justin's chest. He could feel a sharp burn through the fabric of his shirt.

Without another word, Medina vanished from the room, leaving Justin and Caspian alone once more.

"What have you done?" Caspian whispered.

"Oh come on," Justin scorned. "What does it matter what the Goddess of Love does? Her threats aren't exactly dire."

Caspian shook his head. "You have no idea how powerful Medina is. She's the most powerful of our kind awake right now, and she's just cursed you."

"Is that what you call it?" Justin laughed. "Sounded to me like she promised I'd enjoy a quick fling with my soulmate before he leaves. I've always been the love 'em and leave 'em type. If that's her idea of a curse, she needs to up her game a bit."

Caspian scowled and gestured for him to undo his shirt. "Just as I thought."

"What is it?" Justin asked. He squinted down to see what Caspian was staring at and saw a mark that appeared to be some kind of three pronged fork on his chest. He rubbed at it yet it refused to go.

"The mark of the trident," Caspian explained.

"Which means?"

"It means you've been touched by a goddess. Sometimes it's a good thing, that you've been blessed with a gift."

"I take it that isn't what this means today."

"Considering the temper she was in when she left, no. She has marked you to show you've been cursed."

"How bad can it be?" Justin asked.

Caspian sucked in a sharp breath through his teeth. "Very. Medina's curses are some of the worst you can get, and she has just cursed you to find love and lose it. You truly have no idea what this means."

"Well, why don't you explain it to me? Because right now I'm not seeing this as being that big a deal."

"You've never been in love." Caspian sighed and for the first time Justin realized his father had once been in love and very deeply too. "You have no idea what it's like to find the one person who completes you, to know there will never be anyone else who loves you as much as he does. To lose your other half kills something inside you. You can try to move on and find another, yet always you'll remember what it was like when you were in the arms of your soulmate."

"You sound as if you're talking from experience." Justin knew even without Caspian's confirmation that it was true.

Caspian walked toward the window, a faraway expression in his eyes. "It doesn't matter whether it's a year ago, a thousand years or more. You still see his face when you close your eyes, can hear his laughter and ache for his touch. I would never have wanted you to go through such agony, yet now Medina has cursed you to suffer in just such a way."

"Maybe I could apologize to her," Justin suggested. "I still think she shouldn't have butted in, but if it puts your mind at ease, perhaps I could try to smooth her feathers."

"It's too late for a simple apology to set things right."

Before Justin could think of another suggestion, Cari popped into the flat, in much the same way Medina had done.

"What have you done?" she cried, as she threw herself at Justin and wrapped him up in a tight hug. Tears streamed down her face and she began to cry.

"What did you see?" Caspian asked.

Whatever her vision had shown her, Cari was unable to put it into words. She sobbed uncontrollably and Justin wasn't sure he wanted to know the answer to his father's question.

"You have to fix this," Cari begged between hiccups. "You can't lose him. You just can't."

"Lose who?" Justin asked. "I don't even know who this guy is."

Cari sniffled. "Lucas is the one I saw in my vision, but I suspect you already know that, don't you?"

Justin couldn't deny it. Somehow he knew it had to be the visiting merman.

"We'll find a way to sort this out," Caspian promised.

"How about I just avoid Lucas altogether?" Justin suggested.

"And how do you think that'll help?" Cari asked.

"Well, you know what they say about not missing what you never had. If I don't meet Lucas, I won't fall for him, won't have sex with him and won't lose him either. Simple. Avoidance of Lucas equals no way for the curse to come true."

"I don't know." Cari frowned and the expression on her face said she had her doubts about his plan. "Soulmates do tend to find each other. Take it from someone who knows. And like I keep telling you, you can't avoid your destiny."

"Who says it's my destiny to even meet Lucas? There are millions of people who go through their lives without ever meeting their soulmates, and they enjoy perfectly happy and contented lives. Why shouldn't I do the same?"

"Because we want the best for you," Cari said. "That's all we've ever wanted for you. We raised you as our own and hoped one day you would find a soulmate to make your life as wonderful as it could possibly be. Now, thanks to your temper, you'll never know what it means to be truly in love and to share your life with the one person who completes you."

* * * *

Lucas sat in the living room with Jake and the others when the second beautiful woman appeared out of nowhere in front of him. Jake's dog, Treacle, who had previously been sprawled out on the floor near Lucas' feet, gave a loud yelp before running from the room.

Jake glanced up at the stranger and tried to wave her out of the way of the television, which was showing a film they were all enjoying. "Most people call first, or at least knock on the door," he complained.

The woman didn't seem particularly bothered by his comment, though she moved out of the way.

"This is Medina," Finn explained to Lucas. "She's the Atlantean Goddess of Love and one of Jake's distant ancestors. She comes by sometimes to visit."

"To make sure we don't forget about her," Kyle added. "Gods and goddesses gain power from having people believe in them."

Jake snorted. "And when they keep popping in like this, it's rather difficult not to."

"I thought you liked my visits." Medina sat on one of the chairs and crossed her legs. "You're my only real family, Jake. You know I enjoy spending time with you."

"So you keep saying," Jake muttered. "I'm just at a bit of a loss as to why."

"I thought you'd be pleased I now have the power to come and visit. Whenever I'd summon one of you to my temple, you'd complain about it being inconvenient. Now I'm fully awake, it's not necessary to pull you from your lives. I can just pop in for a chat like anyone else."

Jake picked up the remote control and switched the television off. "So, this is just a social visit?"

"Social for you, but business for Lucas. I'm here to help him on his quest."

Lucas sat up straight. "You know why I'm here in England?"

"Of course, and I can help you with your mission. As a goddess, I can locate anyone I choose to and I can tell you everything about Justin from the name of his first boyfriend to the length of his penis."

Jake snorted and shook his head. "I don't see how that will help Lucas find him. Addresses and telephone numbers are much more helpful."

"A little under eight inches," said Medina, as though Jake hadn't spoken.

"I can see how knowing *that* will help Lucas find him," Kyle commented with a fair amount of sarcasm. "What's he going to do? Go round measuring guys' dicks?"

Medina shot him a sour glance. "Of course not. Justin works in an aquarium just a little way down the coast."

"He does?" Lucas gazed hopefully at Jake. "Do you know where that is?"

"Sure. We used to go there on school trips. It's not far. Maybe half an hour in the car."

"It'd be even quicker if we had help from a goddess," Lucas hinted.

Medina smiled. "It would indeed, but I'm afraid my powers are still quite weak from my long rest, not to mention everything I have had to learn to acclimatize to in this modern world. Strange words to learn and peculiar cultures to study. Mortals and their ways and habits have changed so much in the time since I was last here. It's most tiring indeed trying to keep up. While I can transport myself, I'm not so sure I can carry you with me with any degree of accuracy. As Jake said, it's not very far, so I'm sure you'll be able to get there in no time."

"Thank you." Lucas jumped up.

"Where are you going?" Jake asked.

"You aren't going to take me to the aquarium?"

Jake pointed toward the clock. "It's ten o'clock on a Sunday night. The place will be closed. How about I drive you over there tomorrow morning?"

Lucas was disappointed, but he didn't see he had any choice. He supposed one more night—especially one spent in a comfortable bed—wouldn't make much difference. At least now he had a good chance of actually finding Justin. Even though Cari had told him he would find the heir, he had been starting to lose hope in the light of the days passing with no further word from the goddess who had raised the man he searched for.

That settled, Medina focused on Jake. "And how are you coping with your new powers?"

Lucas couldn't hide his surprise. *Jake had powers?*

"Trying to ignore them as much as I can," Jake muttered. "Thanks for asking. Any chance you can take them back from me?"

Medina laughed and shook her head. "Don't be silly. You can do so much good with your powers."

"All they've done so far is cause trouble."

"That's because you're not used to them. In time you'll be more accustomed to them, and you'll be able to spread love all around the world."

Finn snickered into Kyle's shoulder. Lucas wasn't sure what the joke was, unless Jake was the type to be with a lot of different men. He hadn't seen him bring any dates back to the house, though. He seemed to be quite happy being single.

"What powers are you talking about?" Lucas asked.

"Jake is one of my descendants," Medina explained. "When we connected, he inherited a few little powers from me. Nothing dangerous, but things to help the course of true love run smoothly."

"They're a nuisance," Jake complained. "I might say something like 'you're the type to go throw yourself at the next man you meet' and you'd do it without meaning to."

"What a marvelous idea," Medina murmured quietly.

A flash of lightning lit up the room, even though the sky was clear and the forecast didn't predict a storm.

"What have you done?" Jake shot to his feet and strode over to Medina.

"I haven't done a thing. You're the one who spoke the words."

"The last thing we need is for Lucas to go throw himself at the postman or something."

"Oh he won't." Medina gave them a smug smile. "I have a much better idea."

"What. Have. You. Done?" Jake enunciated each word carefully and slowly, but Medina vanished from the room instead of replying.

Lucas cringed under the stares of the other three men. "What just happened?"

"I think Medina might have caused me to put some form of love spell on you," Jake admitted. "I'm sorry. I was just trying to explain how my powers work."

"I don't think it was your fault," Kyle said. "The lightning didn't flash until after she spoke. I think she just had an idea from your words and decided to carry it through."

Jake sat back down in his chair and put his head in his hands. "I should have kept my mouth shut."

"Maybe we're worrying for nothing," Lucas speculated. "I'm not the type to throw myself at anyone, least of all another man."

Kyle and Finn rolled their eyes at each other and shook their heads.

"I'm not!" Lucas insisted.

Kyle chuckled. "Well, we'll soon find out."

"What do you mean?"

Finn took up the explanation. "The powers can't make anyone do something they don't already want to do. If you really aren't attracted to other men, you've nothing to worry about."

"But if you are, you'll be throwing yourself at someone before the week is done," Kyle finished.

"Maybe I'll just stay here until it wears off," Lucas suggested.

"I doubt that'll work. You'll just be putting off the inevitable."

Lucas didn't like the sound of that at all. He just hoped his new friends were wrong and that his own resolve to keep a distance from men would be enough to stop him from making a fool of himself.

Chapter Eight

The next morning Jake drove Lucas to the aquarium so he could finally track down Justin.

"Do you want me to go in with you?" Jake asked.

Lucas peered through the glass doors toward the ticket counter. Jake had given him money for a ticket, and there was a short queue waiting to get in. The woman at the desk smiled and waved the guests through the door behind her with a cheery smile.

"It's a woman at the counter," Jake commented needlessly.

Lucas had not met anyone new since Medina's visit the evening before. He still didn't believe he would be foolish enough to throw himself at anyone. Maybe less determined people fell foul of love spells, but he was not such a merman.

"I think I'll be okay. I'll just go in and ask if Justin's working today. If he is, I'll buy a ticket and ask where to find him."

"What if you... You know...?"

"I'm not going to throw myself at some stranger," Lucas insisted.

"I don't think you understand how powerful the spells can be. You won't be in control of yourself."

"I'm always in control of myself," Lucas argued as he opened the car door.

Jake sighed in frustration. "Okay, suit yourself. I'll wait here until you've asked at the desk. If he's not working today, we'll come back when he is. If he is, and you go in there, you'll have to make your own way back home." He pointed across the road. "The bus back will stop there. You've got enough money for the fare. You need the number eight. Got it?"

"Yes."

"Right. I've got to get to work, so I'll just hold on until you've asked at the counter."

Lucas climbed out of the car and went inside the building.

There were only two people in front of him, an older couple who were talking about seeing the new shark exhibit. Lucas shivered at the idea of sharks being so close to them. He had been lucky not to have encountered many of the creatures during his life. The sea dragons that protected the sunken city by cloaking it in invisibility also made sure no sharks came within the boundaries. He had seen a few sharks during his journey, but he had managed to keep them at a safe distance. He knew the mer clans who lived their lives outside of the city were not so lucky. Shark attacks were the most common form of death for all mer people outside of the protected underwater city.

"Good morning," the lady at the counter — Amy, according to her name tag — greeted him.

"Hello." Lucas gave her what he hoped was a friendly smile. "I was wondering if Justin might be working today."

Amy gave him a quick once-over. "He is, but not if you're here to cause trouble."

"I'm not. I promise." He put his money on the counter. "Can I get a ticket please?"

Amy rang up his purchase and passed him his change and receipt.

"Where in the aquarium is he working today?"

"I'm not sure, but you'll find him sooner or later. He'll be in one of the rooms answering questions at this time. Just follow the route through."

"Thanks."

Lucas pocketed his change and after giving a wave to Jake, he walked through the doors. The dim lighting reminded him immediately of being under the ocean and he found himself feeling a little homesick. He studied each tank as he went through the building. The place didn't seem very busy, and he took his time wandering round. There were a few staff members scattered through the rooms but none of them had the name tag Justin. He avoided eye contact with the men, just in case there was something in Medina's spell. When he found Justin, he would know for sure.

When he finally located Justin, he didn't need the name tag to know who he was. The resemblance to King Nereus was unmistakable. He had the same blond hair, though Justin wore his tied back. The strong jaw was also familiar. In fact the only real difference was the dark brown eyes, which while common for humans, were unusual in a merman. Justin's name tag was merely an additional confirmation.

He approached him nervously. "Hi."

Justin gave him a wide grin. "Good morning," he replied, stretching out the words as he gave Lucas a long and thorough once over that was blatantly flirtatious. "And what can I do for you this fine day?"

Lucas lost the ability to speak in the face of Justin's smile. The borrowed jeans he wore had never felt as tight as they did right now. He tried to gather his thoughts, but the only thing going through his mind was that Justin was the most attractive merman he had ever seen and he wanted him. He pushed his desire aside, blaming Medina's spell and ignoring what the others had told him — the spell wouldn't work at all if there was no attraction to build on.

Justin watched him with an amused smile on his face. Lucas suddenly realized he was waiting for an answer.

Another guest brushed past him on the way to the next room and he stumbled slightly. Justin held his arms out to steady him and the moment his hand touched Lucas' arm, he lost what little remained of his control.

"Come home with me," he begged, right before he threw his arms around Justin's neck and kissed him hard on the lips.

Justin didn't seem to be kissing him back, but when Lucas rubbed up against him, he could feel Justin's hardness pressing back against his own. Justin pulled out of the kiss and tried to set Lucas back a little.

"Sorry, but, as you can see, I'm working at the moment. This really isn't the best time to do this. Maybe you'd like to come back later, after I've finished my shift?"

Lucas reached down between them and squeezed Justin's erection through the coarse fabric. "Want you now. Need you in me."

Justin moaned as he moved Lucas' hand away. "Tempting as you are, I kind of like my job. I don't particularly want to get fired."

Lucas ignored him as he lowered the zip of Justin's jeans and slid his hand inside. "Come to the sunken city with me."

"What did you say?" Justin pushed Lucas away, more forcibly this time and his voice had changed from amused and flirtatious to outright suspicious.

Lucas threw himself at Justin once again. "I've come such a long way to find you. Come back with me. Let me show you the wonders of the ocean."

Justin glared at him. "You're Lucas, aren't you? You're the one my father has sent. Well, now you've found me, you can just leave again. You can go back to Atlantis and tell my father to get stuffed. He didn't want me and my mother twenty-five years ago, and I don't want anything to do with him now."

Lucas could tell Justin was angry, but still he couldn't seem to set aside his desire for him long enough to have a sensible conversation. "I want you to take me... hard. Right here, right now."

"That's not going to happen," Justin snapped. "Now are you going to leave or am I going to have you escorted from the building?"

"What's going on here?"

Lucas jumped as a stranger approached them. He growled at the interruption and clung to Justin.

"This visitor was just leaving," Justin explained.

"Come with me," Lucas pleaded as he pushed his hand inside Justin's pants and squeezed him again, delighted when he felt the flesh hardening to his touch.

Justin jerked back. "Stop that!"

The other man stepped closer. "I'm going to have to ask you to leave," he said as he yanked Lucas away from Justin. He glared at Justin. "In future I'd appreciate it if you didn't bring your personal life to work."

"I didn't," Justin argued. "He just showed up here. I've never even met him."

"You don't expect me to believe that, do you? I come in here to find him all over you and his hand round your dick."

"It's the truth. I've never seen him before in my life, and I'd be happy to never lay eyes on him again."

Lucas struggled against the grip of the man who was taking him away from Justin, but the guard was too strong for him and quickly escorted him out of the aquarium.

The minute Justin was out of his sight, Lucas' mind began to clear. Mortified at how he had behaved, he mumbled apologies to the man and ran from the building.

How could he have behaved in such a disgraceful manner? He'd forced his attentions on a man who clearly had no interest in him at all. Any chance he had of convincing Justin to come to the sunken city had been well and truly blown. How could he ever convince him to even talk to him again, let alone give up his entire life here in England?

Dejected and furious with both himself and Medina for her interference, he walked to the bus stop and sat to wait for the vehicle to arrive to take him home.

* * * *

When he arrived back at Jake's, he dove straight into the pool. He needed to swim to gather his thoughts together. He still couldn't believe he had thrown himself at Justin in such a blatant manner. What must the heir think of him?

He swam for hours, back and forth along the length of the pool. Finally he surfaced to find Jake watching him.

"How long have you been there?"

"A while."

"Why didn't you join me?" Lucas asked, as he swam to the edge of the pool.

"You seemed to want some time alone. I'm guessing the meeting with Justin didn't go as well as you'd hoped."

Lucas snorted. "You could say that. You could also call it a total disaster."

"What happened?"

"I threw myself at him," Lucas admitted. "I don't know what came over me. It was as if I had no control over my actions."

"That sounds like a result of Medina's spell."

"I thought so too, but it makes no difference. It still means the heir thinks I'm some sex-crazed lunatic."

"I'm sure if you explain things to him, he'll understand."

"I'm not so sure. He wasn't exactly pleased to see me when he found out who I was."

Lucas lifted himself out of the water and once he had his legs back he walked over to Jake. "How can a spell make me do something so out of character?"

"Is it really out of character?" Jake asked. "Come on, *really*?"

Lucas knew exactly what Jake hinted at.

"Medina's love spells can't make someone attracted to someone of the same gender if they aren't already, er, that way inclined."

Lucas hung his head. "Even if I were attracted to him, it's not in my nature to throw myself at someone like that."

"That part would be the spell. It doesn't give you feelings that you don't usually have. It releases your inhibitions."

"Are you sure?"

Jake nodded firmly. "I have a few powers that I've inherited from Medina and that's how they seem to work. They're new to me, but I'm learning about them."

The sound of a footfall behind them drew Lucas' attention away from Jake. Finn stood there with a sympathetic expression on his face.

"I'm sorry I gave Medina the idea for the spell," Jake offered. "I need to watch what I say when she's around."

"It's not your fault. You didn't know what was going to happen. I should have had more control over myself."

"You've got plenty of control if you ask me," Finn commented. "You've grown up in the sunken city while desiring other men. It takes a lot of willpower to keep that hidden."

"That's not willpower, that's self-preservation," Lucas muttered.

"It's both. We each had a lot to lose back there if anyone found out about our desires. You even more so than me. I had the protection of being a member of the royal family. Few would have dared to speak out about me for fear of my parents."

"Yet you've lost everything now," Lucas reminded him.

Finn shook his head and smiled. "Not at all. I have everything I ever wanted. You just have to decide what it is *you* want."

"I want to follow in my father's footsteps as a member of the Council."

"Is that what *you* want, or what he wants?"

"Both of us."

Finn sat opposite him and Jake stood to leave. "I'm sorry again."

Lucas acknowledged his apology and after Jake had departed, he waited for whatever it was Finn had to say to him.

"Is your career really more important than finding someone to spend the rest of your life with?" Finn asked.

"The sunken city is my home. I don't want to spend my life swimming the oceans, always looking over my shoulder for sharks."

"You could live on land, like we do," Finn pointed out.

"I don't know. I can see you enjoy living here and I can tell why, but I feel like a literal fish out of water here. I've never had to take human form for so long and it feels unnatural to me."

Finn chuckled, though Lucas wasn't sure he could see the joke. "You'll get used to it, I promise."

"I don't want to get used to it. I just want to find the heir and go home."

"Jake says home is where the heart is. Maybe you need to at least consider the possibility of making a life for yourself away from the sunken city, somewhere you don't have to hide your love."

Finn had a point, but the idea of leaving behind everything he knew and his entire family terrified Lucas more than he wanted to admit.

Chapter Nine

It had been a very frustrating day for Justin. After the merman had groped him in the aquarium, he had been ridiculously hard all day. At lunch time he had ducked into the staff restroom and tried to ease the pressure a little, but he had been interrupted by someone who — rather inconveniently — had insisted on using the facilities. He had called Caspian as he was leaving the aquarium and told him not to come round tonight and to warn Cari, who refused to own any modern technology like phones, to stay away too. He knew his parents would assume he had a hot date lined up and abide by his wishes. By the time he arrived home, he wanted nothing more than to shut the door, whip it out and jack off.

He kicked the door shut and yanked down the zip to his jeans. Only then did he realize he wasn't alone. Medina sat waiting for him. Any thought he had about apologizing to her vanished from his mind at the annoyance of her letting herself into his home yet again.

He hurriedly zipped himself up. "How many times do you have to be told that it's rude to drop in uninvited?"

"So everyone keeps telling me." Medina didn't sound particularly bothered by the fact. "Have you had a nice day at work?"

"What's it got to do with you?" Justin asked.

"Just a simple question. I believe you might have had a visitor today."

"You told Lucas where to find me, didn't you?"

"Yes." Again she didn't appear phased by his question. "Lucas is such a sweetie and just your type."

"I'm not interested in Lucas — or any other merman. I'm perfectly capable of getting laid without your assistance."

Medina chuckled under her breath. "Ah, but you won't be getting laid at all, unless you cooperate."

"Just get out of here," Justin snapped. "As I'm sure you're aware, it's been rather a frustrating day for me, what with a horny merman fondling me at work and no chance of getting off."

Medina didn't move from her seat. "Lucas is your soulmate. The one being in all the world who can make you truly happy."

"I don't believe in soulmates. I think all that stuff is a load of bollocks."

"It doesn't matter whether you believe it or not. He's the only one you'll ever be intimate with again for the rest of your life."

Justin didn't believe a word she said. "I'm sure I can find a suitable substitute for him. He wasn't *that* special." He ignored the little voice in his head reminding him he had flirted with Lucas before he had found out who he was.

Medina stood and walked over to him. She leaned down to whisper into his ear. "Have you forgotten my curse so soon?"

"I don't believe in curses either."

"Maybe not yet, but you soon will, my stubborn merman. From this day forward, you'll never find pleasure with another man. Only Lucas will be able to satisfy you. You'll never be able to orgasm again, unless he is the one who pleasures you."

Justin laughed and shook his head. "You really have no idea about men, have you? I'm sure I can find another man to take the edge off, or failing that, I can just use my own right hand."

"You think you can avoid my curse by staying away from Lucas. You'll soon find out that won't work, but it'll be fun to watch you try. Go ahead, Justin. Try to come without Lucas. You'll soon be hunting him down."

"I don't even know where he lives."

"I can tell you where to find him."

"I don't want anything to do with him or his schemes to get me to go to Atlantis."

Medina vanished from the room, though her voice lingered as she replied. "When you change your mind, call my name and I'll show you where to find him."

Justin waited as long as he could to make sure she didn't pop back in. The thought of her watching him while he jerked off wasn't a pleasant one, though unfortunately it didn't help get rid of the problem.

He sat on the beat-up sofa and freed his erection from the confines of his jeans. He moaned with relief as his cock sprang free. It had been a bloody long day and he had been half hard for most of the duration. Now he ached so badly that he couldn't wait another minute.

He closed his eyes and tried to conjure up the image of a handsome man to daydream about. Instead, the person springing to mind was Lucas. His golden eyes should have given him away as a merman right from the start, but Justin hadn't expected him to be able to track him down.

"Damn it," he muttered as the golden-eyed merman refused to leave his mind. He supposed there wasn't any harm in picturing him while he jerked off. It wasn't like he was inviting him into his home and asking him to bend over for him. That thought made Justin even more desperate for relief. He pictured Lucas, naked and ready for him, kneeling on the sofa with his knees placed wide apart. Justin would take him from behind and pound into that tight arse.

Or maybe he would be the one sitting on the sofa, as he was now, with Lucas riding his dick, moaning all the time as Justin fisted him. He'd cry out his name as he came hard, his cum spurting over his chest. Perhaps Lucas might even come hard enough that he'd manage it without Justin actually touching him.

All the time he thought about what he would do to Lucas, Justin played with his own balls, squeezing them and stroking his length. He could tell he was close to coming, yet he wasn't quite there yet. Considering how hard he had been all day, Justin was a little surprised he hadn't exploded at the first touch, and as he continued to fondle himself, he began to worry something wasn't quite right.

As hard as he was and as desperate as he had been all day, there was no reason at all why he wasn't coming right now. Justin knew exactly where to touch himself to make the pleasure last, as well as which spots made him come hard and fast on the occasions where he couldn't take his time. Yet right now, no matter what he tried, there wasn't even so much as a drop of pre-cum appearing at the tip of his penis. For the first time, he wondered if maybe there might be something to Medina's curse.

Opening his eyes, he glared down at his dick. It jutted out from the nest of dark blond curls just as it always did. The flesh felt the same when he touched it and his heart rate increased with anticipation when he gave himself a long slow stroke. Yet, he was still no closer to coming than he'd been all day.

He tried a few more tugs but nothing seemed to work. He was going through the motions and yet he might as well have been touching an inanimate object.

Giving up for the moment, he opened his laptop on the coffee table and loaded it up. *If all else fails, find some porn.*

It didn't take long to set one of his favorites playing and he sat back to watch and try again.

He fisted his length with a firm hand and gave himself a quick tug. He concentrated on the short film as he continued to touch himself. This particular piece of porn had never failed to get him off before the credits rolled. Usually he came all over his hand before it was a third of the way through, yet today he struggled. The scene moved from the shower to the bedroom and he was still hard and aching. Normally he didn't last through the soapy antics of the two men on the screen. Today he was not getting anywhere. If his favorite porno wasn't helping, there was only one thing for it. He'd have to go out and find a willing man to sink his cock into.

The video finished and he was still rock hard. Frustrated and horny he switched off the computer and went to get changed into more suitable clothes. Even though he didn't usually go out to a club on a Monday night, he felt the situation was dire enough for him to risk being a little tired at work the following day.

* * * *

The club wasn't one of his favorites, but it was the nearest one to his flat and right now that was all Justin cared about.

Even though the time was early there were quite a few patrons already in the club and Justin searched the room for a likely prospect. Too tall. Too short. Too happy. Too angry. Now he remembered why he didn't usually go to clubs on a Monday night. Where were all the decent looking men?

One likely possibility raised his glass in his direction from the other end of the bar. Justin smiled as he sized him up. Maybe he would be open to the possibility of a quickie. The stranger sidled up to him and leaned down to whisper into his ear. His words were slurred and the last thing Justin wanted to hear. "Wanna slide my cock up your arse."

Great, nothing like a drunken top to make the day complete. Justin shook his head and smiled. "Sorry, mate. No one gets in my arse. It's strictly off limits. Now, if you're willing to switch, I might be persuaded."

The guy backed away so far he nearly fell over the bar stool.

"Yeah, didn't think so," Justin said. "Have a good night."

"You too," the drunk slurred before making his way back to his post at the end of the bar.

Justin twisted round on his stool and surveyed the room. He drank his beer as he watched the place fill up, waiting for someone to catch his interest. His breath caught when he spotted a young man in his early twenties with short brown hair. Lucas? The man turned to his friend and Justin realized it wasn't him. He had the same brown hair, worn in a similar style, but that was where the resemblance finished.

He carried on studying the room, but again and again his eyes were drawn back to the brown-haired man near the edge of the dance floor. As horny as he was, Justin was annoyed with himself for not simply finding any willing guy and picking him up. Why was he wasting time searching for who knows what?

"Oh damn it," he finally muttered. There was no point avoiding the inevitable any longer. Only one man in the room held any interest for him, so he might as well see if he wanted to hook up. He finished his drink, placed his glass on the bar and made his way across the room.

The closer he got to his target, the less resemblance he could see to Lucas. By the time he reached his side, he could tell the two men were actually nothing alike. Justin hadn't expected to see golden eyes gazing back at him, yet he still felt a twinge of disappointment when they turned out to be a rather boring shade of brown.

"I told you he was watching you," one of the man's friends whispered loudly.

The man blushed and smiled at Justin. "Hi. Do you want to dance?"

Justin didn't, but he nodded anyway and they headed onto the dance floor.

"I'm Gavin," the man said as they found a space and began to move in time to the music.

"Justin," Justin replied loudly as he tugged Gavin flush against him. The moment their bodies connected, it happened. Like a switch had been thrown, his erection disappeared. He hadn't come, yet he was no longer aching and hard. Instead of bringing him closer to the edge, Gavin's presence seemed to have pushed him back from it.

The same couldn't be said for Gavin. As they ground together, Justin could feel his hardness pressing against his groin. Normally such friction would be enough to have Justin hard in seconds, yet he wasn't even twitching in response.

They finished the dance and Justin made an excuse to leave. He could tell Gavin was disappointed, but the night was still young and he had plenty of time to find someone else. Justin meanwhile intended to return home and try to put a certain merman out of his mind.

"Shit!" The moment he thought of Lucas, he was back to square one. His cock hardened and within seconds, he was in the same state he had been for most of the day. How was this possible?

"I told you." Medina appeared in front of him on the dark street. "Only Lucas will be able to satisfy you from now on. Other men will have the same effect as a cold shower. The moment you get close to them, you'll turn soft and flaccid. Nothing except the touch of your soulmate will ever give you pleasure."

This time Justin believed her. He didn't want to, but the evidence was pretty overwhelming.

"Maybe I'll just go without sex until the curse is over," he suggested.

"It'll never be over," Medina told him. "You're a healthy young man. How long do you think you can go without sex? I don't think you'll last more than a week."

"We'll see about that."

Medina laughed. "Yes, we will. Oh, and just in case you're wondering. Lucas will be having the same problem. Only your touch will ease him, for the rest of his life."

"That's not exactly fair," Justin pointed out. "I'm the one who insulted you, not him."

"All's fair in love and war."

Justin glared at her, but she did nothing except smile and vanish into thin air once again.

"I'm sorry," he shouted after her, hoping it would be enough to appease her. No reply came. He called several times, but the only response he received were some strange looks from passers-by who hurried on their way rather than approach him.

Annoyed and frustratingly hard yet again, Justin made his way home. Maybe a literal cold shower was in order if he was going to make it through the night without getting off.

* * * *

The next day, after discovering cold showers did nothing to rid him of his erection and spending a very restless night, Justin called his father.

"This sounds just like something Medina would do," Caspian said after Justin had finished explaining his predicament.

"Any ideas how I can fix it?" Justin asked.

"Join a monastery?" Caspian suggested.

"Dad!" Justin pressed a cushion into his face as he whined.

"You do know you brought this on yourself, right?" Caspian reminded him. "You're too stubborn for your own good."

"I wonder where I get that from," Justin muttered. "Haven't you got any suggestions on how I get out of this mess?"

"Not really. If you have sex with Lucas, you're destined to lose him and you'll mourn his loss for the rest of your life. If you resist, then from the sounds of it, you have a life of celibacy ahead of you. Not much of a choice."

"What would *you* do?"

Caspian sat quietly for several minutes, studying his glass of whiskey thoughtfully. "I'd go find Lucas."

"Even knowing if anything happens between us, I'll lose him?"

"Yes. Losing him will tear you apart, but maybe you can find a way to save him. Your destiny isn't set in stone."

"That's what Mum says."

"She's right. I believe you have a better chance of defeating this curse if you stick together."

"Better to have loved and lost and all that?"

"I disagree with the sentiment," Caspian replied. "I was thinking two heads are better than one."

"I don't know. I'll have to think about it. Maybe celibacy won't be so bad."

Caspian cringed. "For now, but when the mating season comes, you'll find it a different story."

"What do you mean? What's a mating season?"

Caspian frowned. "I thought your mother talked to you about those?"

"No. What are they?"

"You're a merman. How can you not know about the mating seasons?"

"Apparently quite easily. Care to explain?"

Justin was curious as to what his father was talking about. He knew animals had mating seasons and that his other form was half fish, but he had never heard of such a thing. As far as he was concerned, his sex drive was the same as any other human, at least until Medina had interfered.

"On the summer and winter solstices, mer people go into heat," Caspian explained. "They, and you, develop a fever that can only be broken by a particular form of sexual activity. The method is different for each merman and mermaid."

"What sort of methods?"

"Topping, bottoming, sucking, spanking, whipping — basically anything between two individuals that causes one to orgasm thanks to the actions of the other. Each mer person has a different trigger. Your Lucas, for example, can only come on the night of the solstice when another merman fills his arse with his seed."

"How do you know that?"

"Your mother told me."

"And how does she know?"

Caspian gave him a glance of annoyance. "I didn't ask. Just as I'm not asking you right now what your trigger is. I don't care to know."

"I don't have a trigger."

"You're a merman, so I assure you, you do. You probably just haven't realized it."

"I think I'd know if I went into some sort of sex crazed heat twice a year."

Caspian raised an eyebrow and smirked at him. "I beg to differ."

"What's that supposed to mean?"

Caspian laughed loudly. "You've been sexually active for years now and you're a good-looking man. You've had no problem finding men to share your bed and, forgive me for saying, but considering how bossy you are generally, I'm betting you're just as pushy when it comes to getting your own way in the bedroom."

"The men I sleep with don't have any complaints."

"I never said they did, but you're missing my point."

"Which is?"

"Have you ever noticed on the night of the solstice how you're all hot and bothered and desperate to get laid? No matter what night of the week it falls on, you have this burning desire to find a man to share your bed with. If your trigger is to fuck another man—and no, I don't want to know if it is or not—then you'd just go out and find someone that night, much as you would any other. You wouldn't think of it as being the mating season, you'd just be a regular horny guy who wants to fuck someone to get off."

Justin didn't want to admit to being a pushy top, but his father knew him pretty well. Although he couldn't say for sure, since he wasn't even entirely certain what dates the solstices fell on, he did recall there were occasions, a couple of times a year, when he was particularly desperate to get laid.

Caspian coughed and distracted Justin from his thoughts. "I could be wrong, of course. We both know you've been suppressing your mer side your entire life. It could be that by doing so the mating season instincts have been dampened as well. When was the last time you stretched your fins?"

"How did we get from Medina's wretched curse to my fins?" Justin asked.

"That long, huh?"

"It's been a while, yeah. But I think you were right the first time. I've probably just not realized I'm in some sort of merman heat, which, by the way, is another reason for me to not want anything to do with that part of me. Bad enough I can't go swimming or even soak my muscles in a hot bath."

"There's nothing stopping you from doing either, so long as you're careful to ensure no humans see your tail."

Justin didn't want to have this argument yet again so tried to steer the conversation back to the problem at hand. "I need to come soon or I'm going to go crazy."

"I can tell you where to find Lucas, if you want."

"I don't know. Maybe, if you're right about the mating season, the curse will be broken next solstice?"

"Or maybe it won't, not if Medina has done what I suspect she has."

"What's that?"

"I think perhaps she has put a spell on you that has a similar effect to the mating season triggers. During the mating season, you can only come in certain circumstances. Right now you will only be able to come in a particular way, when you are with Lucas."

"Assuming she's telling the truth about that."

"I don't think she'd have any reason to lie. She wants you and Lucas to get together so her curse will play out the way she wants."

Justin groaned. "Why is this happening to me?"

Caspian snorted. "Because you angered a goddess and didn't listen to my advice."

"Thanks, Dad."

"My pleasure. Now, I'm going to go and leave you to decide what to do."

Caspian disappeared with a crack of lightning. "Show off," Justin muttered.

Turning to his laptop, Justin Googled the dates for the solstices. "December the twenty-first. Okay, that's a little over two months away. How hard can it be to go without sex for a couple of months?"

He glared down at his groin. The hard outline of his cock was clearly visible through his pants. *Two months? I won't be able to manage two bloody hours.*

Chapter Ten

If he didn't know better, Lucas would have sworn it was the mating season right now. He felt unbelievably desperate to feel another man's cock in his arse. He didn't know what was happening to him, but he was extremely frustrated. He had decided to go jogging to work off some of his energy, but when it became clear the exercise wasn't working, he cut his run short and took the quicker route back to the house.

He wondered if his excessive horniness might be a consequence of being on land. Maybe Finn or Kyle could clarify the position. Goodness knows they certainly couldn't keep their hands off each other, so maybe it was a land thing.

When he arrived back at the house, he checked the clock in the hallway and realized Kyle would be at work. Finn should be around, though, so he set out to track him down. When he found the merman, he could barely believe his eyes. He sat straddling Jake on the living room sofa and the two men were locked at the lip.

"What in the world?" Lucas exclaimed before he could stop himself.

Finn jumped and stared at him in surprise. "I thought you went for a run?"

"I did. I thought you and Kyle were a couple?"

Finn glanced at Jake and some silent communication passed between them. Jake patted Finn on the arse and nudged him aside. "Come on in, Lucas. This isn't what it looks like."

Lucas walked into the room with a little trepidation. "What's going on, Finn? Did you and Kyle have a fight or something?"

"No," Finn replied. "Kyle's at work right now."

"And from what I've just seen, you're taking the opportunity to cheat on him."

"No!" Finn shook his head. "Never. Kyle and me are still together, it's just Jake is with us too."

"What?"

Jake nodded. "The three of us are in a relationship together."

Lucas looked from Jake to Finn and back again. In the sunken city, where the mermaids outnumbered the mermen considerably, it wasn't unusual for a mermaid to have more than one merman as a regular lover. Three in a relationship wasn't unheard of, yet Lucas couldn't quite get his head round what he was hearing. There were many men on land, so why did they need to share?

"I'm sorry we didn't tell you," Finn said. "It's kind of difficult to bring it up in a conversation and since you already knew about me and Kyle, we thought perhaps it might be best to let you believe it was just the two of us together."

"We've had a few bad reactions from people who have found out there are three men in our bed," Jake added. "Not that it's anyone's business except ours."

Finn fidgeted in his seat. "We didn't mean to lie to you. It's just not easy being judged all the time, and we didn't want to make things difficult for everyone if you took it as badly as some people do."

Lucas rubbed his chin as he considered what they had said. "I guess it's not really any of my business."

Finn's face fell. "So you don't approve."

"I didn't mean it like that," Lucas assured him. "I'm just trying to understand. I didn't mean to interrupt or upset you."

Jake pulled Finn into his arms and held him close. "It's okay," he murmured. "I've got you and I'm not letting you go."

Lucas smiled as he watched Finn snuggle into Jake's side, much as he did with Kyle in the evenings after they finished work. Somehow they seemed right together.

Jake watched him intently and when he seemed to understand Lucas wasn't going to say anything to upset Finn, he visibly relaxed. "What are you doing back so soon anyway?"

"I wanted to talk to Finn about the mating season," Lucas explained.

"What about it?" Finn asked and there was clear nervousness in his voice. Lucas wasn't sure whether it was because of Lucas discovering him and Jake together or something else.

"Does it work the same on land as it does in the water?"

"Pretty much, except there's no need to swim to land to have sex. Why do you ask?"

Lucas shrugged. "It's strange, but the last couple of days I've felt similar to how I do during the mating season and I can't, you know…"

Finn stared at him blankly "What?"

"Come," Lucas whispered. "No matter what I try, I can't manage it. The only thing I've not tried is being with another man and it's getting to the point where I'm wondering whether I should go and find one just to ease the pressure."

"How long have you been like this?" Finn asked.

"Since Monday."

"The day you went super horny and threw yourself at Justin," Jake surmised.

"Yeah." Lucas half wished he hadn't told them what had happened at the aquarium.

"What's your trigger?" Finn asked.

Jake frowned at him. "Isn't it bad manners to ask a practical stranger something like that?"

Finn shrugged. "Not really. Mermen are very sexual creatures."

"Really?" Jake asked sarcastically. "I hadn't noticed."

Finn smacked him on the chest. "Idiot. I just thought if Lucas doesn't want to go out on the pull on his own, maybe we can help him."

"You don't think there're enough men in your bed?" Lucas asked.

Finn waggled his eyebrows. "It's a big bed, but no, that's not what I meant."

"You're thinking of the chest, aren't you?" Jake asked.

"Yes. Maybe there's something in there Lucas can use."

"What are you talking about?" Lucas asked.

Finn shot him a wicked grin. "Humans have a lot of rather interesting shops that sell some pretty unusual toys."

Jake snorted. "And Finn is fast becoming an expert on quite a few of them."

Lucas was confused. The sunken city had a market place where the mer people bartered for services, trinkets or rare and expensive foods, but in reality they didn't need much and had no real shops. He had visited several shops since his arrival in England, but he couldn't think of anything he had seen to assist him with his current problem.

Finn jumped up and hurried to the door. "Come on. I'll show you."

Lucas followed him out of the living room and up the stairs. He had been in Finn's bedroom before, though only once, during his quick tour of the house. Now he looked at the bed with the eyes of someone who knew more than two men occupied it each night.

"It's okay," Finn said. "You don't have to be uncomfortable about the three of us. We're the same people we were yesterday. You just know something else about us that you didn't then."

Lucas blushed. "At least the bed appears to be big enough for you all."

Finn laughed. "It certainly is."

Lucas watched while Finn walked to the end of the bed and opened a large wooden chest. If he had still been expecting to see bed linen or clothing inside, he would have had something of a surprise. Inside the chest were various boxes, bags and packets.

"These are all new," Finn explained. "I don't really enjoy going into the city — that's where the shop is — so we bought a bunch of stuff all at once. The ones we use are kept over there." He pointed to the drawers at the side of the bed.

Lucas stepped closer and knelt down on the floor beside Finn. "What is all this stuff?"

Finn grinned. "Adult toys. So, what *is* your trigger?"

Lucas hadn't thought his face could heat up any more than it already had. He was sadly mistaken. "Being fucked by another man."

Finn gave him a sympathetic pat on the arm. "There's no need to be embarrassed. That's Kyle's trigger too, and he doesn't care who knows about it. You want to know what mine is?"

"Fucking someone?" Lucas guessed.

"Nope, guess again."

"Being fucked."

"Strike two."

Lucas frowned, not sure what to suggest next. He had seen several mermen having sex with each other, but those he had seen had all been having pretty much the same sort of sex.

"Spanking," Finn said before Lucas could make a third guess.

"What?" Lucas wondered if he had misheard.

Finn picked up one of the toys and swatted the air with it. "I get aroused when another man takes his hand — or a paddle like this one — to my arse. I can come from being spanked and during the mating season, that's the only thing that can make me release."

"Doesn't it hurt?"

Finn smiled. "Not as much as going through the mating season without coming at all."

Lucas knew all about that sort of suffering and he had the deepest sympathy for Finn, who it seemed had been through the same ordeals he had.

"Let me see what we have in here to help you." Finn turned back to the trunk and rummaged through the boxes. "Ah, there it is. I knew we had a spare."

Finn pulled out a long box with a delighted grin. "Here you go."

Lucas took it cautiously. "What is it?"

"The answer to your prayers," Finn replied. "Well, it won't do you any good on the solstice, but the rest of the time it should do."

Lucas studied the box closely. "Is this what I think it is?" He had never heard of such a thing, but the picture on the side of the package was pretty clear.

"If you think it's a fake cock for you to shove up your arse, then yes," Finn told him. "Just don't let Treacle near it. Stupid mutt sees one of these and thinks it's a bone. We've already lost two to the crazy animal. I just hope he's buried them somewhere in the garden and they aren't going to suddenly appear when we have guests."

Treacle, who must have heard his name mentioned, appeared in the doorway with a yap.

"No," Finn told him firmly. "Your toys are downstairs." He shut the chest firmly and pointed back out of the door. Treacle seemed to realize he wasn't going to get his nose into the forbidden trunk, hung his head and wandered back out of the room.

Finn stood and stretched. "Let me know if it's too big or too small. We can get you an alternative if you don't mind waiting a few days."

"I'm sure this will be fine. Thank you."

"You're welcome," Finn replied.

They walked out of the room and over to the top of the stairs.

"I'll just..." Lucas waved toward the guest room.

Finn laughed. "Have fun. I'll be downstairs with Jake. Hopefully Treacle hasn't stolen my place on his lap."

Lucas practically ran to his room and closed the door behind him. The few clothes he had thrown on before going for his run were tossed aside. He climbed onto the bed and sat in the center. He opened the box and after reading the instructions, he began to prepare himself. He already had a supply of lube. The others had given him that, along with the clothes and some money. They had known, as he had soon discovered, that mermen on land were extremely horny creatures, who couldn't seem to go for more than a day or two without coming.

This was the longest period of time Lucas had been human for, and right now he couldn't seem to concentrate on anything apart from the need to orgasm.

He put aside the fake cock for the moment and grabbed the lube. He prepared himself as best he could, easing two then three fingers into his arse to stretch himself. It wasn't enough to satisfy him, but he hoped Finn's toy would be.

His hands were clumsy in their eagerness and he fumbled as he placed the hard, flesh-colored toy between his legs. He closed his eyes and relaxed his muscles enough for the thick head to enter him.

"Ah," he moaned lightly as the familiar sensation of being breached began.

It was slow going and he suspected he hadn't used enough lube in his desperation to do this. He reminded himself that back on the island there was no such thing as lube and despite the slight discomfort he was experiencing now, it was nothing compared to being taken roughly by Otus, a merman who half the time didn't even bother to use a little saliva to ease his partner.

Lucas groaned as he pushed his way in. He used one hand to grasp his erection and stroke it. He needed to come so badly. He squeezed his balls, stroked his length and ran his fingers over every sensitive inch of his penis. Yet, not a single drop of cum appeared at the tip.

Leaving his dick alone again, he shifted his attention to the fake one in his arse and pushed it in a little more. If this worked, perhaps he could take one of these wonderful toys back to the city to use during the mating season. He was sure he could find a place to use it where no one else would see. That way he could come without ever having to risk being caught with another merman. Finn hadn't seemed to think it would work on the solstice, but Lucas considered he had nothing to lose by at least giving it a try.

With a final loud groan that Lucas suspected could be heard throughout the house, the fake penis was fully seated within him. The toy was both longer and wider in girth than Otus' member and Lucas knew he had never been this full in his life.

Once he had become accustomed to the feeling, he began to move the cock, easing it out an inch or two before sliding it back again.

As he worked it, he closed his eyes and the moment he did, an image of Justin popped into his head. He saw the long blond hair of the merman and the teasing smile he had given him before the heir had realized who Lucas was.

He licked his lips as he tried to remember the taste of Justin's. The heir hadn't made any effort to kiss him back, though. He wondered what kisses would be like if he actually kissed someone who participated and kissed him back. He had never kissed Otus and quite frankly he didn't want to. Justin on the other hand was the most kissable merman he had ever laid eyes on.

He slid the phallus in and out, searching for the spot which Otus only occasionally managed to find. Not that his lover had shown any interest in ensuring Lucas found his pleasure. He had only ever been interested in making sure he broke his own fever. Thankfully for

Lucas, his fever had always broken the moment another man's heat filled his arse. He didn't need anything more.

If only it were so easy today. Lucas was becoming a little concerned he still wasn't any closer to coming than he had been before his talk with Finn. If he had been feverish as well he'd have genuinely thought himself in the middle of the mating season. Only the lack of a burning fever convinced him this wasn't the case.

He groaned and screamed out a cry of pleasure as he finally found his sweet spot, yet even that stimulation didn't make him come in an instant like it had before. Again and again he aimed for the same place. He stroked his penis as he fucked himself harder and harder, hitting his target again and again.

His moans of pleasure soon became cries of frustration as he realized this wasn't working. His state of arousal was as uncomfortable as it had been during the mating seasons where he had not taken a lover.

Tears streamed down his face and his arms ached from working the phallus. He dropped his arms to his sides and stared down at himself in defeat.

His penis rose hard and aching with still no sign of cum. The fake cock remained in his arse and he clenched around it. He felt full, stimulated and on the verge of his orgasm, yet he had felt the same way all day. It was as though, no matter what he did, he was still in the exact same position he had been in when he had woken that morning.

What was he doing wrong?

He changed position, even though he began to suspect it would make no difference. He had already managed to hit the spot that should have sent him soaring. What more could he do?

Still, he was reluctant to give up so soon, and he tried another stance, this time easing himself down onto the phallus, hoping it might do the trick and fill him a little more, enough to send him over the edge.

With another loud groan of satisfaction, he threw back his head and let loose a scream of pure frustration when he realized the change of position made not the slightest bit of difference.

Finally, Lucas removed the phallus and put it to one side. His arse ached and it was starting to genuinely hurt from his attempts to come. Resting his head in his hands, he wept.

Chapter Eleven

Justin had never been so sexually frustrated in his life. His problem was compounded by a certain goddess who seemed to be making it her mission to increase his torment. Justin had long since lost any interest in being polite to Medina and had resorted to alternately ignoring her and swearing at her in an effort to get her to leave him alone. Neither method worked. The latter seemed to amuse her.

"Why don't you just fuck off?" Justin complained. He made a valiant effort to keep his voice down so he didn't disturb his neighbors.

Medina laughed. "Why would I do that when we're having so much fun?"

"You call this fun?" Justin hadn't even been able to pull his jeans over his erection this morning.

"Why don't you just go to him and put the two of you out of your misery?" Medina asked.

"You know damn well why."

"You'd rather see Lucas suffer this way?"

"You keep saying that, but for all I know, he might be perfectly okay and not living the life of the sexually frustrated."

Medina smiled and waved her hand. "Take a look for yourself."

Justin staggered a little as an image of Lucas appeared in front of him. It was hazy, like a poor form of hologram, but it was definitely him.

"As my powers return, the images like this will improve," Medina told him. "Until then, this will have to suffice."

Justin wanted to tell her to switch it off, yet he couldn't seem to find the words. Nor could he take his eyes off what he saw in front of him.

"Isn't he gorgeous?"

Justin nodded mutely. The merman who had been sent to find him knelt on a bed with his legs spread wide.

"Do you see what he's doing?" Medina murmured right into this ear. "Take a close look between Lucas' legs and tell me what you see."

He tried not to do as the goddess suggested—he really did—but the temptation was too much to resist and he let his gaze drift down. He took in every single detail of the other merman's form. His smooth chest was completely hairless. Justin knew from discussions with his parents that mermen were mostly smooth skinned and very few had chest hair. He himself was equally hairless and had always been drawn to men who were similarly smooth. He licked his lips as he imagined running his tongue over Lucas' chest, sucking on those brown nipples, maybe even biting them a little. Would Lucas like that? He had a feeling he might.

The flat stomach without a single ounce of fat was also common in mermen who lived their whole lives in the sea. His mother had harped on at him about exercise and dieting during his teen years. She had worried that his lack of the constant exercise the other mermen had would cause him to become overweight. He hadn't, even though he refused to swim for exercise, instead preferring to run or go to the gym.

Justin knew Lucas had probably never set foot in a gym, but his entire life had been spent swimming rather than riding around in cars and other equally lazy forms of human transport. He could see the strain of Lucas' muscles as he moved his arms in a way that made it clear to Justin what he was doing.

Lucas' penis was hard and purple and the perfect size for Justin to take in his mouth. He stepped forward, forgetting for a moment Lucas wasn't actually in his flat, and that the Goddess of Love was.

Lucas had one hand round his dick and the other grasped a dildo. Justin could only see part of the phallus since it was well buried inside the other merman's arse. His cock ached at the idea of taking the place of the sex toy and being the one to fuck Lucas.

He remembered the hardness of Lucas' erection rubbing against him in the aquarium. It had taken every bit of self-restraint he had to pry the merman off him before he lost his job for inappropriate behavior.

"He's thinking of you," Medina murmured.

Justin jumped. He had completely forgotten she was in the room. "You don't know that for sure."

"Oh, but I do. I can hear the thoughts of any man or woman—mer or otherwise—when they are in the throes of passion, and that pretty little merman right there is thinking about you. Maybe you should go to him and show him what it's like to be fucked by a merman who knows what he's doing."

"I'm sure he has plenty of mermen willing to fuck him."

"Lucas has been a little unlucky in finding a suitable merman."

Justin tried to turn away from Lucas to face Medina, but it took too much effort. "What do you mean?"

"The merman he usually takes as his lover during the mating season has no care for Lucas' pleasure. He takes what he needs and leaves."

"He does?" Justin practically growled the words and he faced Medina at last. "What sort of merman would be so callous?"

Medina waved her hand again and the vision of Lucas on his bed vanished. Justin gave an involuntary whine of disappointment, before he realized another vision was forming in its place.

This time he saw what appeared to be trees and vegetation unlike anything found in England. Lucas held onto the branch of a tree as another man took him from behind. Justin's heart clenched at the expression on Lucas' face. The merman was obviously trying to hold back his tears and clearly wasn't enjoying the experience at all.

"This was a couple of years ago," Medina explained. "The summer and winter solstices are the only times Lucas allows himself to be fucked, and only when he has already suffered through several mating seasons without release. His lover — and I use that word very loosely — cares nothing for Lucas. In fact, he despises him because Lucas has a position in the palace that he envies."

Justin stepped forward and raised his hand to Lucas' face. The tears were flowing freely now. "Why does Lucas put up with such treatment?"

"You have never gone through a mating season without coming. What you feel right now is a mere shadow of that pain. Lucas has gone through much worse than this."

"And yet you let him suffer needlessly because of your curse," Justin reminded her.

"I'm not the one causing him his current pain," Medina replied. "That would be solely on your shoulders. If you want to end his torment, all you have to do is go to him right now and fuck him like you both want."

"If I fuck him, you said I'll lose him."

"Yes, but if you don't, neither of you will ever come again."

"And you call yourself the Goddess of Love," Justin muttered.

"Love, lust and romance," Medina reminded him. "As well as everything else in between. Do you give in yet?"

As Justin watched the events from the past the image faded and he nodded reluctantly. Someone had to show Lucas sex didn't have to be the ordeal it had apparently been for him.

"Excellent." Medina smiled as she took him by the arm.

A moment later he stood alone in front of a large unfamiliar house. "A little warning would have been nice," he muttered. The light mocking laughter told him she had heard him.

"Can I help you?"

Justin jumped and spun round. The man who had crept up behind him stared at him curiously. "Who are you?"

"I live here," the man replied. The man looked him up and down no doubt taking in the fact he wasn't wearing a shirt or shoes on what was a chilly autumn day.

"I'm here to speak with Lucas," Justin explained. "I thought he lived here."

"Ah." The light seemed to dawn in the man's eyes. "Let me guess. You're Justin, right?"

"How did you know?"

"I'm Kyle, formerly of the sunken city of Atlantis and now of right here. I'm guessing you're King Nereus' lost son?"

"That man is not my father," Justin snapped. "I've never even met him."

"Met him or not, he's the man who fathered you."

"He's not the man who raised me. Caspian did that."

Kyle snickered, though he quickly tried to cover it up. "Sorry, I just can't see Caspian as the fatherly type."

"Why not? He did a damn sight better job than King Nereus."

"No offense. He just doesn't seem like the sort of man to have much to do with people generally, let alone children."

Justin bristled with indignation. "What would you know? How much time have you spent with him? A few minutes when you came here to England?"

Kyle raised his hands in surrender. "Sorry. Like I said, no offense meant. I'll take your word for it. Come on. Let's go find Lucas. I'm sure he's around here somewhere, and if not, well…he doesn't tend to stray very far."

Justin let Kyle lead him into the house.

"I'm home," he called out. "Lucas, are you around?"

A naked stranger with blond hair nearly as long as Justin's walked into the hallway and squeaked. "Kyle!" he squealed as he covered his dick and ducked back through the doorway. "You could have warned me you were bringing a friend home."

Kyle laughed. "I didn't bring him home. I found him on the step. And he's mer, so you don't have to hide. I'm sure he's seen it all before."

Justin wondered whether it was worth explaining that in fact he didn't spend his entire life wandering around starkers. He decided against getting into that particular discussion, especially since he was, as was quite obvious, dressed in precious little himself. Kyle's assumption may have been inaccurate, but he couldn't exactly blame him for jumping to it.

The blond stepped back into the hallway. "You're mer?" he asked cautiously.

"Unfortunately," Justin muttered.

The merman tactfully ignored Justin's comment. "I'm Finn."

"This is Justin." From the way Kyle introduced him, Justin could tell he had been a topic of conversation within the house.

Finn's knowing smile confirmed Justin's suspicion. "So, that's why you were calling Lucas instead of me."

"Yeah, have you seen him?"

"He's in the pool." Finn waved toward the back of the house. "Or he was the last time I saw him. I haven't seen him since he dove in, so presume he's still there."

"This way." Kyle directed Justin through the house. "We've got a great pool here, and it's actually thanks to Caspian that we have this place."

"That doesn't surprise me," Justin replied.

As he stepped through the door, Justin saw Lucas was still in the pool. He swam under the water with his face toward the bottom.

"Just dive in and give him a poke," Kyle suggested. "I'm going to get something to eat, so I'll leave you to it."

Justin opened his mouth to say something, but Kyle had already disappeared back out through the door.

"Dive in?" he said to no one. There was no way on Earth he was getting into the water. "Lucas," he called.

The merman either ignored him or didn't hear him. He suspected it was probably the latter.

Lucas propelled himself through the water with a speed that would run rings round any Olympic swimmer. The room didn't have any natural light and there appeared to be specialist blinds hiding the pool from the outside world. There was no illumination at all, yet his vision was perfect as he watched the merman swim length after length of the huge pool. The golden fins of his tail matched the golden eyes that had raked over him with such wanton lust at the aquarium.

He tried calling again, but Lucas still didn't hear him. When raising his voice didn't work he knelt on the edge of the pool and tried splashing the water to get his attention. It took quite a few attempts and nearly falling in head first, but finally Lucas realized he was no longer alone and came to the surface.

"It's about time," Justin complained.

Lucas looked at him curiously. The lust had gone from his eyes, yet there was still something there Justin couldn't quite place. "Why didn't you just come in and get my attention that way?"

"I don't swim," Justin explained.

Lucas laughed. "Don't be ridiculous. Every merman can swim."

"I didn't say I can't swim. I said I don't."

With a graceful dive, Lucas disappeared under the water and reappeared at the edge of the pool near Justin a second or two later. "You're serious, aren't you?"

"Very."

"But why not?"

"I don't like to."

"But you're a merman." Lucas stared at him with utter confusion. "I can't imagine not wanting to swim. It would be like not wanting to breathe."

"I've no interest in swimming."

Lucas shook his head in obvious disbelief. "You don't know what you're missing."

Justin knew exactly what he was missing, but he hadn't come here to discuss his issues with his fins. "Can we talk?"

"If you want," Lucas said. "But first, let me apologize for the way I acted at the aquarium. I don't know what came over me."

"It's not your fault," Justin assured him. "You were under a love spell."

"I know."

"The Atlantean Goddess of Love is determined to bring the two of us together and will use any underhanded method she can to bring that about."

"So I gathered," Lucas interrupted. "Medina came here the day before I went to the aquarium. I should have just stayed away, but I didn't believe in spells."

"But you do now?"

"Can't really deny it, considering how I threw myself at you." Lucas leaned his arms on the edge of the pool and rested his head on them. He gazed up at Justin with wide eyes. "I'm sorry."

"It's all right."

"Maybe we could start over," Lucas suggested. "Pretend we never met before today."

Justin nodded and Lucas heaved himself up out of the water. Justin jumped back as Lucas' fins brushed against his bare shin. He had never seen another merman in his half fish form before and while he hated his own fins, he could still appreciate the beauty of the merman reclining before him.

"I don't remember all of what I said to you," Lucas admitted. "I just remember throwing myself at you. Did I even get round to explaining why I'm here?"

"I know why you're here," Justin replied. "You want to take me to Atlantis."

"Yes."

"It's not going to happen."

"What? That's it? You're not even going to consider the possibility?"

Justin sat sideways on a nearby lounger. "My home is here, on land. I don't swim and I have no desire to give up my entire life to go flippering off to Atlantis on a whim. If my birth father wants to meet me badly enough, he can bloody well make the effort to swim here himself."

"King Nereus is a very busy man. He can't leave the city for the length of time it would take to travel here."

"Then he can't want to see me that badly, can he?"

Lucas was rapidly drying out from his swim and as Justin watched, his fins vanished and his legs and feet appeared, along with his long, hard cock. The erection reminded Justin why he was actually here and he realized while they had been talking, his own desire had been tempered. Now it returned, as fiercely as before.

"Do you believe in curses?" Justin asked quietly.

"Not really," Lucas replied. "Why do you ask?"

"Because I've been cursed and I'm afraid you're the one that's going to pay for it if I can't figure out a way to break it."

Lucas stood and walked over to sit beside Justin on the lounger. "That's better. I much prefer being at the same height, don't you?"

"Um yes, I guess. Did you hear what I said about being cursed?"

"Yes. I assume you're going to explain what you mean."

Justin met Lucas' eyes. "Medina has cursed me to find love, only to have it taken from me forever after a short time."

"Why would she do that?"

"Because I pissed her off. She's also made it so neither of us can come unless it's through the actions of the other."

Lucas suddenly appeared far more interested in the conversation than he had been. "Are you telling me the reason I can't come — no matter what I try — is because you angered a goddess?"

"Yes."

Lucas hit him, hard, in the chest. "I've been going through a nightmare the last few days and it's all your fault."

"I'm right there with you," Justin muttered. "Nothing has worked, not even picking up another guy. In fact that was the only thing that made my hard on disappear. Pity it came back as soon as I left the bloke."

"You were going to have sex with another man?" Lucas asked.

"Of course I was."

"Oh."

"Bloody hell. You had to be the jealous type, didn't you?"

"I'm not jealous. I just… Oh shit, I *am* jealous, aren't I?"

"Maybe a little," Justin teased. "But so am I. Medina showed me visions of you trying to get off and also with another merman. I wanted to tear his hair out, and not just because of the way he was treating you."

"You saw me with Otus?"

"Otus. Is that his name?"

"Yes."

"Is it serious between you two?"

Lucas shook his head. "No, of course not. Homosexual relations are forbidden in the sunken city, and I have my career to think about. We just use each other during the mating seasons."

Justin realized everything Medina had told him had been true. Lucas had never known the pleasure to be had from making love because for him sex had never been anything more than finding release as quickly as possible.

"Do you think if we fucked it would break the curse?" Lucas asked. "I'm kind of desperate to come right now and I can see you are too."

Justin scowled at his crotch and could clearly see the outline of his erection through the thin fabric of his shorts. Lucas was right about that. If he didn't come soon he thought he just might explode. There was only one problem.

"If we have sex, we trade one problem in for another. We get to come, but then I lose you."

"You said the curse was that you find love and lose it."

"Yes." Justin wasn't sure where Lucas' mind had wandered. The merman seemed to be considering something, but he had no idea what.

"Sex doesn't have to mean love."

Justin knew Lucas was right, yet he had a feeling they couldn't bypass the curse quite so easily.

Lucas stood and gestured for Justin to undress.

"Are you sure about this?" Justin asked as he shed his shorts and stood naked before the merman's increasingly hungry gaze.

"I want to come and if this is the only way then, yes, I'm sure."

Justin sat back down on the lounger, this time sitting on it properly with his legs stretched out in front of him.

Lucas climbed on top of him and straddled his thighs. "Fuck me."

With a care he knew Lucas had never experienced before Justin tugged him closer and drew him into a kiss. Lucas pulled back almost immediately. "What's wrong?"

"It's just sex," Lucas reminded him. "We don't need to kiss when that's all it is."

Justin stopped himself from saying the words that he wanted this to be more. He had never wanted anything other than casual relationships. Yet when he gazed into Lucas' intense gaze, he couldn't seem to remember his unspoken vow to keep other men at a safe distance. Then again, the primary reason he had stuck with no strings relationships was because he didn't want any man to get close enough to discover he wasn't entirely human. Lucas already knew exactly what he was. He wouldn't hand him over to some government laboratory. If he even knew about such things he wouldn't want to draw the authorities' attention to either of them.

"But I want to kiss you," he finally admitted.

"You didn't at the aquarium."

Justin drew Lucas closer. "That day didn't happen, remember?"

He brought Lucas' lips to his and this time when they kissed, they both participated equally. Their tongues touched, hesitantly at first, then with a firmness that soon became greedy.

Lucas' penis brushed against Justin's stomach and he felt the dampness of his cum against his skin. His own dick, which had been aching for days, was likewise finally doing what it was supposed to. As they kissed, he felt his balls draw back and he realized they didn't even have to be fucking for him to come. All it took was Lucas' touch to bring him to the edge. He had been so close since their last encounter, it didn't take much at all.

He thrust his hips a little, though his movements were hampered by the merman straddling him. His dick brushed deliciously against Lucas' bare buttocks as he wriggled around, trying to find a comfortable position on the not-entirely-suitable pool lounger.

He told himself it was just sex, yet he didn't believe it any more. He didn't know if it was Medina's magic or something as corny as love at first sight, but whatever it was, he was lost to the feelings swarming through him.

Lucas clung to him, his knees on either side of Justin's hips. He rubbed up against him, each gentle thrust causing his cock to hit Justin's stomach.

Justin drew out of the kiss and raised a finger to Lucas' lips. "Suck," he ordered.

Lucas obeyed him immediately, taking the digit between his lips and wetting the finger with his saliva. Their eyes were locked together the whole time and Justin found himself lost in the golden gaze.

"I'm going to finger-fuck you," he explained, causing Lucas to suck even harder. "I see you like the idea."

He brushed his middle finger against Lucas' lip before pushing it inside to join the other.

Finally, when Justin considered them ready, he removed his fingers from Lucas' mouth and reached round toward his arse.

Lucas keened as Justin used his dry hand to part his cheeks before easing the wet digits inside his anus.

The merman pushed back against the intrusion. "More," he begged. "Please, Justin. It's been so long."

"How long?" Justin was curious as to whether Lucas was really as inexperienced as Medina claimed.

"Not since the summer solstice," Lucas answered, his voice already breathless. "Please, Justin. Make me come."

Justin wasn't sure how any man could go that long without sex, especially one as gorgeous and responsive as Lucas appeared to be. "Soon," he promised.

As he explored Lucas with his fingers the merman lost the ability do anything more than moan as he rocked against him. Justin's dick strained toward Lucas, but he didn't want to take the merman as roughly as he was used to. To do so would only prove all men were like his former lover. Justin didn't want to see tears in Lucas' eyes, unless they were ones of joy.

Lucas came suddenly with a cry of surprised joy. His cum sprayed Justin's chest and neck.

"That's it," Justin crooned. "Come for me."

Lucas collapsed on his chest, Justin's fingers still buried in his arse. Justin's erection lingered and it seemed he had been wrong in his assumption that he could come just from kissing the merman in his arms.

When Lucas had recovered himself a little he sat back and saw Justin was still hard. "Can I suck it?" he asked. Justin could hear the nervous note in his question.

"Have you ever given someone a blow job before?"

Lucas shook his head. "No. The mer don't really do such things."

"Then how do you know about blow jobs?"

Lucas chewed on his lip before whispering his answer. "I saw Finn doing it to Kyle once. They seemed to enjoy it. I won't if you don't want me to."

Justin tilted Lucas' chin up. "Oh I definitely want you to. Just mind the teeth."

Lucas looked over toward the pool. "Can we do this over there?" he asked.

"What do you mean? In the water?"

Lucas rose. "The floor isn't exactly comfortable. You can sit on the edge of the pool while I'm in the water."

"Are you sure?" Justin didn't think it would be any more comfortable in the water as on the lounger or kneeling on the floor.

"I'm sure." Lucas ran and dove into the pool, transforming as soon as he was submerged.

Justin stood on the edge for a few moments before he sat. His legs dangled in the water, but he retained his human form. "You aren't planning on dragging me in there, are you?"

Lucas swam over and ran his hands up Justin's shins and along his thighs. "If I did that, I couldn't do this," he pointed out, right before he leaned in to lick along the length of Justin's penis.

Justin nearly fell in the water anyway at the feel of Lucas' tongue on his dick.

Lucas wrapped his wet fingers round his balls, squeezing them slowly. Justin held onto the edge of the pool with a death grip. He wrapped his legs round

Lucas' back and held him close. He didn't even squirm when his feet felt the scales of Lucas' tail beneath them.

Despite Justin's lack of faith, Lucas maintained his position in the pool with ease. He hovered in place as he licked and sucked at him, his tongue leaving no spot untouched as he explored him thoroughly.

Justin didn't know how he had held back from coming as long as he had. After the magically prolonged erection, he had truly believed he would be coming at the very first touch. Much to his relief, he wasn't shooting like a teenager watching his first porno. It was a close call, but he managed to draw his orgasm out. At least he hoped it was his doing and not yet another result of Medina's meddling.

Lucas' brown hair appeared so perfect between his legs. Justin sighed and brushed his hand through the damp locks. "That's it," he encouraged. "Feels so good."

It felt good until the moment Lucas took him in his mouth. Then it felt absolutely amazing. The merman sucked his cock as vigorously as he had sucked his fingers just a short while before.

Justin smiled down at Lucas when the merman gazed up at him with those steady golden eyes. "My eyes are golden too," he felt the need to say. He could see the confusion on Lucas' face and felt the need to elaborate. "I wear contact lenses so people don't stare."

Lucas' expression told him he understood. Caspian always did a good job when he gave mermen who came to shore the knowledge they would need to survive on land.

With a loud sucking noise, Lucas pulled away from his dick and Justin gave a moan of disappointment. Lucas hoisted himself out of the water. His fish tail remained in the pool as he braced his arms on the tiles.

Justin leaned into the kiss he knew was coming but Lucas surprised him once again. He moved back far enough that Justin couldn't quite reach him without risking toppling into the pool. "I know you want to kiss me, but it's not going to happen."

"Why not?" Justin asked. "Didn't you like it?"

"Yes, but the next time I kiss you, I want it to be under the water."

"I told you I don't swim."

"I know, but I'm telling you that's what I want."

"Why is that so important to you?"

Lucas nipped his earlobe before he answered. "My mission is to bring you to your father. My first hurdle is going to be getting you into the water at all, and if my kisses entice you into the pool, I'm willing to hold them back as bribes."

"Did anyone ever tell you you're very devious?"

"My brother tells me all the time." Lucas lowered himself down into the water and took Justin's dick back into his mouth.

Justin realized he knew very little about the merman who had been sent to find him and that he shouldn't underestimate his resourcefulness in getting his own way. He wanted to tell him to leave because he had no intention of being manipulated into going to Atlantis. Yet, he didn't say the words. He simply sat there as Lucas sucked him with renewed purpose.

They could argue about Atlantis later. Right now all Justin wanted was to come in the sweet mouth of the merman who pleasured him so thoroughly.

His balls tightened once again and this time Justin knew nothing would stop him going over the edge. One more lick from Lucas in just the right spot and he shot down the merman's throat. His body shook from the force of his orgasm. He couldn't recall a time when he had come so hard. Lucas drank down everything he gave him, licking the sensitive flesh over and over until he had cleaned up every last drop of cum.

"Let me taste," Justin begged, but when he leaned down, Lucas swam backward into the center of the pool with a teasing grin.

"You know what you need to do if you want that," he called from his position well out of Justin's reach. "Let me see those golden fins."

Justin shook his head. "That's not going to happen. I'm the most stubborn man you're ever likely to meet."

Lucas laughed and splashed water with his tail with enough force to spray Justin with a few drops. "I think I'm up to the challenge."

Justin brushed away the water and stood. "We'll see about that," he said, and he found himself eager to spar with the merman who had been sent to find him.

Chapter Twelve

Lucas watched Justin from the water. He didn't expect him to simply dive into the pool and into his arms, yet he still felt a wave of disappointment when Justin refused to do so.

A part of Lucas was shocked at his own behavior since Justin had walked into the room. This time he couldn't even blame Medina's spell. He was in total control of his own actions. He would never have dared behave in such a manner back home. He had too much to lose. Yet here in this faraway land he was free of anyone who might see him and report his tendencies back to the king. He threw his inhibitions to the wind and let himself enjoy the pleasure of the touch of another man for the first time in his life, without fear of repercussions.

He did wonder what the king would say if he were to discover his heir was another lover of men. Prince Finn had been forced to hide his desires when he had lived in the sunken city, though the rumors had still flown around, and he had done a pretty poor job of concealing his feelings for his bodyguard. If King Nereus were to discover Justin was similarly inclined, he would be far from happy.

A movement near the doorway drew his attention and he saw Kyle poke his head in. When the merman clearly saw he wasn't interrupting anything, he stepped inside. "We're about to have dinner if you two want to join us."

Lucas glanced over at the clock on the wall. He couldn't believe how much time had passed since he had first entered the pool in an effort to swim off his frustration. He nodded and swam to the edge. "Are you staying?" he asked Justin.

"Please do," Kyle said. "There's plenty for everyone, and I must admit we're all a little curious about you."

"I'm just a regular guy," Justin insisted. "Nothing special. But I would like to stay to dinner."

Lucas couldn't keep the grin off his face that Justin wasn't bolting out of the door as soon as he had got what he wanted from him.

"There's no need to dress," Kyle told them. "Only Jake wears clothes round here and we're slowly breaking him of the habit."

Justin laughed as he picked up his shorts. "I've been raised as a human, and I happen to prefer wearing clothes." He pulled the garment on and walked toward the door. Lucas mourned the covering of what happened to be a surprisingly pert arse, and resolved to break Justin of his own habit of clothes before much longer.

Lucas himself remained unclothed as he grabbed a towel to dry himself off before joining the others in the dining room.

Jake, he quickly discovered, was the cook amongst them and he had clearly been working hard in the kitchen for a while.

"Did you have a nice time in the pool?" Finn asked with a blatant wink at Lucas.

Lucas flushed as he recalled the doors had been open the entire time and no doubt Finn and anyone else in the vicinity would have been able to hear his shameless moans as he begged Justin to fuck him.

"Finn," Jake warned. "It's not nice to tease the guests."

"I don't mind," Justin, the traitor, piped up. "We had a very nice time in there. Thank you for asking. You should try it some time."

Finn laughed. "Oh we already did. I love sucking Kyle as he sits on the edge of the pool, as Lucas knows."

Justin choked a little as Lucas flushed bright red at the realization Finn had watched them together and, even worse, had spotted Lucas observing him with Kyle.

"Are you sure you're a merman?" Finn asked Lucas. "Most mermen don't get embarrassed by this sort of stuff."

"They probably do," Jake teased. "It's just oversexed little devils like you who don't."

Finn stuck two fingers up at Jake who merely laughed and blew him a kiss.

"So, Lucas," Justin said. "What do you do in Atlantis, besides run errands for the king?"

Glad for a change of subject, Lucas took a bite of his meal before answering. "I don't really run errands for King Nereus. This is the first time he's ever asked me to do anything. Usually I work with my father while he's training me on what his job entails. One day I hope to take his place as one of the senior advisers to the king. Right now I'm just a junior adviser."

"What do you advise him about?"

"The law."

"This would include the law that says gay sex is wrong?" Jake asked.

Lucas squirmed. "Yes, that's one of our laws."

"Bit of a moral dilemma for you, if you ask me."

"What do you mean?" Lucas had a feeling he knew exactly what Jake meant, but he had to ask.

Jake gave him a stern look. "Telling others they can't be with the ones they desire, but secretly doing the same thing."

Lucas bristled. "I don't agree with that law and neither does my father."

"And yet you enforce it when you don't uphold it."

Lucas hung his head. Jake was right. He should have spoken out, yet it was easy to say so from this safe distance away.

"Leave him alone," Justin suddenly snapped. "You don't know what it's like there any more than I do."

"I know a damn sight more than you," Jake barked back. "Kyle and Finn have told me all I need to know about the place."

"Please don't argue," Finn said. He placed his hand on Jake's and squeezed his fingers. "I'm sure it isn't any easier for Lucas to live as a gay merman in the sunken city than it was for me."

Jake gave Finn a loving smile and kissed him lightly on the lips. "Okay, I'll drop the subject."

They turned back to their plates and carried on eating. Lucas watched Justin from the corner of his eye and saw the other merman studying him closely. "Thank you," he mouthed to Justin.

Justin smiled back at him and squeezed his leg under the table. Lucas' cock, so recently spent, rose again in anticipation of getting a little more attention after being starved of the same for so long.

They finished the meal quietly, each man lost in their own thoughts. For Lucas, his thoughts centered on the merman next to him—the one who had not removed his hand from his thigh and who even now inched closer and closer to his dick. He reached down and took Justin's hand, moving it away from temptation.

Kyle seemed to realize something was happening under the table and gave Lucas a sly grin. Lucas smiled back timidly. He felt so welcome at this table, in this house and on land generally. For the first time, he seriously considered the possibility of staying in England and not returning to the sunken city. Would Justin want to see him again if he made a home for himself on land? He thought perhaps he might.

They were just finishing the meal when Justin made a sound as though he were choking. Lucas leaned over and was about to pat him on the back when he realized he had been mistaken. He wasn't choking at all.

"Is he having a vision?" Finn asked. He sounded as surprised as Lucas was.

"I think so," Lucas replied as he took Justin's hand. The merman didn't squeeze his fingers or do anything to acknowledge Lucas' presence. His eyes remained unseeing for several minutes until he came back to them.

"Are you all right?" Lucas asked.

Justin stared at him with unexplained horror in his eyes. Then he threw himself into Lucas' arms, shaking uncontrollably at whatever he had seen.

Lucas held him for several minutes, gesturing for the others to give them a minute or two of privacy. They left the room, leaving the two of them alone. "Are you okay?" he asked again.

"Yes," Justin whispered. "I hate it when that happens."

"You were having a vision, weren't you?"

Justin nodded.

"Can you tell me what you saw?"

"I'd rather not talk about it, at least not yet."

"Okay."

"You aren't going to insist on my telling you what it was?" Justin pulled back to stare at Lucas with mild surprise.

"You'll tell me when you're ready to. I'm guessing you inherited this little talent from your mother."

"Yes." Justin snorted. "Both of them. My visions come from my birth mother, but my foster mother—the Goddess of Prophecy, and Caspian's sister—has taught me how to control them. Or at least she's tried to teach me. I'm a poor and stubborn student apparently. How did you know I was having a vision and not some sort of fit?"

"I've seen the Oracles have visions before. They look as you did when they're seeing something. I didn't realize you had their gift."

"But you knew who my mother was."

"Yes, but she, just like all Oracles, was blind. You seem to have perfectly normal vision, at least as far as I can tell. You're also in human form, when the Oracles only ever have their visions in their mer form."

"I have perfect eyesight," Justin confirmed. "Never had a problem with them, apart from the whole visions thing, which thankfully doesn't happen too often."

Lucas wondered why Justin was different to the Oracles in the city, before he realized he already knew the answer to his question. Justin had been born an Oracle because of who his mother had been. He was truly unique in that respect for no other Oracle in living memory—at least to Lucas' knowledge—had ever given birth to or fathered a child. The Oracles were forbidden to have sexual relations with anyone for a reason and that reason was sitting right beside him. A child of an Oracle would inherit their powers.

"Did you know Oracles are forbidden to have sex?" Lucas asked.

"Bit late for that," Justin teased. "Both for my mother and me."

"Do you know why it's outlawed?"

"Because no one in Atlantis is allowed to enjoy sex?" Justin asked sarcastically. "No, I don't know, nor do I care. I'll have sex when I want and this discussion is doing absolutely nothing to convince me to come with you to this underwater prison."

Lucas knew he wasn't exactly doing a lot to help his case, but he felt Justin at least needed to know the truth. "A long time ago the Oracles were allowed to have sex and give birth to children. One female Oracle and one male Oracle had a child together. That child could see both the past and the present, because that is what her parents could see. Her children inherited her gifts, and one of those children was a boy who mated with an Oracle with the power to see the future. Their child had the power to see everything, the past, present and future."

"Sounds like quite an interesting power to have."

"It drove the poor mermaid mad. She took her own life and since that day, sexual relations between Oracles has been strictly forbidden. Over time, the descendants of the Oracles have died out and now only true Oracles — that is, those who received their powers directly from the Goddess — remain. At least until you."

"Well, I don't intend to have any children unless they're adopted, so I doubt I'll be fathering any more freaks like me."

Lucas supposed he had a point, but it didn't change the fact that what they had done was forbidden. "I still shouldn't have had sex with you."

"It was already forbidden, since we're both men. What does it matter if it's also forbidden because I occasionally see something of my future?"

"You see only your own future?"

"I can see you're trying to change the subject, but yes, I only ever see my own future, boring as it may seem."

"I'm sure your life is anything but boring," Lucas teased. "But now you see why your mother couldn't stay in the city when she found she was pregnant."

"I never blamed my mother for what she had to do. I blame my father. He was the one who got her pregnant and sent her to her death. Even if they couldn't be together, he had a responsibility to her. He should have at least kept her safe."

"He has a responsibility to his people as well," Lucas reminded him.

"She was one of his people," Justin argued. "But he sent her away when she was at her most vulnerable. You've traveled here from Atlantis. You know how long the journey took, as well as how dangerous it can be. She was pregnant and blind. Can you even imagine how difficult it must have been for her?"

Lucas nodded as Justin broke down right before his eyes. "I'm sorry," he whispered as he took Justin in his arms and held him tightly.

"He should have been there for her," Justin sobbed. "He should have been there for both of us."

"He wants to be there for you now," Lucas said. "He really does."

Lucas felt Justin shake his head rather than saw it. "More likely he wants something from me."

146

"He needs an heir and like it or not, by virtue of your birth, you *are* his heir."

"He can have other children. Let one of them be his prodigy and I'll just live my life here on land. I've never had any interest in my mer heritage, and I don't intend to start raking up the past now."

From the way Justin quivered in his arms, Lucas had a feeling it was too late for that. The past had already come back to haunt him.

Lucas led Justin out of the dining room and toward the stairs. Jake hovered nearby and Lucas gave him a nod to indicate they were okay.

Upstairs, he took Justin into the guest room and led him to the bed.

"I thought it was forbidden," Justin reminded him.

"It is."

Lucas took the lube from the bedside table and tossed it to Justin, who caught it one-handed. "Fuck me."

Justin looked down at the lube and Lucas could see he was tempted by his offer, but instead of taking him up on it, Justin shook his head and threw the lube back to him. "I think maybe this is a bad idea."

"What do you mean? I thought you enjoyed what we did earlier?"

"It was fun, but it doesn't mean I want a repeat performance. Medina's 'can't come' spell seems to have been broken, so let's just call it a day and go our separate ways. You go back to Atlantis and I'll go back to my life."

"That's it?" Lucas could barely contain his anger at Justin's casual rejection. He had really believed they had formed a connection during the last couple of hours. How had he misjudged things so badly?

"Like I said, it's been fun," Justin told him. "But we both know this isn't going to go anywhere, so we might as well quit while we're ahead."

Lucas glared at him before turning his back. "Fine, go and fuck off back to your perfect life."

Justin didn't reply. He simply left.

Justin could tell he had offended Lucas as well as hurt his feelings. He was considering changing his mind when the vision of what he had seen crossed his mind once again. He knew he couldn't let this go any further. He gasped involuntarily when he recalled his panic of being under the water in an unfamiliar place. If he stayed with Lucas, then he would end up there before much longer. He couldn't take the risk. Better to end things now and alter his destiny before it couldn't be avoided.

When he arrived home several hours later after a long, barefoot walk, then hitching a lift for the last part of the journey, he was cold, dirty and annoyed. Neither of his parents had shown up when he'd shouted for them to give him a lift home and he cursed Medina with every foul name he could think of for putting him in such a predicament. It wasn't unusual for his parents not to come when he called. He knew they could only hear him when they were in the same realm and both of them spent a lot of time in the realm of the immortals. Still, he wasn't happy about the situation.

He just hoped leaving Lucas behind was enough to divert his fate. Even so, he worried that putting this distance between them wouldn't be enough.

Chapter Thirteen

The next morning Justin woke up with another bad case of morning wood. He had been dreaming about Lucas and the merman's talented mouth. Unfortunately that mouth was some miles away and not wrapped around his dick.

All Justin had was his imagination and his hand, so he wasted no time in putting both of them to use.

It didn't take long to realize he wasn't coming and was, in fact, in the exact same predicament he had found himself in the last few days.

"Medina!" he shouted. "Get here right now, you fucking bitch!"

"How rude," Medina commented as she appeared at the end of his bed. "It would serve you right if I ignored such an order."

"Why can't I come?" Justin demanded, gesturing to his erection.

Medina gazed around the room with an annoying expression of innocence on her face. "I don't see Lucas here."

"That's because he's not," Justin snapped. "Can you just answer the damn question?"

"I just did." Medina offered him a deceptively sweet smile. "Lucas is the only one who can make you come. I already told you that."

"Lucas *did* make me come, yesterday. What's the problem now?"

Medina clucked her tongue at him. "Justin, Justin, Justin. Such a foolish mortal."

"Can you get to the point and tell me what the fuck is going on?"

The goddess' gaze hardened. "Lucas is your soulmate and I have bound the two of you together in such a way that neither of you can come unless it is through the actions of the other. I'm fairly sure I already explained this to you."

"And I already told you, Lucas made me come yesterday."

"Let me explain to you in words you can—hopefully—understand." Medina stepped forward and poked him in the chest. "You and Lucas will *never* be able to come unless it is with each other. This isn't a curse. It's your life from now on. He's your soulmate. You and he will never know satisfaction unless it's together. As soulmates, you shouldn't even want another. Is that clear enough for you?"

"Are you telling me I can never have another lover?"

"That's right."

"And I can't even jerk off?"

"At last, the mortal seems to finally understand."

Justin pushed the goddess, who stumbled in surprise. "Undo what you did or I swear I'll…"

"You'll what?" Medina laughed. "You dare to threaten me. Have you learnt nothing?"

"You can't do this. You have to undo it. This is intolerable."

Medina faded out slightly so Justin's pokes to her body passed straight through her. "If you think it's bad now, just wait until you've gone through a few mating seasons without being able to fuck someone."

"Just undo it!"

"It's irreversible," Medina stated before vanishing completely.

Justin's phone rang and when he looked at the screen, he saw it was his father. "Where were you last night?" he asked.

"And good morning to you too," Caspian answered. "I was off world, why, did you need me?"

Justin sat on the edge of his bed and sighed. A moment later both his parents appeared in his room. He quickly covered himself with the sheet.

"What happened?" Cari asked.

"Medina's curse is permanent," he explained. "She's made it so I can only ever come if it's with Lucas."

"That's not a curse," Cari told him. "That's a bonding of souls. It's part of the marriage ceremonies she used to perform back in ancient times. She wanted to be sure no couple she personally joined together could ever insult her gift of love by cheating on their other halves."

"It might not be a traditional curse, but the effect is the same as if it was."

Cari patted his knee consolingly. "Lucas is still here on land and just a few miles away. All you have to do is go to him."

"He wants me to go to Atlantis."

"Maybe you should go," Caspian suggested. "It might be good to face your father."

"You're my father."

"You know what I mean."

Justin shook his head. "I can't go to Atlantis, and I can't get involved with Lucas. If I fall in love with him, then I'll lose him forever."

"Oh, honey." Cari rubbed his arm with one hand while wrapping her other arm round his shoulders. "It's too late for that. I see your love for him shining in your eyes every time you say his name."

"I don't want to be in love with him or anyone else."

"We know you've kept men at a distance because you don't want them to find out about your fins," Caspian said, "but Lucas is a merman himself. There's no reason for you to stay away from him."

"Lucas is a lovely merman," Cari added. "He and you could have a wonderful future together."

"I thought I was cursed to lose him."

"You are, but curses can be broken, and last night I decided to meditate and focus on your future."

"What did you see?"

"You know I can't tell you, but I will tell you I saw two distinct paths your life can take. One is the cursed life we all want you to avoid, and the other is a life of joy and love with Lucas."

"Here on land?"

"Stop fishing," Cari scolded. "Just know we're watching out for you and we want you to be happy."

"It would make me happy if you told Medina to butt out of my life and made her undo her curse."

Caspian sighed. "I'm afraid neither of us have that sort of power. Just try to learn from this and next time a god or goddess shows up here, try not to insult them."

"What am I going to do?" Justin asked.

"You're going to go to Lucas and work this out together," Cari told him. "Now, what are you waiting for?"

In the blink of an eye, Justin went from sitting on the edge of his own bed to sitting on the edge of Lucas'. "Mother!" he complained. Even Medina hadn't transported him to the next town completely naked.

Cari's soft chuckle echoed through the room and he knew she wasn't the least sorry for what she had done. He looked at Lucas. The merman was stretched out on top of the covers. He had one arm flung out and the other above his head. Although he was fast asleep, Justin could see he was very aroused and, like Justin, would be waking up with a serious case of morning wood.

There were shadows under Lucas' eyes and Justin guessed he had spent a restless night. He hoped he hadn't been the cause of it, even though he suspected that might be the case.

Justin slowly crawled up the bed and settled down beside Lucas. When he woke up, they would have to talk about what they were going to do, and it was a conversation he dreaded. It didn't help that they hadn't exactly parted on good terms the night before.

Lucas stirred in his sleep and rolled toward Justin. Even though he knew Lucas wasn't aware of what he was doing, Justin couldn't stop the smile of contentment at the sight and feel of the merman curling around him. He fit in his arms perfectly and Justin didn't want to let him go. His parents were right. There was no real reason to keep Lucas at a distance. Unlike the other men he had been with, there was no secret he had to keep from him. Maybe they could make this work.

Of course there was the whole issue about Lucas wanting to take him back to Atlantis, a place Justin had no intention of going. He couldn't see the appeal of the place for Lucas either. Yes, his family were there, but what sort of life did he have if he had to hide who he was? Justin knew all about that since he had been hiding his whole life.

Perhaps he might be able to persuade Lucas to stay here with him, especially when he explained they needed each other, thanks to Medina's bonding spell.

Lucas made an adorable snorting noise as he burrowed even closer to Justin. He could tell when the merman began to stir and braced himself for Lucas' astonishment. He supposed he shouldn't have been surprised to see his anger as well.

"What the fuck are you doing here?" Lucas asked as he jumped back from Justin as though his skin burned.

"We need to talk," Justin explained quietly. He raised his hands in a gesture of peaceful surrender, but it quickly became obvious Lucas was in no mood to listen to what he had to say.

Lucas climbed off the bed and glared at him. "I think you said enough last night. Now get out so I can get ready to leave."

"Leave? Where are you going?"

"Home."

"Atlantis?" Justin stood and moved toward the door, effectively blocking it from Lucas.

"Yes, Atlantis. I need to go and report back to the king that I've failed in my mission. The sooner I get it over with, the better."

"You don't have to leave," Justin said. "You could stay here, at least for a while."

Lucas shook his head. "What for? There's nothing for me here."

"I'm here."

Lucas turned his back to him and walked over to the window. "You didn't want me last night."

"That's not true." It wasn't. Even as he'd been walking out of the door, he had wanted to crawl into bed with Lucas and lose himself in his body.

"You said we should quit while we're ahead," Lucas reminded him.

"I was wrong. I'm asking for another chance. Please reconsider."

Lucas appeared to be thinking it over and Justin waited patiently until he had made his decision.

"I can't stay here forever." Lucas finally faced him again. "Even if I choose to live on land with you, I have to go back to the sunken city to let my family know of my decision and to report back on my mission."

"I know."

Lucas watched him steadily for several long minutes. "Why did you change your mind?"

Justin gestured to their groins, where they were each sporting impressive erections. "The main reason is this little problem."

"What do you mean?"

"It's permanent," Justin explained. "Medina's spell has bound us together for the rest of our lives. We can never get off again unless it's with the other."

"What?" Lucas gaped at him in horror.

"I'm sorry, but she made it pretty clear that from now on it's you and me or celibacy."

"I understood what you said," Lucas snapped. "Are you telling me the only reason you're back here is because you need me for sex?"

Justin flinched at Lucas' renewed anger. "It's not just me. You're equally affected by this."

"That's not the point. You made me think you'd changed your mind about being with me, when the only reason you want me to stick around is so you can have sex whenever you want. Well, maybe I want more than that for a reason to stay here."

"You think you can go through a mating season without sex?"

"I already have. I've gone through several in a row and they get worse each time, but I'm not going to stay with someone who's only with me because he has no other choice."

"It's not that I don't want you. I do. But you have to see we aren't exactly a good match. You live in Atlantis, and I don't even swim."

"You're missing the point. You're saying you want me to stay on land just so you can use me for sex."

Justin didn't think he would have put it quite like that, but it was clear there would be no reasoning with Lucas. "Fine, you think you can go without sex for the rest of your life, try it. Give me a call when you change your mind."

"Get out!" Lucas yelled.

Justin turned to leave before he remembered he was in an even worse state of undress than he had been the day before. "Er…"

"What?" Lucas snapped impatiently.

"Do you think I might be able to borrow some clothes?"

Lucas looked him up and down with a clear question in his eyes.

"My mother sent me here," Justin explained. "I hadn't got dressed yet and she thought she was being helpful."

"Oh." Lucas' lips twitched and it was obvious he was trying to hold in his laughter.

Justin felt the laughter bubbling up inside him and when Lucas finally let loose a tiny suppressed snort of humor he couldn't hold back any longer.

They laughed until tears ran down their faces and just when they thought they were getting themselves back under control, they started all over again.

Finally they seemed to get hold of themselves. Lying on the bed, side by side, they stared up at the ceiling. Justin couldn't face Lucas for fear it would start him off again.

"What are we going to do?" Lucas asked, with no trace of the earlier humor in his voice.

"I don't know," Justin admitted. "I don't exactly like the idea of becoming a monk."

"What's a monk?"

Justin frowned at him. "Sorry, I forgot Caspian's knowledge implants don't include things like other religions."

"There are other religions besides the Atlantean one? Why didn't Caspian give me the knowledge of those if I was going to need it?"

"There are many religions, but Caspian and his ilk don't want to foster belief in other pantheons instead of their own," Justin explained. "Anyway, I'm not religious at all, which seems a bit weird when you consider I've been raised by an Atlantean god and goddess. You'd think I would at least have faith in their religion."

Lucas rolled onto his side and rested his head on his arm. "So, what's a monk?"

"It doesn't matter. I didn't mean a literal monk. Caspian's knowledge implants don't always take into account modern slang either. All I meant was I don't relish the idea of never having sex again."

"Me neither," Lucas admitted. "Especially during the mating season."

"Is it really bad to go through a solstice without having sex?"

"Yes, and it gets worse each time. I can usually go a few without getting off, but then the pain gets worse and I give in rather than suffer any longer. If we really are tied together this way, then I guess we have some painful times ahead of us."

"I guess we do."

Lucas played with Justin's hair a little as they each thought things over. "Maybe we could help each other out until we decide what we're going to do," he suggested.

"You're desperate to get off right now, aren't you?" Justin teased.

"Is it that obvious?"

Justin shifted his body slightly and nudged Lucas' penis, which was just touching his hip. "You can't hide it any more than I can."

"I can't concentrate while I'm this horny," Lucas admitted with a sheepish grin. "I don't usually get it this bad outside of the mating season."

"I'm not usually this desperate either."

"You think it might be Medina's spell?"

Justin twisted round to look Lucas in the eye. "No."

Lucas blushed and Justin knew he had heard the unspoken words. They wanted each other pretty badly, with or without the interference of the Goddess of Love.

"Can I kiss you?" Justin asked.

Lucas smiled and shook his head. "No, I'm holding you to what I said yesterday. My kisses are being held back until I get you into the water."

Justin sighed dramatically. "Fine, have it your way. I'll join you in the pool, but just this once."

"Really?" Lucas sat up and bounced eagerly on the mattress.

"If I must."

Justin grabbed Lucas to yank him down on top of him. "I really don't see the appeal of being half fish." He wrapped his legs round Lucas' back and brought them closer, their aching shafts rubbing together between their bodies.

"That feels so good," Lucas moaned as they moved slowly together. He buried his face in Justin's neck as they quickened their pace.

"We couldn't do this if we were in our other forms," Justin pointed out.

"I know, but we can be so much closer in other ways when we're under the water."

"I like being close this way."

Lucas whined into his ear and Justin tightened his legs round him. "So close."

"Come for me, Lucas," Justin demanded. "Let me feel your heat."

Lucas bucked in his embrace and Justin felt the hot flood of his release between their bodies. His own penis, which was already right on the brink, reacted to the heat of his lover's seed and his orgasm hit him hard. He screamed out his pleasure as Lucas collapsed across his chest.

They held each other as they rode out the tremors of their release. Justin ran his hands up and down Lucas' back, cupping his arse and squeezing the flesh.

"Later I want you in there," Lucas whispered.

"I can't wait."

"But first we're going to clean up and go for a swim."

Justin groaned. "You're not going to let that go, are you?"

"Never. I can't believe you don't want to be in the water all the time."

"I can't believe you think it's so bloody wonderful."

Lucas tweaked one of his nipples. "Don't knock it until you've tried it."

Justin slapped Lucas' hand away playfully. "Are you sure you don't want to just stay in bed for the day?"

Lucas tilted his chin as though he was considering the idea. "Tempting as you are, I want to kiss you and I'm a man of my word. You're not going to get a kiss from me until you're in the water."

Justin rolled Lucas onto his back and knelt between his legs. "Are you sure you don't want to change your mind?"

"If the promise of a kiss is the only thing that will get you in the pool then no, I'm not going to change my mind."

"Why is it so important to you that I go for a swim?"

Lucas took hold of Justin's hands and held them tight. "I'm not giving up on my mission just yet. The first step to getting you to come with me to the sunken city is to get you into the water and I'll do whatever it takes to accomplish that."

"A quick swim in an indoor pool is a far cry from the ocean."

"I know."

Justin wasn't sure he liked the determination in Lucas' eyes. The stubborn set of his jaw was far too familiar for his liking. He hoped he wasn't making the biggest mistake of his life by agreeing to transform for the first time since he had been a child.

Chapter Fourteen

Finn and Kyle were in the pool when Lucas and Justin walked into the room. Finn splashed at Kyle with his silver fins, while Kyle used his own silvery blue ones to retaliate. Neither of them appeared surprised to see Lucas with Justin.

"I don't think they know I went home last night," Justin whispered as they approached the edge of the pool. "I didn't see them as I left."

Lucas waved to the others before facing Justin. "Are you ready?"

"As I'll ever be," Justin replied with a dubious glance over Lucas' shoulder.

Lucas smiled and even though he knew he was showing off he flipped backwards into the pool, cutting neatly through the water with barely a splash. He surfaced with a grin and crooked his finger at Justin.

Justin didn't move from his spot on the tiles.

"Do I have to come over there and force you in?" Lucas called.

Justin inched forward the tiniest of steps. He seemed scared and for the first time, Lucas wondered if maybe he had made a mistake in suggesting this.

Lucas shot under the water and darted to the edge of the pool. "You don't have to do this. I thought you were just being stubborn, but it's not just that, is it?"

Justin looked at him and crouched down so they were closer to eye level. Lucas glanced back over his shoulder and saw both Kyle and Finn were under the water at the other end of the pool. Neither of them would hear what he said. "Is it that you're scared of the water?"

Justin shook his head. "No, I just don't like my fins."

"Why not?"

"I just don't. I never have."

"But they're a part of you, just like your arms and legs. How can you not like them?"

"Most humans dislike some part of their body, whether it's their nose, ears or arse. I don't like my fins."

Lucas didn't know what to say. He didn't want to force Justin into the pool, but if he couldn't get him to even transform, what hope did he have of persuading him to return with him? "I don't want to make you, not if you really don't want to."

Justin looked along the edge of the pool toward the shallow end. "Damn it, I can't believe I'm doing this just for a kiss."

"You don't have to."

Justin stood and walked over to the steps. He made his way slowly down them until the water came up to his knees. Lucas swam across to join him. "Are you sure about this?"

"I'm not a coward," Justin replied as he sat on one of the higher steps and let the water cover the lower half of his body.

Lucas watched his lover's legs disappear from sight and his golden fins appear. He wanted to touch Justin so badly, but he didn't want to startle him or sending him fleeing from the water.

Finally, Justin opened his eyes and stared down at the lower half of his body. "I don't see what's so special about having bloody fins."

Lucas took hold of Justin's hand and was delighted when Justin let him tug him fully into the pool. They were still in the shallow end, but at least they were both in the water.

"I'm not sure I like this," Justin admitted as he floundered a little. "I'm not used to being in the water. I'm not even sure I remember how to swim."

"You're a merman," Lucas reminded him. "Swimming comes as naturally to us as breathing. Just try to relax and get used to your fins."

"Easy for you to say," Justin muttered. "You make it look easy."

Lucas held Justin afloat as he guided him toward the deeper end of the pool. "See, it is easy."

"I better get a lot more than a single bloody kiss after all this," Justin complained.

Lucas had almost forgotten about their bargain, but with Justin's reminder, he pressed their lips together. He felt Justin relax in his arms and so he guided him under the water.

"Are my kisses worth it?" he whispered into Justin's mind.

Justin jerked a little. *"What the fuck?"*

Lucas didn't let him break the kiss. He wrapped his arms around Justin and guided him down to the bottom of the pool. The pool was pure fresh water, unlike the salty sea. Lucas could taste nothing except Justin's flavor as he swept his tongue into the merman's mouth. *"Tell me what you want me to do?"* he communicated to Justin.

"Tell me how you're doing that," Justin replied.

"It's how we communicate underwater," Lucas explained as he broke their kiss so he could trail kisses down Justin's chest. *"Have you never done that before?"*

"I try to avoid being underwater as much as possible."

"But surely your parents let you swim when you were a child?"

"Yes, but I didn't like it much, so they stopped forcing me."

"They never spoke telepathically to you?"

"Yes, but they're gods. I guess I didn't realize it was a mer thing too."

Lucas suckled on Justin's nipple as he ran his hands over his fish scales, causing him to shiver a little. When he brushed his fingers over the sensitive patches around his pectoral fins, Justin quivered in his arms as though he was in the throes of an orgasm. *"Like that?"* he teased.

"So sensitive," Justin gasped.

"Your fins are beautiful," Lucas told him. *"You have a whole new area of pleasure to explore."*

Justin blinked down at him. *"Kiss me."*

Lucas moved back up Justin's body and lowered himself on top of him so they were face to face. He let his own fins gently brush against Justin's and enjoyed watching the surprised pleasure on his face. *"There's only one problem with being in this form,"* he explained. *"We can get as close to orgasm as we like, but we can never actually come."*

"Surely fish get to come," Justin pointed out. *"Pretty sure all the baby fish out there mean they must be getting some."*

Lucas chuckled. *"But we're only half fish, remember? And whoever divvied up the parts made it so we only have our sex organs when we're in human form."*

"The gods are cruel bastards," Justin complained.

"Maybe, but at least we get human sex." Lucas pushed Justin's long wavy hair from his face and kissed him again. Their tongues brushed together, mimicking their fins. When Justin rolled him onto his back and took charge, Lucas wondered if he might have been wrong in his belief about sex. He was pretty sure he was ready to come right now, regardless of which form he was in.

As bossy as he had been about getting Justin into the water, Lucas had nothing on Justin when he took charge of the situation. He dragged Lucas upright and their kiss transformed into something fierce and primal. Their teeth clashed together as they clawed at each other, desperately seeking more than they could get in their present forms.

"I want to fuck you," Justin said. *"I want to bend you over and take you from behind until you scream with pleasure."*

Lucas moaned into the kiss. *"Tell me what else you want to do,"* he demanded.

"I want to lick you all over, including that delicious hole I ache to fill. I want to hear you cry out my name when I thrust my cock into your sweet arse."

"Please!"

"I want you in my bed, your legs spread wide, while I fuck you with that dildo you used when you were trying to get off. I want you to fuck yourself while I feed you my dick."

Lucas' heart rate increased and when Justin twisted him round so his arms were pinned against the floor of the pool, he thought he would collapse from the excitement and anticipation.

"You know what else I want?" Justin whispered.

"No."

"I want to take you under the water."

"*It's not possible,*" Lucas reminded him.

"*Maybe it could be,*" Justin explained. "*You've been to the aquarium. Did you see the tunnel under the sea where the visitors get to experience being underwater?*"

Lucas couldn't remember seeing such a tunnel, but he had left in something of a hurry and had not completed the tour.

"*I want to take you in there,*" Justin explained.

"*You'll get fired.*"

"*Not if we wait until after it's closed.*"

"*You can get inside?*"

"*No, but I know someone who can help out in that regard.*"

"*You don't mean your parents?*"

"*Yes. Why not? Don't you like the idea?*"

"*What are you planning on telling them? That you want them to break you into the place so you can have sex there?*"

"*Yeah, that about covers it.*"

"*But they're your parents!*" Lucas broke their kiss so he could try to concentrate on the conversation he had somehow lost track of without realizing.

"*My parents are immortals with the power to read minds. There would be little point in lying to them. Honesty is the best policy when it comes to dealing with my parents.*"

"*I guess,*" Lucas muttered, even though he wasn't entirely convinced this was a good idea.

Justin tweaked one of Lucas' nipples. "*I thought you'd be all for it. Especially considering how you threw yourself at me when you met me.*"

"*I thought we agreed that day never happened.*"

Justin grinned. "*Maybe I would prefer to remember the feeling of your lips on mine as your hard cock rubbed up against me. No amount of denim can hide an erection the size of yours. So, how about we take a trip to see the fishes?*"

Lucas could tell Justin really wanted this and he found himself nodding his agreement. "*On one condition.*"

Justin gazed at him questioningly. *"And what would that be?"*

"That you at least consider coming back to the sunken city with me. Even if it's just a quick visit for you to meet my family."

"They could come here if they really wanted to meet me."

Lucas decided not to push the issue too much. *"Just think about it."*

Justin kissed him again. *"Okay, I'll think it over, but I'm not making any promises. There's a difference between a swim in a pool and a long and dangerous journey through the ocean to a place I don't want to go in the first place."*

"Thank you," Lucas replied as they continued to roll around on the bottom of the pool.

They spent the next few hours swimming this way and that as Justin became accustomed to his fins and Lucas introduced him to all the sensitive spots he knew about.

Chapter Fifteen

Cari had done exactly as Justin had suggested she would and deposited them inside the aquarium after the place had closed for the day. She had assured them the alarms had been disabled and they would not be picked up by the surveillance cameras.

"Interesting parents you have," Lucas commented as Justin took him on a private tour of the place. "I notice she didn't say anything about how we're going to get out of here when we're ready to leave."

"She'll stay in this realm until I give her a call," Justin explained — at least he hoped she would. It wouldn't be the first time something had distracted her and resulted in him being landed in hot water.

Lucas didn't question him and they walked hand in hand through the aquarium. "How it is someone who professes to hate the ocean works in an aquarium?"

"I don't hate the ocean," Justin insisted. "I just have no desire to go swimming in it. There are a lot of dangerous creatures out there, not to mention a lot of pollution."

"It's not so bad once you're away from the land masses and the shipping routes," Lucas explained. "Well, the pollution isn't anyway. The dangerous creatures are all over, except in the sunken city, of course."

"What keeps them away from Atlantis?" Justin asked. "I would have thought a city full of mermen and mermaids would be ideal feeding grounds."

Lucas laughed. "It is, if they could only get past the sea dragons."

Justin frowned as he tried to figure out what animal Lucas was referring to. He had never heard of a sea dragon, though he imagined it had to be a pretty large and fearsome creature if it kept things like sharks away from the city. "I'm guessing we call them something else."

"No, you don't," Lucas replied. "The sea dragons are native to the city and aren't found anywhere else in the world. Humans don't know of their existence."

"Are you sure? If they're that big, surely they must have been spotted at some point in the past."

"They have the power to make themselves and their surroundings invisible," Lucas explained. "They keep themselves, the city and all the inhabitants within hidden from the world."

"Is that why no one has discovered the location of Atlantis?"

"Partly. That and the fact most humans are searching in entirely the wrong place anyway." Lucas let go of his hand as something caught his eye and he wandered across the room to peer into one of the tanks.

"You like sea horses?" Justin asked.

"I like most creatures of the sea," Lucas replied. "These ones are quite rare in my part of the ocean, though. I never saw this breed before."

"Understandable. There's a hell of a lot of water out there."

Lucas nodded and they carried on walking through the aquarium. Justin tried not to go through the building at a run, but his pace grew considerably faster as they neared the tunnel under the shark tank. When they finally arrived, they stopped at the edge and watched the sharks for several minutes.

"So many mer people have been lost to shark attacks," Lucas whispered. "I've been lucky to grow up in the sunken city, but those in clans outside the city lose many of their friends and family."

"They are beautiful but deadly," Justin agreed. "Though these ones aren't exactly man-killers."

"I still don't like them too much," Lucas muttered.

"We can go home if you like," Justin suggested. "We can go back to my flat instead."

Lucas offered him a smile and shook his head. "No, I'm okay. I don't want to wait any longer to feel you inside me. You and your mother have gone to so much trouble to get us in here that we might as well make the most of the opportunity."

Justin drew in long breath as Lucas lifted his borrowed T-shirt up and over his head, tossing it to the floor. He pushed his jeans down and kicked them out of the way. Since they hadn't intended to do any walking other than inside the building, neither of them had bothered to put on shoes. They weren't wearing underwear either, something which Lucas wasn't accustomed to and Justin hadn't seen the point of bothering with.

With trembling hands Justin unbuttoned his shirt and slid down the zipper of his trousers. "I *really* hope she managed to fix the cameras," he admitted. As a goddess who wasn't exactly familiar with modern technology, it wouldn't be entirely unexpected if she managed to screw up that part of the job. He guessed he would find out if his boss fired him during the coming week. Pushing the thought aside, he tried not to worry about it.

Lucas leaned back against the glass wall of the tunnel and watched him as he undressed. He stroked his cock to life as he waited for Justin to ready himself.

Justin had come prepared with plenty of lube and he used a liberal amount on his shaft before tossing the rest to Lucas. "Get ready for me," he ordered.

Lucas didn't need telling twice. He coated his fingers and reached between his legs to insert them into his arse. He moaned as he fingered himself and the sounds were music to Justin's ears. His own dick twitched in eager anticipation and he had to remind himself to take his time. He wanted Lucas to enjoy what they were about to do. The last thing he wanted was for Lucas to compare him to his former lover and find him coming up short. Otus had cared nothing for Lucas' pleasure and Justin intended to wipe those memories clear from Lucas' mind.

"I'm ready," Lucas finally said and his voice was husky with desire.

Justin stepped close to him and gestured for him to face the tank. "Lean over and place your hands on the glass," he ordered. Lucas obeyed him immediately and spread his legs a little. Justin moved them a little farther apart and eased his butt cheeks open wide.

Lucas gave a small whimper as Justin slid a lube-coated finger between his buttocks and found his hole. Lucas pushed back against the digit with a whine of pleasure. "I'm ready, Justin. I need your cock."

Justin could tell Lucas had certainly stretched himself a great deal and his hole was slippery with lube. He could always stop if it wasn't enough, but with Lucas begging to be fucked, he couldn't hold back any longer. He took himself in hand and stroked the hard flesh before stepping up against Lucas' back. He pressed himself against Lucas' arse and leaned down to whisper into his ear. "Can you feel how hard I am for you?"

Lucas pushed his arse backwards. "Fuck me, Justin. Please fuck me."

Justin couldn't resist teasing him a little longer and he spread Lucas' buttocks once again, this time keeping them apart and pressing the head of his dick up against the red pucker of Lucas' anus.

Lucas moaned and his hands slid on the glass.

"Leave your hands there," Justin ordered. "Don't move them until I say you can."

"Just fuck me," Lucas demanded. "I need you in me, need you to fill me."

"Soon, Lucas, soon," Justin promised. He reached down and ran his finger over the tip of his cock, gathering up the bead of pre-cum that had gathered there. He held it in front of Lucas' lips. "Taste how much I want you."

Lucas obediently licked the cum from his finger. "More."

"Greedy," Justin teased, though he was more than ready to come and had enough seed dripping slowly from his dick that he could oblige Lucas' desire to feed him more.

Lucas sucked his fingers clean, straining to get every last drop as Justin took his fingers away.

"I'm going to fuck you now," he told him as he focused his attention on Lucas' arse once more.

Lucas keened as Justin ran his dick along the crease from the small of his back and down between his cheeks. When he pushed the head inside, Lucas panted as he made an effort to relax his muscles.

"It's okay," Justin murmured as he reached round and took Lucas' wilting erection in his hand and stroked it back to life. "Just relax and let me in."

Lucas closed his eyes and took a deep breath. "Otus just used to push his way inside."

Justin caressed Lucas' penis with one hand and his stomach with the other. "I'm not Otus. I saw how he took you and that's not me. I want you to enjoy it when I'm inside you. I want you to come from the feel of my dick in your arse."

"On the solstice I come from the feeling of being filled with another man's seed," Lucas reminded him.

"I know, but I want you to feel that same way tonight too. Sex is supposed to be fun, not an ordeal you have to go through."

Lucas nodded and finally began to relax around him. "Give me more."

Justin pushed in a little farther and this time Lucas opened himself to the intrusion. "How are you doing?"

"Good," Lucas replied. "It's good."

With a grunt of satisfaction, Justin pushed the rest of the way inside and held his position while Lucas grew accustomed to him. He reached for Lucas' penis once more and found it half hard. He took him in hand and brought him to full hardness again. Lucas alternated between pushing back against his cock and thrusting his own dick into Justin's hand. He moaned loudly, though no one except the creatures of the sea were around to hear them.

"That's it," Justin encouraged. "Let me hear how much you enjoy this."

"Justin, please," Lucas moaned. "Fill me up. Let me feel you come inside me."

"Soon," Justin promised. He hoped not too soon, but he was so close he wasn't sure he would last much longer. He pulled out a little before pushing back inside with shallow thrusts.

Lucas clawed at the wall of the tank while the sharks swam overhead in the dimly lit room.

Justin released Lucas' erection, causing the merman to cry out with dismay. He placed his hands on Lucas' hips to hold him steady as he deepened his thrusts. He changed his angle slightly and found the spot he searched for. He hit it with the head of his cock and Lucas screamed out his pleasure.

"That's it." Justin moaned loudly. "Let me hear you."

Lucas screamed again. "Oh fuck!" he yelled as he came, his cum spraying the glass wall of the tunnel in a long line. He clenched around Justin's dick and the pressure sent Justin spiraling toward his own orgasm. He released his seed into Lucas' arse as he cried out his name. His legs felt weak and he thought he might lose his balance, but somehow he managed to keep his feet.

"I've made a mess of the glass," Lucas whispered, his voice sounding sleepy.

"We'll clean it up," Justin managed to reply.

Still locked together in their intimate embrace, Justin eased the two of them down to the floor. It wasn't comfortable at all, but he didn't want them to separate just yet.

"How do you feel?" he asked.

Lucas moaned contentedly. "Wonderfully full."

They stayed on the hard floor, side by side, still joined, while they savored the feeling of being together.

"The sharks keep looking at us," Lucas whined.

"Let them," Justin muttered. "There's nothing for them to see here except two men who just fucked each other senseless."

Lucas chuckled and the movement made his arse clench again. Justin felt his dick begin to harden once more. He moved his hips a little and Lucas' laughter became moans of pleasure.

Justin took hold of Lucas' penis and found it too had become hard again. He tugged his length and it only took a few strokes before he felt the heat of Lucas' cum spilling over his hand once more. He held Lucas through his second orgasm, then licked his seed clean from his fingers.

He was close to coming again himself and when Lucas clenched and quivered around him, it triggered his own release. He didn't come as hard as he had the first time, but Lucas' tremors sent him over the edge once again.

They lay in each other's arms for a long time, silently watching the sharks circling above them. Justin was utterly spent, though he could feel Lucas' cock against his thigh. His merman was completely insatiable. He reached between them and took Lucas in hand, cupping his balls and lightly squeezing and stroking him.

He was so lost in thought he didn't notice the warning signs that he was about to have a vision. His sight disappeared in an instant and he heard Lucas' squeak of surprised pain when he accidentally gripped his penis too tightly. He had just enough awareness of Lucas to relax his grasp, but then the world around him disappeared completely.

He was under the ocean again and he tried not to panic as he had done back at the dinner table the night before. He had never had two visions so close together and this one took him totally by surprise. He could see through the murky waters that he wasn't alone in the underwater world. Lucas swam up to him and wrapped his arms around his neck.

Justin had to admit it wasn't so bad under the ocean when he had a sexy merman like Lucas in his arms. He held him close and kissed him deeply.

"*Love you,*" Lucas whispered into his mind right before he disappeared from his arms.

Justin spun round, trying to see where Lucas had gone. When he saw him, he screamed, though no sound came from his mouth while he was underwater.

There was no mistaking what he saw before him. Lucas' dead body floated in the water a short distance away.

"*No!*" he screamed.

"Justin, Justin!" Lucas' voice came to him as though from a distance and while Justin could hear him he couldn't see him yet. It always took a few seconds for his sight to come back after having a vision, and while he didn't think it usually took this long, it did seem to be coming back.

"I'm okay," he said, trying to reassure Lucas when all he wanted to do was throw himself into his arms and remind himself that Lucas was very much alive and well.

"Was it another vision?" Lucas asked.

"Yes."

"What did you see?" Lucas rubbed Justin's arm comfortingly and Justin took his hand to maintain his anchor in the real world. "Can you tell me this time?"

Justin shook his head. "I really don't want to talk about it."

"Maybe it would help."

Justin didn't see how it would help Lucas at all to know he had just had a vision of his death.

"Was it the same vision you had at dinner?" Lucas asked.

"No, this one was different."

"But both scary, yes?"

Justin nodded.

"You know you can tell me anything," Lucas told him. "We're in this together now, aren't we?"

Justin didn't want to tell Lucas what he had seen, but perhaps a partial truth might be in order. "I think you're in danger if you stay with me."

"Are you trying to send me back to the sunken city again?" Lucas asked. "Because I'm not going anywhere without you."

The last thing Justin wanted was for Lucas to return to the underwater city, especially since he was fairly certain Atlantis was where he was destined to meet his death. Though maybe it was only if Justin went there with him. Justin only ever saw his own future in his visions. If he refused to go to Atlantis then perhaps Lucas could go home safely.

"I'm not leaving you yet," Lucas whispered before he kissed him tenderly. He ran his hands over Justin's body, soothing him with his kisses and his touch in a way no one else had ever managed.

Justin held him tight. "I need to go talk to my mother. Can I come to you later?"

"I thought we were going back to your place?"

"Maybe another time," Justin replied.

"I could come with you to see your mother," Lucas suggested.

Justin shook his head. The last thing he wanted was for Lucas to find out what he had seen in his vision. He reluctantly eased his way out of Lucas' embrace and they cleaned up any trace of their presence.

"Mum!" Justin called.

Cari appeared a moment later. "Did you have fun?" she asked before she caught sight of Justin's face. "Oh, darling, what's wrong?"

"Can you send Lucas back to Jake's and us to my flat?"

Cari nodded and thankfully didn't try to argue with them.

* * * *

Justin arrived back in his flat a moment later.

"You had another vision, didn't you?" Cari said. "What did you see this time?"

"Lucas, dead, in Atlantis."

Cari paled and sat on the sofa. "Are you sure?"

"Yes. I guess when Medina said I would lose him forever, she was taking no chances of my finding him again."

"Even the most powerful curse can be broken if you know how," Cari assured him. "I've seen Lucas' future, just as I have seen yours. I've seen the two of you happy together."

"Was that before or after Medina cursed me?"

"Before."

"And what do you see if you look now?"

Cari closed her eyes. "I see two possible futures ahead of you. One of misery, with Lucas dead."

Justin pressed on. "And the other?"

"The two of you blissfully happy together."

"Where? Here or in Atlantis?"

Cari chuckled and opened her eyes. "You never give up, do you? I'm not going to tell you what to do. You have to make your own choices."

"I have no idea how to break this wretched curse," Justin complained. "I think I should send him back to

Atlantis without me. If I do, he should be safe. I'll still have lost him, but better we're alive and celibate than for Lucas to die."

"Mermen aren't made for lives without sex," Cari pointed out. "You're amongst the most sexual creatures on the planet. Your sex drives are quite remarkable."

"So I've heard," Justin muttered. "It's not like I want to go the rest of my life without getting off, but if the other option is for Lucas to end up dead, then I don't see we have any choice."

"You need to find a way to break the curse, rather than simply trying to avoid it. Then you need to face the truth and take the advice I've been giving you all your life. Embrace your destiny instead of running away from it."

"Screw destiny. All I want to know is how to save Lucas when he's been cursed to die."

"Curses aren't destiny, they are a way of deliberately and maliciously causing someone's path to stray from what fate intended. You need to find a way to put your lives back on track."

"I tried apologizing to Medina," Justin reminded her. "It didn't exactly work."

"You didn't *exactly* mean it, though, did you? Perhaps a proper and heartfelt apology might be a little more effective."

Justin wasn't sure anything would appease Medina at this point, but with Lucas' life hanging in the balance he was willing to try anything.

"Medina!" he called, trying to keep his voice and tone as polite as possible.

The goddess appeared in the room a moment later. "You called me." She had a rather bored expression on her face.

"Yes," Cari said while Justin tried to gather his thoughts together. "Justin has something to say to you."

"He does?" Medina glared at him as though he were something she had trod in.

Justin tried to keep his temper under control by counting to ten under his breath. "I'm sorry for the way I spoke to you," he offered. "It was uncalled for, and I'm truly sorry for my behavior."

Medina didn't seem to be appeased. "Why should I believe you?"

One... Two... Three... Cari nudged him in the arm and he stopped counting again. "I've seen what will happen to Lucas, thanks to your curse. He doesn't deserve to die just because of me."

Medina stared at him in surprise. "You have the sight?"

Justin nodded. "I see events in my own future, and I saw myself witnessing his death."

Medina faced Cari. "You gifted your foster son with your powers?"

"No, he inherited those from his birth mother, an Oracle. I merely guide him and try to teach him how to control them."

"A monumental task with this merman, no doubt," Medina offered consolingly before turning back to Justin. "My curse is not a killing curse. Lucas was sent here to find you. I believed your stubborn nature would prevent you from leaving with him, thus you would lose him forever since Lucas has made his home in Atlantis and has extremely strong ties to the city."

"I saw him dead."

"I don't doubt your word." Medina tapped her lip as she paced back and forth across the room. "This is not what I intended. Unfortunately I don't have the sight of

Cari, and I'm unable to see how my curses play out when I inflict them. I only intended you and Lucas to be parted."

"So your intention was simply for the two of us to spend our entire lives sexually frustrated?"

"Yes. I didn't intend for Lucas to die as a direct result of the curse. This development could harm my own reputation amongst the gods."

Justin frowned at the goddess, who clearly only cared about herself.

"My powers are to bring lovers together and to teach those who scorn love the true value of it—not to kill. If it were to become known that my curse caused the death of an innocent…"

"You wanted me to lose him forever," Justin reminded her. "This is your curse playing out in the most final way possible."

"I realize that," Medina snapped. "Now, let me think."

"Can't you just undo your curse?" Justin asked. "I've apologized to you and you've admitted Lucas isn't to blame for any of this."

"A sacrifice," Medina suddenly declared with a snap of her fingers. "You will travel to my temple and make a suitable sacrifice, then the curse will be lifted."

"What sort of sacrifice?" Justin asked. "I'm not killing anyone and I include animals in that."

Medina stared at him in horror. "I don't want blood— animal or human—messing up my temple. The sacrifice should be personal to you. I'm sure you'll think of something suitable."

Justin had no idea what she had in mind. "Okay, where's your temple? Greece?"

"Why would my temple be in Greece?" Medina asked. "I'm not a Greek goddess, I'm Atlantean."

Justin closed his eyes as he realized his mistake. "Please tell me it's not in Atlantis."

"Of course it's in Atlantis," Medina replied, as though speaking to a child.

"Why can't I make this sacrifice here?" Justin asked.

"Or don't make the effort," Medina said. "I'm sure you and Lucas will be very happy together, for the little time you have left."

With those parting words Medina vanished from the room.

"She's done this deliberately," Justin complained to his mother.

Cari sighed. "If you're referring to the temple, then no, she is right. To break a curse takes a lot of strength and we are at our most powerful in our temples. I have my most potent visions when I visit the ruins of my own temple. Medina is more powerful than I, but even she has her limits, especially after sleeping for so many centuries. Curses strengthen over time and while she might have taken back her curse at the start with just an apology from you, it's probably too late for that now."

"Great. I guess I'm going to Atlantis, whether I want to or not."

"Maybe you'll like it there," Cari suggested. "You've seen nothing of the world from which you came. It's long past time you did."

"I just want to go in, break the curse and leave again. Can you or Dad send me there now?"

Cari shook her head. "I don't think that would be a good idea."

"You aren't going to make me swim there, are you?"

"Yes, I think I am. You have no idea what sacrifice is expected of you, and the journey will give you time to consider that, as well as learn more about the world you come from."

"I can't believe you're going to make me swim there."

Cari smiled and gave him a peck on the cheek. "You might find you enjoy it. If you need me or your father when you're in Atlantis, go and visit one of our temples and call for us. We might not be able to hear you otherwise."

"I thought you could hear me wherever I am on Earth, provided you're in this realm?"

"Usually, yes, but Atlantis is the one exception."

"Why's that?"

Cari rose to leave. "The sleeping gods are waking and they're being quite noisy about it. Unless you call to us from our temples, we may not hear you above the waking masses."

Chapter Sixteen

Justin ended the call to his boss with a sigh of resignation. He was pretty sure he wasn't going to have a job to come back to after his trip to Atlantis. Telling his manager that he needed a bit of time off for personal reasons had been fine. Explaining the bit of time would be at least three months and would have to start immediately had gone down like a lead balloon.

He tossed his phone into the glove compartment of his car and faced Caspian. "Don't scratch the car when you take it back to my place."

Caspian rolled his eyes. "Yes, I heard you the first time, and the second, and the third. Anyone would think you didn't trust me to drive it."

"I don't," Justin said. "I haven't forgotten the last time, when it got impounded."

"That wasn't my fault. The car was under my control the entire time."

"You were in the back seat," Justin reminded him. "Talk about back seat driving."

Caspian climbed out of the car and wandered down toward the sea. Justin followed him. Lucas already waited on the beach.

"Anything else you need before you go?" Caspian asked.

"I think I've got everything covered."

"Then I'll leave you to go explain your decision to Lucas. Have you decided what you're going to tell him yet?"

"Not a clue."

"Well, good luck and remember, if you need me or your mother, go to one of our temples and call us. We'll hear you from there and come to you."

"Thanks."

Justin hugged his father, who stood stiffly in his embrace. Caspian just wasn't the hugging type.

"Get out of here," Caspian mumbled gruffly.

Justin gave him a final pat on the back then hurried down the beach toward Lucas. Caspian followed after him at a more leisurely pace.

Lucas stared at him in confusion. "Isn't it a little cold to be wandering around in only a pair of shorts?"

"I didn't want to ruin any of my clothes," Justin explained. "These boxers are probably going to get trashed as soon as we go into the water."

Lucas gave the crashing waves a dubious glance. "You want to go swim in the sea? After all the fuss you made about even getting into the nice clean pool?"

"Yeah, about that…"

"What about it?"

"I've changed my mind about going to Atlantis."

"You have? Why?"

Justin didn't want to tell Lucas about the curse or his vision of his death, but he knew he would need some sort of explanation for his sudden change of mind. "I had a vision of myself in Atlantis." It was the truth, as far as it went. "Since it's pretty clear I'm going to be there one day, I guess there's no point in my putting off the inevitable."

"And you want to leave now?" Lucas asked. "Just like that?"

"Why not?"

Lucas gaped at him. "I guess there isn't any reason why we shouldn't leave, but what about Jake and the others?"

"I'll make sure they know what's happened," Caspian assured them. "Now I would suggest you leave immediately if you're going. I'm keeping you shielded from the prying eyes of humans, but I'm not going to stand around here all day."

Lucas quickly shrugged out of his clothes and tossed them at a bemused Caspian. "Can you take them back to Jake's house? They loaned them to me."

"Please," Caspian muttered with a roll of his eyes.

"Please," Lucas repeated. "Sorry. I'm still a bit stunned."

Justin fingered the hem of his boxers.

Caspian held out his hand. "Fine, since it seems I'm the designated laundry man, you might as well hand them over as well."

Justin stripped them off and tossed them to his father, who grumbled under his breath about the things he got stuck doing, thanks to his bloody sister.

"Ready?" Justin asked Lucas.

Lucas nodded and ran into the sea. Justin, after a moment of hesitation, followed him into the water.

He had a brief moment of panic when the sandy bottom vanished from under his feet as his tail and fins appeared. Lucas had apparently anticipated his reaction and was at his side immediately, ready to calm him and help him.

"It'll be easier when we're away from land," he promised. "Come on under the water before someone with a set of binoculars spots us out here and sees more than we want them to."

Even though he didn't need to, Justin took a deep breath and dove under the surface.

Lucas was a strong swimmer and he dragged Justin along with him as they swam away from land and the waters grew deeper and darker.

"Your eyes are designed to be able to see in the dark as well as in the sunlight," Lucas explained. *"They'll adjust to the lack of light at the bottom of the ocean within a few seconds."*

"I've never really had trouble seeing in the dark, even on land," Justin recalled. *"Never really thought about why, but I guess that would explain it."*

Lucas smiled at him and let go of his hand so Justin could swim under his own power. The loss of connection hit him in a way he hadn't anticipated.

"We're heading south?" Justin asked. Even if they weren't touching, Lucas' voice in his head would keep their connection alive.

"Southwest," Lucas confirmed. *"It'll take us about six weeks to get there, maybe a little longer since you aren't used to traveling great distances, swimming or otherwise."*

"Are you saying you don't think I can handle the trip?"

"No, but I think you'll struggle after a week or two of near constant swimming. Your body will adjust to being in this form for longer periods of time, but you'll still tire as much as you would if you were constantly exercising on land all day, every day."

"Will we get to sleep?"

"Yes, when we can."

"That doesn't sound too promising."

"You'd rather sleep in places where danger lurks? Get eaten by sharks while you're taking a nap?"

"Fine, we'll sleep when you say so," Justin agreed.

Lucas' laughter echoed through his mind. It helped to ease Justin's fears a little, yet he still fancied every dark shape in the distance was a shark, eager to take a bite out of him. Lucas teased him as he jumped at every little movement, but Justin noticed when they did come across some sharks, Lucas made sure to give them a wide berth. Even after they had made a short detour to collect the spear Lucas had hidden before coming to land, they erred on the side of caution.

Justin's stomach growled as the day progressed. Unfortunately they couldn't bring any food with them on the journey. They didn't wish to litter the ocean with wrappers, and few foods would last in the sea. He trusted Lucas would be able to feed him as they made their way to Atlantis, after all, Lucas had lived his entire life under the ocean.

"When do we eat?" he asked when his stomach rumbled for the fourth time in a matter of minutes.

"Hungry?"

"Yes, aren't you?"

"Not really, but I ate a large breakfast this morning. Jake is a great cook and he's been spoiling me. Human foods are so wide and varied."

"What do you eat normally?" Justin asked. *"And don't tell me seaweed."*

"Only if I have to," Lucas replied. *"We may have to eat some on our journey. There'll be some long stretches of seabed where there's not much else growing."*

"Yuk!"

Lucas laughed again. *"In the sunken city we have farms of sea fruits that you won't have heard of since they only grow far underwater. You'll love them."*

"Sounds boringly healthy."

"You won't see any fat mermen when you get there," Lucas said with a teasing smile.

"They all as hot as you?"

"Maybe," Lucas replied with a grin. *"I can't say I've got any complaints about the scenery."*

Lucas pointed down toward the seabed. *"Come on. Let's go see if we can scrounge up some food for you."*

Justin didn't think he could see anything even remotely edible in the direction Lucas pointed. He guessed he had to trust Lucas' judgment, and hope his lover hadn't got the type of sense of humor where he would feed him things that were totally revolting just to see the expression on Justin's face.

Lucas laughed again and nudged him toward something between the rocks that at least seemed to be green. *"I promise I won't poison you."*

* * * *

They traveled swiftly through the waters, using the currents to speed their journey as best they could. Justin had a feeling he was slowing Lucas down a little, even though he did his best to keep up. The days and nights blended into one another. Justin quickly lost track of how long they had been swimming without the sun and the moon overhead to mark the passing of time.

Lucas took charge of them both and Justin found he liked the bossier Lucas he was coming to know. Lucas encouraged him to keep going when he thought he couldn't swim for another minute, and when they finally stopped to rest, Lucas always let Justin sleep first, while keeping watch for danger. Justin slept, curled up against Lucas and when they swapped places, Lucas remained equally close to him.

Even though Justin no longer needed Lucas' hand in his to guide him in the right direction, he found himself aching for Lucas' touch anyway. With fingers entwined, they swam toward their destiny.

They passed the time while traveling, talking and learning everything they could about each other and the worlds they came from.

Lucas told Justin about his family and the older brother he clearly adored. Justin in turn told Lucas about what it had been like being raised by two immortals who had little concept of human needs. He assured him Caspian and Cari had done a good job bringing him up, but there had been a few incidents that none of his human friends could possibly understand. Things like Cari pulling him out of school whenever she foresaw him catching some human illness from his classmates. The teachers simply didn't accept things like 'he might become ill' as sufficient reason for his absence.

Justin learned about Atlantis and the laws which governed the city of mer people. Lucas seemed to know every law that had ever been written for the mer people, which made sense since he was in training to take over his father's position as a senior adviser to the king on all matters relating to the law. The only law Justin really worried over was the one Lucas made sure to remind him of frequently, the one that would prevent them being together as soon as they passed the boundaries into Atlantis.

With each passing day they grew closer. Justin fell a little deeper in love with Lucas and he was certain the other merman felt the same way. The idea of stepping away from him when they arrived at their destination didn't sit right with him at all. He could no more deny his feelings for Lucas than he could deny his own mer heritage.

Justin didn't know whether to be excited about seeing Atlantis or to dread it.

* * * *

Even though he had not felt the cold chill of the ocean, Justin was surprised when he felt his temperature rising in the middle of December. *"I think I'm coming down with something,"* he told Lucas as they swam closer to their destination.

"It's the mating fever," Lucas replied. *"The solstice is tomorrow."*

"Have we been swimming that long?" It didn't seem as long as all that, but if the mating season really was so close, they had to have been.

"Time flies when you're having fun," Lucas teased as he rammed into Justin from the side and tackled him.

Justin laughed as they playfully swam in circles around each other. *"Fun though this is, what are we going to do tomorrow?"* he asked.

"Have sex," Lucas replied with a grin. *"Lots and lots of very dirty sex. It's been too long since we were on land."*

"You're telling me," Justin muttered. *"I've never gone so long without sex since the day I discovered what my dick was for."*

"We'll make up for it tomorrow," Lucas promised. *"There's an island not far from here where we can go."*

"Is that the island your people use during the mating season?"

"No. The people of the sunken city use a large island and tend to separate off in groups of age. After all, no one wants to have sex knowing their parents are just around the corner doing the same thing. The island we use is big enough that

the generations can separate out. This island we'll use is several days out from the city. I met up with a clan of nomads on my journey to England and they told me this is the one they use when they're in the area. They won't mind us joining them."

"*Wait a minute!*" Justin swam to an abrupt halt. "*Just how many mer people use this island?*"

"*A fair few. Why?*"

"*And they're all there together at the same time?*"

"*Of course. The fever hits us all at once.*"

"*And they're all having sex on this tiny island?*"

Lucas frowned at him in confusion. "*I thought you understood the mating season and how it works.*"

"*I do, or at least I think so. I just hadn't realized we would practically be having sex in public.*"

Lucas' laugh drifted through his mind before his lover could hold it back. "*Is that what you're worried about?*"

"*You're not worried about people seeing us together?*"

"*Homosexual relations are only forbidden in the sunken city. The law is one of the reasons why some clans refuse to take shelter in the city. There were several men in the clan I met who were clearly lovers. You have nothing to worry about.*"

"*You're missing the point. It's not the gay sex that's bothering me. It's the public sex.*"

"*They'll be too busy breaking their own fevers to worry about us,*" Lucas promised. "*Now come on or we might not even reach the island in time and since it's the only one around here, we wouldn't want that.*"

Justin followed Lucas as he led the way to the island. They swam the rest of the day, steadily climbing upwards until they broke through the surface and breathed air for the first time since they had left England.

Lucas swam into his arms and they kissed in the moonlight. When they had to pull back to get some air, Justin realized he missed kissing underwater, where there was no need to worry about the lack of oxygen.

"Come on," Lucas urged. "We can sleep on the beach."

Justin didn't relish the idea of getting sand into places where it would no doubt be uncomfortable, but after sleeping on the floor of the ocean for so many nights, he considered the beach to be something of a step up. He would still prefer his bed and each time he found himself unable to sleep, he cursed his parents for refusing to send him instantly to Atlantis.

They collapsed on the beach and as they dried off, their legs returned, along with two rather obvious erections.

"I'm too tired to even jerk off," Justin commented as he gazed up at the stars. He didn't think the sky had ever been so clear.

Lucas' only reply was a loud yawn as he draped himself across Justin's body. They tangled their legs together, feet rubbing against shins as they tried to get comfortable.

Justin was still awake when Lucas began to snore. In the morning they would have the energy to seek relief. Justin couldn't wait until he was buried in Lucas once again.

* * * *

Justin woke to the pleasant sensation of someone's lips round his cock. He opened his eyes to see Lucas sucking him intently.

"That won't be enough to get me off today," he reminded him. "Only being inside that tight arse of yours will do it for me."

Lucas eased back with a long lick along his length. "Once the fever is broken, we'll be able to come any way we like, but for now, I'm just getting you ready. In case you hadn't noticed, there aren't any shops round here and we didn't bring any lube with us."

"Oh, yeah." Justin had completely forgotten when mermen traveled light, they didn't take anything with them at all. "Don't you have any oils or something you use instead?"

"Not that I know of. If there is something, Otus certainly never used it."

Justin growled under his breath. "When I meet this Otus I'm going to make sure he regrets the way he treated you."

"Please don't start picking fights?" Lucas asked. "It doesn't matter anymore. All that matters is you and me, right?"

Justin liked to think so, but from all he had heard about Atlantis, he wasn't sure their relationship would survive long there. He hoped he could break the curse quickly and be safely back in England before the next mating season came round. He knew he couldn't put off telling Lucas about his vision for much longer.

Oblivious to the direction Justin's thoughts had gone in, Lucas straddled him and slowly lowered himself down onto Justin's erection.

Justin held Lucas by the hips as he gracefully moved up and down, slowly and gradually taking him inside. He let Lucas set the pace, knowing he had never had the opportunity to do so during the mating season. He had always been taken roughly without any care for his pleasure. This time would be different. Justin would let Lucas take charge and take what he needed from him.

Lucas' hands felt hot against his chest.

"Feels so good," Lucas moaned. "Love you so much."

Justin's heart soared at Lucas' words. He wanted to say them back, but he felt the need to wait until they had finished making love. He didn't want Lucas to doubt him the first time he spoke the words. He needed him to know it wasn't just the passion and heat of the moment talking.

Lucas, who apparently had no such reservations, repeated his declaration as he slowly fucked himself on Justin's penis.

Justin's fever raged, but he felt close to coming and knew instinctively that the moment he came, buried deep inside his lover, it would recede for the season.

Lucas clenched around him and Justin came with a long moan of pleasure, filling the merman with his seed. Lucas' hands, still on his chest cooled as his own fever broke the moment Justin released inside him. Lucas cried out as he followed him over the edge, his cum spraying Justin's chest and chin in a wide arc.

"The fever's gone," Lucas said, though Justin didn't need telling. It had disappeared the moment they had orgasmed.

Justin pulled Lucas down to lay across his chest. "I love you. I just need you to know that."

"I already knew," Lucas replied with a chuckle. "I've known for a long time."

"Do you have prophetic tendencies too?" Justin teased.

"No, but you wouldn't be here with me if you didn't."

"We're bound together," Justin reminded him. "Medina has made sure of that."

"I like being bound to you," Lucas admitted. "I can't think of anyone else I'd rather be forced to have sex with."

"Me too," Justin said as he held Lucas in his arms.

"If you didn't love me, we'd still be in England with me trying to convince you to make this journey."

Justin tensed. He had to tell Lucas the truth. He couldn't keep it from him any longer. "There's something I have to tell you."

Lucas must have sensed the change in his tone and he gazed up at him with those mesmerizing golden eyes. "What is it?"

"I wasn't exactly truthful about my reasons for coming to Atlantis."

"You don't want to confront your father and draw a line under your past?"

"Yes, but that's not why I decided to come here. I could go my whole life without doing that, but since I'm going to Atlantis anyway, I do want to speak to him."

"Then why did you change your mind?" Lucas asked. "Was it for me?"

"In a way."

"What do you mean?"

"Do you remember in the aquarium?" Justin asked.

"You're not talking about the fucking in the tunnel, are you?"

"No."

"Then I guess you mean the vision."

Justin sighed and nodded. "I saw the two of us in Atlantis, and you were dead."

Lucas faced paled and Justin wondered if maybe he had been too blunt in telling him in such a manner. "I died?"

"Yes."

"In the sunken city?"

"Yes."

Lucas smacked him on the chest, hard. "And you're taking me back there? Are you fucking crazy? Why didn't you chain me to your bed in England and keep me there?"

Lucas stood and put some distance between them.

"We have to go to Atlantis to break the curse," Justin explained. "Medina told me she could lift the curse and save your life if I went to her temple in Atlantis and made a suitable sacrifice."

"What sort of sacrifice?"

"I haven't figured that part out yet."

Lucas gave him an annoyed grimace. "Are you planning on figuring it out before or after I die?"

Justin followed Lucas as he stalked down the beach, kicking at the sand. "Lucas, wait!"

Lucas rounded on him and shoved him in the chest. "You should have told me."

"I know. I'm sorry, but I didn't want you to know what I'd seen. I didn't want to scare you."

"Bit late for that," Lucas snapped. "You sure know how to put a blight on a perfectly good day. Here was me thinking we'd spend the day making love here on the beach and instead we're having our first big fight. Great."

Justin half wished he hadn't told Lucas the truth. "I don't want you to die."

"That makes two of us." Lucas' voice broke and he appeared to be on the verge of tears. Justin gathered him into a tight embrace and held him as he broke down. "Let's turn round and go back to England."

"We have to break the curse."

"You said I'd die in Atlantis, so we don't go there."

Justin couldn't say no to him. "It's okay, we'll go back. I'm sorry. I should have thought this through. We'll go home."

He had barely finished his sentence when his vision clouded and the beach disappeared. This time he didn't see Atlantis in his vision. He wasn't underwater and there wasn't a fin in sight. He was in his human form and he held Lucas in his arms. Blood poured from a wound on Lucas' head and even though Justin tried to stem the flow, there was nothing he could do. The light in Lucas' eyes dimmed as he tried and failed to save him.

This time his sight took even longer to be restored after the vision. When it did, the first thing he saw was Lucas' concerned face in front of him. "What did you see?" he asked.

"Your death," Justin whispered.

"In the sunken city?"

Justin shook his head. "No, in England. When I agreed to take you back there, it altered the place of your death, but not the ultimate outcome."

Lucas appeared defeated. "We have to go to the sunken city, don't we?"

"I think so."

"Can we at least put it off until tomorrow?" Lucas asked.

Justin took Lucas back into his arms. "We had plans for today," he reminded him. "We should stick to those plans, I think."

Lucas dragged him down onto the sand and they spent the rest of the day making love. Thankfully for Justin, they saw no other mer folk on the island, the clan Lucas had met apparently having left the area for the moment.

Neither dared to voice the thought that maybe this would be their last chance to partake of such pleasures.

Chapter Seventeen

Justin wasn't sure where this huge city was, but he was surprised he couldn't see it yet. Lucas had assured him they would be arriving within the hour, yet he couldn't see a single structure ahead of him.

"Are you sure we're close?" he asked for what had to be the fourth time.

Lucas nodded and quickened his speed. *"The city is invisible, remember?"*

"But surely we'll see the place when we're close enough?"

"It'll become visible when we've passed the sea dragons."

"And how are we going to get by them when we can't see them?"

"One of the guards will see us approach and bring us in." Lucas pointed ahead of them. *"There. See?"*

Justin focused toward where Lucas pointed and sure enough, a merman appeared ahead of them. *"Are you sure we aren't going to be eaten by one of these dragons?"*

"The dragons don't eat mermen," Lucas assured him. *"Though they're still dangerous to us if they get out of control."*

"Does that happen often?"

"Not very. Come on. Calder will show us in."

"Is he the merman ahead of us?"

"Yes. He's the leader of the guards."

"He looks pretty fierce."

"He can be, but he's a good merman."

They swam up to the guard and Justin noticed Lucas put a little distance between them as they drew near. Lucas had told him all about the laws of the city, but he still felt the loss of his lover's hand against his back and his fingers entwined with his own as they had been for much of their journey.

"Lucas," Calder greeted them with a smile. *"How did your mission to the northern clan go? Everyone is eager to hear your report."*

"But no one knows about my mission, save for the few mer people I told." Lucas couldn't hide his surprise.

"They do now. The king explained in the last Council meeting how you had swum north to enter into talks with the queen's people. Everyone is eager to hear how things are going. They hope the queen and Prince Finn will come back to the city soon."

Justin suspected it would be a cold day in hell before Finn swam back to Atlantis and while he wasn't entirely sure where the queen had disappeared to he had heard enough to suspect she too lived in England, probably fairly close to her son.

"And who's this?" Calder asked as he casually pointed his spear in Justin's direction. *"An emissary from the north?"*

"Not exactly." Justin wasn't sure how they planned on introducing him to the general population.

Calder studied him closely and Justin squirmed under the attention.

"He bears more than a passing resemblance to the king."

"They share a bloodline," Lucas explained.

Justin snorted, but refrained from commenting. He suspected everyone would discover his identity soon enough, and since his features were apparently similar to those of the king, there would be no hiding his parentage for long.

Calder didn't question Lucas. He guided them past the huge dragon that watched them carefully as they swam past. Justin felt his stomach do flips as the creature became visible and behind it the city of Atlantis. He had never seen an animal of such an enormous size. Even the whales they had passed on their journey were dwarfed by comparison. The scales on the back of the dragon were burnt orange in color, while its belly was a more yellowish hue. Its front legs were short, with wickedly long claws. What would have been rear legs on a land animal were large fins on the dragon. It had a long snout and when it opened its mouth, Justin could see fangs that looked as sharp as knives. The eyes of the creature were brown and looked almost human. Justin suspected intelligence lingered in their depths. Around the dragon's neck was a thick collar. Justin wondered how the mer people had ever managed to capture the dragons and how they held them in the city. The creature didn't appear remotely tamed and far more hazardous to his health than any number of sharks. He was relieved when it disappeared behind him.

Atlantis lay ahead of him, huge and sprawling, though the nearest buildings appeared to be in ruins.

"We'll report to the palace first of all." Lucas pointed toward the large structure situated in the center of the city and atop a large hill.

As they approached the building, they passed more and more of the mer people, all of them going about their daily business.

"There don't seem to be many children." Justin had only seen two amongst the increasingly large crowds of mer people.

"The number of births falls each mating season," Lucas explained. *"We're a dying race and no one seems to be able to discover the reason why. It's a regular topic of discussion at the council meetings."*

"Too many gay mermen?" Justin suggested with a laugh.

"I don't know, but that's why the law forbidding same sex relations was made. Someone thought that might be the problem, though the law certainly isn't the cure."

Justin could tell his joke had fallen flat and they swam on in silence for several minutes.

"The king and the Oracles are the only ones who know what my true mission was," Lucas told him as they neared the palace. *"Until you've spoken with your father I would suggest we simply say you're related to him and leave it at that."*

Justin nodded and followed Lucas through the archway into the palace. The building seemed to be in a far better state of repair than many of those they had passed. It also appeared to be a hive of activity with many mermen and mermaids swimming in and out. *"It seems very busy."*

"It always is at this time of day," Lucas explained. *"The king should be holding audience now and those who wish to speak to him will be here to do so. We'll have to wait in the queue until we can take our turn."*

Justin let Lucas lead the way and they took their place in the line of people. Neither merman said much as they waited to be called. As the line moved forward, Justin's nervousness grew.

Eventually they arrived at the front of the queue and a few minutes later they were called into the audience chamber.

Lucas swam toward the king with Justin following close behind. Justin watched Lucas bow low and followed his example.

"Lucas." King Nereus greeted him with a smile that grew even wider when he focused his gaze on Justin. *"Welcome back to the sunken city, which I believe your companion knows as Atlantis. I trust you both had a safe journey."*

Lucas nodded. *"We did indeed. It's good to be home once more."*

"I'm sure your family are delighted to have you back."

"I haven't seen them yet," Lucas replied. *"I came straight here to report to you."*

King Nereus smiled at him again. *"Then I won't keep you long. I can tell your father missed you during your time away. As a father who has also been parted from his son, I can recognize the signs in another."*

To anyone else present in the room, it would sound as if the king was missing Prince Finn, but Justin had a feeling the words had been for his benefit.

The king waved them both closer to his throne. *"And who have you brought back with you?"* he asked.

"This is Justin." Lucas beckoned Justin forward.

The king studied him carefully. *"And what brings you to the sunken city?"*

Lucas swam forward again. *"Justin would appear to be a relation of Your Majesty. I saw the resemblance between the two of you almost at once."*

The king nodded thoughtfully. *"Since I have never seen a good reflection of my own face, I'll have to take your word for that."* He turned to Justin again. *"As kin, you are most welcome here."*

Justin bowed again. *"Thank you, Your Majesty."*

"We will talk privately later," King Nereus assured him. *"Lucas will show you the way to my private quarters. Wait*

for me there until my audience this morning has concluded. Lucas will show you to the guest suite later."

Lucas swam backwards from the king with a grace Justin envied. Although he was quite capable of swimming in a forward direction, the backward swimming was another matter entirely.

"I'd rather stay in your bed than the guest suite," he commented to Lucas as he too bowed to the king.

Suddenly he heard a cacophony of voices in his head, all speaking at once and saying the same thing. *"Lover of men."*

He glanced over to Lucas and saw his face was a mask of horror. He reached out to touch him but the merman recoiled from his touch. *"What's the matter?"*

"You just told everyone in the room you want to share my bed," Lucas snarled. *"Even though we use sponges to sleep on here, I'm quite sure there isn't a merman present who didn't understand your meaning."*

"I thought I was just speaking to you."

Lucas flipped round and swam away through the archway. Justin glanced over his shoulder at the king. He expected to see anger on his face, or at least censure, but instead he was surprised to see his features set in a thoughtful expression.

Keeping quiet seemed to be the best course of action and he silently followed after Lucas.

Justin didn't want Lucas to be angry with him. His brief tastes of the merman's temper back in England and more recently on the island had been more than enough for him. He wished he could take back what he had said, but it was too late. Underwater communication was still relatively new to him and he was frustrated with himself for making such an embarrassing gaffe. They had met no other mer on their way to Atlantis and Justin had had no clue his thoughts were being transmitted on all frequencies, rather than privately to his lover. He didn't know how he was going to repair the damage he had done, or if he even could.

* * * *

Lucas deposited Justin in what he referred to as the receiving room and quickly left with a promise to return later in the afternoon. His manner was abrupt and blunt and Justin flinched as Lucas swam from the room, leaving him to wait for the king to join him.

Justin didn't have to wait long. King Nereus swam into the room a short while later. He dismissed his guards, leaving Justin and the king alone.

"Welcome home, my son," the king said as soon as they were alone.

Justin bit his tongue rather than reply as he wished. He didn't consider himself to be the son of the merman before him and Atlantis was not his home.

"You are new to your mer form," the king continued.

"Yes."

"I can tell. You have yet to master the skill of sending your thoughts to an individual, rather than to anyone in the vicinity."

"I've been raised on land," Justin reminded him. He refrained from adding the words 'because of you', but they hung in the air anyway.

"I know, and I don't blame you for your ignorance. We will ensure you are appropriately schooled as soon as possible."

Justin nodded, but he was curious about something. *"Aren't you going to say anything about what you heard?"*

"You mean your remark to Lucas about sharing his bed?"

"Yes."

"I assume Lucas has explained to you the laws here forbid sexual relations between two mermen."

"He did tell me." Justin wondered if he was already in trouble because of his careless remark.

"You have been raised on land and are unaccustomed to our ways. Your words to Lucas may be explained in this way, yet…"

"Yet what?" Justin asked as the king's voice trailed off and he seemed to become lost in his thoughts.

"I raised another son who, like you, craved the touch of a merman."

"You're talking about Finn?"

"Prince Finn, yes," King Nereus confirmed. *"I made many mistakes with him and he is now lost to me. I don't wish to repeat those errors with you."*

"What do you mean?" Justin was surprised by the king's words as well as his tone. He seemed to harbor some regrets, rather than being the virtual tyrant he had been led to believe.

"I need an heir, someone who will one day take my place as ruler of the sunken city. You, my firstborn son, should be here at my side."

"I won't live in a closet," Justin stated firmly.

"I don't know this word, closet."

Justin tried to think of the mer equivalent. Even though he had been raised to be fluent in many languages, including that of the mer people, some words simply had no translation. *"It means I don't want to hide who I am."*

"I think it would be best not to tell everyone you are my son right away."

"That's not what I meant," Justin explained. *"I'm gay – or a lover of men, as your people say – and I won't hide that part of me."*

"For the moment, I think it would be best if you did."

"For the moment?" Justin asked.

"*Until you have decided whether you wish to live here permanently. I hope you will, but I won't force you to do so.*"

Justin nodded, relieved he wasn't expected to decide straight away. "*I don't know if I want to spend my life here in Atlantis. This is all very new to me.*"

"*That's understandable,*" King Nereus replied. "*You have much to learn about the city and what we have to offer you.*"

"*I have a life back in England,*" Justin reminded him. "*I have a job, a home, friends and family.*"

The king waved his concerns away. "*You would have a job here, a home and I am also your family. As for friends, you already know Lucas, and I'm sure you will soon have many more besides him.*"

Justin could tell the king was firm in his belief that now he had arrived in Atlantis, he would want nothing more than to stay and begin a new life. Justin didn't know what sort of life would be ahead of him if he stayed in the underwater city. All he wanted was to find a way to break Medina's curse and swim back home. Until he found an answer to what sort of sacrifice Medina wanted from him, Justin figured the best way to go about things would be to go along with King Nereus' plans.

"*Perhaps we could have a trial period of my living here,*" he suggested. "*It's all very different and there's a lot for me to get used to.*"

"Wonderful," the king exclaimed. "*I'll send someone to fetch Lucas so he can show you to the guest quarters. I'm afraid it would be entirely inappropriate for you to share his sleeping quarters.*"

"*I understand.*"

King Nereus patted him on the shoulder and guided him to the archway. "*I'll let the palace staff know you can have the run of the palace and they are to answer any questions you have about the city. I hope you will find you*" *like it here and that I'll soon be able to formally introduce you to everyone as my son and heir. In the meantime, we'll simply say you're kin who has come to the sunken city to learn about life here."*

The king waved over a young mermaid swimming at the far end of the hall. *"Go find Lucas and have him show Justin to the guest quarters."*

The mermaid bowed and swam off at speed.

"Well, I have work to do," the king explained. *"I'll leave you to get settled in and we'll talk more tomorrow."*

The king swam off and Justin waited for the mermaid and Lucas to return. Eventually the mermaid appeared, but the merman with her, while bearing some resemblance to Lucas, was not his lover.

"I'm Halcyon." The stranger greeted him with a smile. *"I'm Lucas' older brother and one of the liaison officers for those who are new to the city. I'll show you to the guest quarters."*

The mermaid swam away, leaving Justin with Lucas' brother. *"I thought Lucas was going to show me to my room?"*

"He was, but he's been away several months now and our parents are reluctant to let him out of their sight so soon after his return."

"He's not in trouble, is he?" Justin hoped his words in the audience chamber hadn't also resulted in Lucas getting into trouble with his parents.

"Your thoughts are spilling over to me," Halcyon warned him. *"Though to answer your questions, yes, Lucas' parents have heard about what you said to him, and that is the reason why he is with them now, rather than showing you to your quarters."*

"Then I have got him into trouble?"

"Not really. I already knew my brother desired men and when I heard what had happened, I spoke to our parents to help smooth things over. They are discussing the matter with

Lucas and coming to terms with things. I suspect they might have known something of his inclinations already, no matter how vehemently he denies them."

Halcyon seemed a nice enough merman and Justin wondered how much Lucas had told him.

"He told me very little, though I don't need to hear him say the words to be able to figure out the two of you are lovers," Halcyon replied. *"You really need to work on projecting your thoughts properly before you get yourself into a lot of trouble."*

"I'm starting to realize that. Any tips on how I go about that?"

Halcyon frowned. *"We learn how to communicate privately or publicly from when we're children. Mostly it's just a question of focus. You'll figure it out soon enough."*

"I hope so."

"In the meantime, just try to keep those naughty thoughts about my little brother to yourself."

Justin laughed at Halcyon's teasing and was still chuckling away when they arrived in the guest quarters.

"I'll make sure Lucas knows where to find you," Halcyon promised.

"Thank you."

Halcyon nodded to him and departed, leaving Justin alone for the first time since he had left England. More than anything he wished Lucas was with him while he became accustomed to the city. He hoped he saw him soon and that he could repair the damage his ignorance had caused,

Chapter Eighteen

"You can't avoid him forever," Halcyon told Lucas.

"I'm not avoiding anyone," Lucas replied. *"I've got a lot to catch up on now I'm back home."*

"Justin seems like a pleasant merman," Halcyon commented. *"Handsome too."*

Lucas ignored him.

"Where did you meet Justin anyway?" Halcyon asked.

"He's a member of the queen's clan," Lucas lied.

"Really? Then why is he so inept at communicating with his mind? The queen never seemed to have that sort of difficulty. If I didn't know any better, I'd say Justin had lived his whole life on land, rather than in the water."

Lucas couldn't meet his brother's eyes. He had never been able to successfully lie to Halcyon.

"He's got an interesting swimming style too," Halcyon continued. *"Like he's not quite used to his fins."*

"Do you have a point you want to make?" Lucas snapped.

"Who is Justin really?" Halcyon countered.

"I told you. He's a merman from the queen's clan and kin of King Nereus."

"Yeah, so you said. But what's the truth? Or perhaps I should take a guess and see how close I am?"

"You think you're so smart. You tell me."

Halcyon appeared way too pleased at Lucas' challenge. *"I think Justin grew up on land. I believe he is some relation to the king — there's too much of a resemblance for him not to be — but that's the only part of this I believe. I think you've been to land to track him down and bring him back here. I also think you and he are lovers."*

Lucas glared at his brother. *"I told you already, I won't risk my career by breaking the laws I'm supposed to uphold."*

"Those laws only apply to those who live in here in the city. When you found Justin, you weren't here. You've known him intimately, I can tell."

"What makes you so sure?"

"Because you've changed since your return. There's something in your eyes that tells me what you've found with Justin is more than just sex to release the pressure during the mating season. I think you're in love with him. What I don't understand is why you brought him back here, instead of staying with him. Care to explain what in the world you were thinking when you made that spectacularly stupid decision?"

Lucas should have known his brother would have figured things out. *"We had to come here,"* he admitted. *"Even if it's only for a little while. There's something we have to do. When that's sorted, we're going to decide whether we stay here or go back to Justin's home."*

"And where would that be?"

"On land, like you guessed."

"And what is it you have to do?"

"Break a curse."

Halcyon laughed, just as Lucas suspected he would. Halcyon didn't believe in curses or magic. Lucas used to be like him, but he knew better now. *"Are you serious?"* he finally asked when he noticed Lucas wasn't laughing along with him.

"Very."

"And once this curse is broken, you'll be leaving, yes?"

"I don't know, which is why nothing can happen between me and Justin now we're here in the city. If we decide to stay here, I don't want to have ruined my career before it's even started."

"There's more to life than work," Halcyon reminded him. *"Maybe Justin is worth giving up your career for."*

"Maybe he is, but until we've made our decision, I'm going to do what I've always done."

"Don't you think you should tell Justin why you're avoiding him?" Halcyon asked. *"It's been two days since you arrived and I'm sure he's wondering why he hasn't seen you once in that time."*

"I've been busy."

Halcyon raised his hands to the ceiling in despair. *"You can't avoid him forever, no more than you can avoid accepting who you are and what you want."*

* * * *

Lucas didn't see Justin until the first convened Council meeting since their arrival. They were situated at opposite sides of the room, and Justin's eyes focused on him more often than not. Thankfully for Lucas, no stray thoughts broadcasted from Justin to the whole room. Unfortunately there was a voice in his head he didn't want there. Otus, guarding the archway directly behind Lucas, had been keeping up a constant litany of chatter from the moment the meeting had begun.

"Did you let him fuck you last season?" Otus asked. *"Was he better than me? Did he take you hard – the way you like it – or was he lacking in technique?"*

It took every bit of willpower for Lucas to remain silent.

"Everyone's talking about you, you know?" Otus continued. *"They think you'll be dismissed from your post before the next solstice. That's what happens when you let men fuck you. It shows you're weak and easily led. No lover of men has ever dared to aspire to the lofty height of senior adviser to the king, and you won't either. Everyone will be watching you next mating season. They'll hear you beg to be fucked and any respect they had for you will be gone."*

Medon, another trainee, who sat in the meetings like Lucas, seemed to realize Lucas was communicating with someone and decided he too would chime in with his opinion. *"Your lover can't keep his eyes off you. You might want to remember that as someone who hopes to be in charge of our laws, you should be one of those who keeps them."*

Lucas tried to shut the two of them out, but it became increasingly difficult, the longer the meeting dragged on.

"Why don't you join the gatherers?" Otus suggested. *"There are several of them who would like a go at that arse of yours. I suppose it's been selfish of me to keep it to myself all this time. But now your secret is out, I'd be happy to share it with the others."*

"Enough!" King Nereus' bellow echoed through the minds of everyone present.

Lucas wondered what he had missed.

The king pointed his trident at Otus. *"You, guard, leave this room immediately."* He then focused his attention on Medon. *"You too. Get out."*

Lucas waited for the king's anger to turn to him, yet it didn't. There had always been rumors that the reigning king of the sunken city was able to read the thoughts of anyone who had sworn allegiance to the city. Lucas wondered if that was what had happened here.

"Yes, Lucas," the king's words came into his mind. *"Now, if you could concentrate on the matters at hand."*

Lucas nodded, even as he worried about what he might have been thinking at any time he had been in the king's presence.

"Concentrate," King Nereus snapped.

Lucas made an effort to put his worries from his mind and the meeting continued to conclusion without any further outbursts or interruptions.

After the meeting had concluded, Justin made a beeline for Lucas. It seemed there would be no more avoiding him.

"Where have you been?" Justin asked. *"I've been hunting all over for you."*

"I've been busy. There's been a lot to catch up on. Lots of important work to do."

"More important than going to Medina's temple and breaking the curse?" Justin asked. *"You know, the curse that means you're going to die – and probably fairly soon."*

Lucas shook his head. *"We can go there now, if you want."*

Justin agreed and they set off across the city.

"I was expecting more homophobic wankers here," Justin commented.

Lucas stared at him in confusion. Justin guessed Caspian hadn't included that particular colorful expletive in Lucas' vocabulary. *"Idiots,"* he amended.

"There are plenty of those," Lucas told him.

"I didn't say there weren't any, just that I haven't seen them."

"Give it time and you will," Lucas muttered. *"Do you know why King Nereus ordered those two mermen from the room?"*

Justin wondered at the change of subject. *"I assumed they were talking to each other instead of concentrating on the meeting."*

"They were mocking and goading me."

"I'm sorry, but surely they're not typical of all mer people."

"They're typical of those who live here. All I ever wanted was to do my job and make my father proud. As a homosexual merman I'll only bring him shame and I'll never be able to take a place on the Council."

"We don't have to stay here," Justin reminded him. *"We can return to England as soon as the curse is lifted."*

Lucas nodded. *"I know, but you have to understand that leaving everything I've ever known is a huge decision."*

"I know. But once the curse is broken, we'll have to decide where we're going to spend our lives."

"Speaking of curses, here we are." Lucas gestured to the structure in front of them. *"Medina's temple."*

The place appeared deserted, as though no one had set foot or fin inside for centuries. Justin suspected that might actually be the case. Were it not for the statue of the goddess, he would not have believed they were even in the right place.

"Most mer avoid the temples," Lucas explained.

"But you don't."

"As children, Halcyon and I used to play in the ruins. We would swim through them all as we hid from each other and the other youngsters of the city."

"Sounds like fun."

"It was. These are the public temples. There are private ones underneath the palace, but I don't know where Medina's would be. Hopefully she will come to this one."

"Medina!" Justin called. *"We summon you here."*

The goddess appeared immediately. *"I see you have made it to Atlantis. How are you enjoying your visit here?"*

"It's okay," Justin replied. *"We're here to ask you to lift your curse."*

"Really, Justin, have you forgotten our agreement? A sacrifice must be made before I can do that."

"I've lost my job by coming here to Atlantis."

Medina laughed. "Jobs are easy to come by, especially for a bright young merman like you. A true sacrifice is something which cannot be replaced. What else do you have to offer me?"

Justin glanced at Lucas, who shrugged. He clearly had no idea either.

Medina vanished, though her presence lingered a little longer. "Summon me again when you're better prepared. But don't leave it too long. Time is already running out."

"We could try the Oracles," Lucas suggested. "They might be able to see you make the sacrifice and tell you what it is."

Justin didn't have any better ideas, so he followed Lucas out of the temple and to the home of the Oracles.

They too lived in a temple, though theirs was far better kept than that of Medina. The only place more luxurious in Atlantis, so far as Justin had seen, was the palace itself.

"We shouldn't really be here," Lucas told him, "not without permission of the king. Only the royal family are permitted to consult the Oracles without his authority."

"Aren't I included in that family?" Justin asked.

"I guess."

"Or we could go and ask for permission if it makes you more comfortable?" Justin suggested.

"He'll want to know why and King Nereus doesn't believe in curses. If he asks about our visit, let's just say you came here to ask about your mother. As she was an Oracle herself, it's only natural you would wish to talk to those who knew her."

The Oracles were waiting for them when they arrived. Lucas introduced them to Justin who hoped they could assist.

Ula turned to the servants — or were they guards? — present in the room and waved them away. They each bowed respectfully and swam out of the room. Perhaps they weren't guards after all.

"Why did you send them away?" Justin asked.

"Our servants are here to help us with things we cannot do without our sight," Delwyn explained, *"but they also report everything they hear to the king."*

"Everything?"

"Yes. They didn't used to, but Mallea, the king's adviser who reports on us, has asked for far more detailed reports in recent months. They wish to know the name of every merman and mermaid who has visited us, what they have asked us and what our replies have been."

"That sounds really intrusive."

"We're used to it," Kai said. *"Though, as you can see, our spies are happy to leave the room if we request they do so. Their loyalty is to us first and foremost. They will no doubt report that you have visited us, but they will not say anything about the reason why, because they will not know. They will make something up if questioned directly."*

Justin chuckled at the idea of the Oracles getting one over on the king.

Ula swam forward and embraced Justin. *"Welcome, my brother."*

"Brother?" he asked.

"Not literally," Ula confirmed. *"But as one of us, you are most welcome here."*

"Can you help us?" Justin asked. *"Can you see what we must do to appease Medina?"*

Ula shook her head. *"Medina is a powerful goddess. Her powers exceed our own and we can see nothing of her plans."*

"She's blocking you?"

"Yes."

Justin sighed. *"Then I guess we'll have to figure out what the sacrifice is on our own."*

"Were you to hone your powers, you might see for yourself," Kai suggested.

"I can never see my future on command," Justin explained.

"That's because you reject your powers rather than nurturing them."

"That's what my mother — my foster mother, that is — says."

Delwyn nodded. *"The Goddess of Prophecy is correct."*

"You knew about Cari?" Lucas asked. *"Why didn't you tell me before I left? It would have saved me quite a bit of time."*

"Before you left, Justin was shielded by those more powerful than us. We knew Cari had been present at his birth, but not what happened afterwards. We could tell he was protected, but that could have been from a distance and not necessarily by Cari. Now that Justin is here, standing before us, we can see more, though not what you would wish us to see."

"If Justin wishes to find answers through visions, he must open his mind to them."

"I don't like having visions," Justin complained. *"They're a nuisance."*

Ula laughed and shook her head, her long aquamarine hair floating around her like a cloud. *"For as long as you think like that, you'll never see anything more than those visions which force themselves into your mind."*

"I just want to know how to stop the vision of Lucas dying coming true."

"Events are already on course for that eventuality unless you can figure out a way to appease the goddess."

"I have an idea," Delwyn interrupted. *"Lucas, ask Justin the question you most want answered."*

"*What do you mean?*" Justin asked.

"*Our powers are greatest here in our temple. As an Oracle, your powers should also be amplified. Direct questions to us can trigger visions. Perhaps a direct question to Justin can do likewise.*"

Lucas turned to Justin. "*What sacrifice does Medina want?*"

Delwyn's suggestion certainly worked. Justin's sight vanished as the vision came to him. Medina stood before him while Lucas' corpse floated to his right.

"*You seek answers in the wrong place,*" Medina told him.

Then the vision was over. Justin waited for his sight to be restored and this time he was certain it took longer than usual. He remained blind for several minutes before Lucas' concerned face formed before him.

"*Did it work?*" he asked.

"*I saw Medina,*" Justin said. "*She told me I'm searching for answers in the wrong place.*"

"*She means you won't find what you're looking for in a vision,*" Ula explained. "*It also confirms our suspicion that she is blocking us from seeing your sacrifice.*"

"*Are you all right?*" Lucas asked him. "*I need to get back to work, but if you're still shaken, I can make my excuses.*"

"*I'm fine. It just took a little longer than usual for my sight to come back. You go back to work. I'm going to stay here a little longer.*"

"*You wish to know about your mother,*" Delwyn accurately guessed. "*We'll tell you what we know of her with pleasure.*"

Justin let Lucas leave and turned to the Oracles. He wondered what they would have to say about the mermaid who had lost her life bringing him into the world.

"*What do you wish to know first?*" Ula asked. "*I have all Daphne's memories from the moment she came into her powers until the night she held you in her arms.*"

Justin didn't know what he wanted to know specifically and he didn't answer immediately.

"*She loved you very much,*" Ula whispered. "*After she left here, her one goal was to protect you. She called out to our goddess for help.*"

"Your *goddess?*" Justin asked. "*I didn't think the mer people worshiped any gods.*"

"*Most don't,*" Ula agreed. "*At least not any more. But a long time ago, when Atlantis first fell below the waves, mer people and Atlanteans lived in harmony together. They told us of their gods and how they called on them in times of need and thanked them for their benevolence. The mer adopted those gods as their own. Then one day they seemed to stop hearing our prayers. Only a few mer continued to pray to any of them, but Cari, the Goddess of Prophecy, watches over us still and the Oracles have always called on her. Unlike many of her kin, she has not deserted us.*"

"*Cari raised me,*" Justin told them. "*She was a good mother to me, even though she knew nothing of bringing up a child, let alone one who was mer.*"

Ula smiled. "*We thought she might have been raising you, but we could not tell Lucas of our suspicions in case we were wrong. I saw Cari through your mother's eyes when you were born. After she passed, we could not see you at all. We were sure you were being hidden by someone more powerful than us and Cari was our best guess. She could, however, have shielded you while leaving you amongst humans, or mer who have chosen to live on land.*"

"*She was a mother to me and her brother Caspian was my father.*"

"*The God of Justice,*" Delwyn said.

"*Yeah, that's the one.*"

"*He is another god the mer have continued to call out to, though perhaps not intentionally. When they cry out for justice, they are calling to him, whether they know it or not.*"

"*They were good parents to me. I just wish I had known my mother.*"

Ula patted his hand, though Justin had no idea how she knew where to reach. "*At least you're now getting the opportunity to know your birth father.*"

"*I don't want to know him,*" Justin snapped. "*He abandoned my mother to fend for herself and I hold him solely responsible for her death.*"

Ula sighed. "*I can see why you would think that and I don't seek to change your mind, but you must be aware of the laws in the sunken city about Oracles.*"

"*That they can't have sex? Yes, I know about that. It makes no difference. He still had a responsibility to keep her safe and he didn't.*"

"*Prince Nereus, as he was then, also had a responsibility to his father and his people. He could not have left with Daphne. They would have called out every guard to track him down. As it was, they sent a great many after Daphne, and only her visions of the future and the protection of our goddess kept her safe. They didn't call off the search until some time later when I arrived here, and they realized she had passed from this world. With the prince gone with her, they would never have given up their search.*"

"*I'm not saying he should have run away with her. But why couldn't he have admitted to what they had done and let her stay here?*"

"*Because he feared you might be put to death,*" Ula stated simply. "*Oracles are forbidden to have children. It is one of our most harsh laws, but it is there for a reason. If it were to be discovered that the heir to the throne had impregnated an Oracle, we truly don't know what would have happened to the prince and Daphne, but there is little doubt you would not have been allowed to live.*"

"*That's barbaric!*" Justin exclaimed.

"We agree, though it would have been no more so than the abortions that the humans you were raised amongst largely condone."

Justin hadn't thought about it in those terms. One of his former colleagues, a teenager who had worked a couple of holiday seasons at the aquarium, had faced the tough choice of whether to keep her unborn baby or not. She had chosen not to and he had not judged her for it.

"Your parents made the best choice they could for you," Ula explained. *"They wanted you to live and hoped because you were born to only one Oracle parent, you would not inherit more than one of our powers. Those who have more than one Oracle in their line see more."*

"Lucas told me something about this, but I don't understand. Why don't they allow Oracles to have relationships, just not with each other? Or only with Oracles who have the same power?"

"Because our descendants all inherit our powers. If they were to allow any of us to have relations, it's only a matter of time before one is born who has more than one power. Think about it, say you were to have a child with one of the mermaids."

"I'm gay," Justin interrupted.

"Yes, we know, but for the example I'm explaining, suppose you weren't. That child would also inherit the power to see into the future. Then suppose Kai here were to have a child of his own with one of the mermaids. That child would inherit his gift to see events taking place in the here and now. Any grandchildren would have the same ability and their children as well. Soon there would be so many Oracles it would be impossible to stop them from forming relationships with each other, and sooner or later, there would be those born who see more than we do and it would drive them insane, just as it did our sister of so long ago. It's far easier to simply keep the

three of us celibate and avoid the problems in later generations."

"But you could stick to the Oracles who have the same powers you do?"

Ula nodded. *"They could, but when one of my predecessors was asked that very question, many years ago, he replied that it would split the mer into four factions and tear us all apart. There would be those that see the future, the past and the present, and those who see nothing at all. Instead of working together, as we do now, the Oracles would end up fighting each other and those without powers would suffer as well. The mer have lived in peace for as long as we can remember. We have never fought amongst ourselves. We hope to never do so and if the law helps to keep our peaceful existence then who are we to argue?"*

"It doesn't exactly seem fair that you can't have relationships," Justin said.

"You are an Oracle too," Kai reminded him. "Sexual relations are forbidden for you as well."

"I'm not giving up sex," Justin replied. "I love Lucas and I want to take him away from this place as soon as I've figured out how to break the curse."

"You don't think maybe you should stay here a little longer before you make that decision?" Ula asked. "You may find the sunken city has a lot to offer you, if you give it a chance."

"I could never live in a place where I'm not allowed to be with the one I love."

All three Oracles smiled at him with almost eerie similarity.

"What?" Justin asked.

"Of all mermen, King Nereus is the one who understands the dilemma you are in better than any other, and unlike when he was in the same situation, he is now in a position to change the law."

"I thought you said the law about Oracles was never going to be changed?"

"It won't be," Ula agreed, *"but few know you are an Oracle. Unlike us, you have your sight and no one in the sunken city knows you have the power to see the future. It is only your love for men that is a known problem and the law relating to homosexuality is totally different from the law relating to Oracles. That law may one day change."*

"Do you think so?"

Ula smiled again. *"Perhaps, but if you leave as quickly as you intend to, you'll never know."*

Justin supposed they had a point. He could bide his time here and see how things went. It wasn't as though he could leave before he'd broken the curse anyway.

The Oracles spent the rest of the day talking to Justin about Daphne. They told him stories about her greatest visions and how she had prevented several disasters which could have befallen their people thanks to her gift.

They also told him repeatedly about her love for his father and the king's love for her. Justin didn't doubt their love for each other, but it didn't change his mind about his father. As sympathetic as he was to the position his father had been in, he still believed he could have done more to keep the mermaid he loved safe.

* * * *

Justin swam around the city for a long time, thinking over what he had learnt about his parents. He now had a better understanding of the positions they had been in. He could see now there was no way his mother could have stayed in Atlantis and his parents had no opportunity for a life together. He just wished his father had made other choices.

As he wandered, lost in thought, he began to hear the sounds of clashing metal, though the noise was dulled by the water. As he drew near, he also heard shouts in his mind. Someone was certainly adept at projecting his voice a great distance.

"Marin, watch where you're aiming that thing!"

Justin swam closer, keeping a careful eye open for whatever it was Marin was apparently aiming.

The barracks were one of the largest buildings he had seen so far in Atlantis. Justin actually thought they might be even bigger than the palace, though he couldn't say for sure. Outside in the yard area there were numerous mermen, each holding spears as they faced each other.

Calder, their leader, stood to one side and Justin realized he was the one shouting at the recruits.

"What are you trying to do, tickle each other? Put some force into it."

Justin leaned on the wall as he watched the sparring. The spears appeared crude but deadly.

He wondered what they were training for. From everything he had been told, the mer people were a peaceful race. They didn't make war on each other and the only predators they faced were those outside the city. With the sea dragons protecting the mer people of Atlantis from anything that came near, he didn't see the point of their spears, unless they planned to use them on the dragons themselves. Then again, having seen the dragons' teeth and fangs for himself, he guessed it was better safe than sorry.

A growl from nearby alerted Justin to the presence of one such beast. He glanced up to see the huge black dragon with a long snout, snapping its teeth in the direction of one of the guards, who was making a valiant effort to steer the creature in another direction to that which it wanted to go. A second guard ducked out of the way of a swipe of the dragon's claws, only to be sent head over fins by the animal's tail as it became increasingly agitated. It circled over his head and appeared to be far larger than the one he and Lucas had passed on their way into the city. Justin wondered how the guards were able to control such a fearsome monster and resolved to keep his distance from them as much as possible.

Turning his attention back to the drills, he saw Calder waving his hands in the air in frustration. *"Marin, what did I tell you about protecting your eyes?"*

Marin, a merman with an unusual two-toned set of fins in shades of dark and light blue, hung his head in shame. Justin didn't hear his reply, if he made one at all.

"Try again," Calder ordered. *"You're not leaving here today until you get it right."*

Marin faced his sparring partner and they began again. When the other merman's spear nearly took off Marin's ear, Justin had a feeling the hapless merman would be there for the night.

The drills continued for a long time until finally Calder started releasing mermen from their duties with pats on the shoulders or backs and words of praise for a job well done. One by one they left the yard until finally only Marin and his sparring partner were left.

"Go on, Arin," Calder told the clearly exasperated merman. *"I'll take over from here. You've done a good job today."*

Arin nodded and smiled at the compliment, before disappearing inside the barracks.

"What about me?" Marin asked. *"Haven't I done a good job?"*

Calder rolled his eyes upwards as though praying for patience. *"If we had been under attack today, you'd be dead ten times over, if not more."*

"No I wouldn't," Marin replied as he leveled the spear at his commanding officer.

"You'd have lost an eye, an ear and been gutted as well."

Marin shook his head. *"You know that's not true."*

Justin saw Marin's stance was far more sure than it had been earlier in the drills and he wondered if the merman was really inept or whether he actually could handle the spear as well as the other recruits.

Calder pointed his own spear at Marin. *"All right. You think you can handle yourself. Let's see you prove it."*

Justin watched as Calder and Marin sparred and he realized Marin was actually far better than he appeared and countered Calder's thrusts with ease. Marin's smaller stature and quick movements were put to good use as he ducked and evaded each of Calder's attacks.

Then, with one sharp movement Calder used his tail to catch Marin and throw him off balance. Taken completely by surprise, the smaller merman tumbled backwards and the spear slipped from his fingers.

"That's not fair," Marin complained. *"You cheated."*

Calder grinned down at him. *"You have to be prepared to fight dirty if you want to join the guards."* He held out his hand to Marin who took it, but instead of letting Calder pull him back into an upright position he yanked him down on top of him.

Justin snickered quietly. Calder hadn't seen that move coming. His amusement bated when he realized Calder and Marin weren't separating. In fact, from what he could see, they were getting closer, a little too close for two straight men to be comfortable with.

The kiss was quick and if he hadn't been watching them so closely, he might even have missed it entirely.

Just before he turned away he saw the nervous glances Calder cast toward the barracks before he quickly eased away from Marin. Justin had no doubt the two mermen were in a relationship together and were, thanks to the law of their city, being forced to hide their feelings for each other.

That wasn't the type of life he wanted for himself. He had known plenty of men who lived in the closet for various reasons and he didn't want to join their number. He didn't want to live like Calder and Marin were doing, constantly watching over their shoulders in case the wrong person saw they were more than just friends.

Chapter Nineteen

Justin sat behind the king as the Council convened for their weekly meeting. The king had again explained Justin's presence by telling the others he was there to see the workings of the sunken city. No one questioned the king and in fact there were several other mermen and mermaids present to see the meeting.

Justin had expected the meeting to be rather a boring event, but things took a lively turn when Telys—the merman reporting on the city structures—mentioned a curse. At first he thought Telys referred to the curse he and Lucas were trying to break, but it quickly became clear this was not the case.

"There is no curse!" King Nereus shouted. *"And I've told you before that I don't want the meeting time wasted with such nonsense."*

"What curse is he talking about?" Justin asked, hoping his voice went to the king and not to everyone in the room. He seemed to be getting better at projecting his thoughts correctly, but occasionally he still slipped up.

The king turned to him briefly. *"Later."*

Justin acknowledged the word with a single nod and the meeting continued on as normal.

Afterwards the king took him aside so they could speak privately and without distraction.

"*I don't know if there is a curse,*" King Nereus admitted, "*but it's appearing more and more likely there might be. The longer we go on this way, the more mer people begin to believe.*"

"*Do you believe in curses at all, or is it just this one you don't believe in?*"

"*I'm not a fanciful man, and curses only hold power over those who believe in them.*"

"*Humans don't believe the mer exist,*" Justin told him. "*They think we're myths.*"

"*Humans are largely foolish creatures, wrapped up in their own lives with no thought for any other beings.*"

"*You're missing my point. They don't believe in us because they have not seen us with their own eyes. Just because you haven't seen proof of this curse, it doesn't mean it isn't there. What is the curse exactly?*"

King Nereus sighed. "*For centuries now there have been rumors about a curse that is bringing about the end of our people. No one knows where the story originated, but they believe the Atlantean Goddess of Fertility has cursed us. They believe this is why our mermaids find it hard to conceive and our numbers drop every year.*"

Justin tried to hide his surprise at the goddess the king referred to. Although he had never met her, he was familiar enough with the Goddess of Fertility to know she was the mother of his foster parents. As far as he knew, she was sleeping, as Medina had been before someone had woken her. Could his foster grandmother's curse—if such a thing existed—still be effective while she remained in stasis?

"If there is a curse, I have no idea how to break it," the king continued. *"If we're really cursed, I doubt the mer can survive for more than a handful of generations."*

* * * *

After he left King Nereus, Justin made a beeline for his father's temple. If anyone knew the truth about the curse, it would be his father.

Caspian appeared at his call. *"How are you enjoying Atlantis?"* he asked.

"It's not so bad, but I can't wait to come home. I just need to find a way to break this damn curse."

"I'm sure you'll find a way to appease Medina soon enough. As interfering as she can be, the one thing the Goddess of Love cannot resist is a happy ending."

"Great, I just wish I could see one for me and Lucas."

Caspian sat on the steps in front of his statue and gestured for Justin to join him. *"Are things all right between you two?"*

"I don't know any more. I thought we were becoming closer and yet now we're here, he seems to be distancing himself from me."

"But you know your relationship is forbidden here."

"Yes, but it's hard being back in the closet when I want to be with him. Anyway, that's not why I called you here."

"What's troubling you?" Caspian asked.

"There's talk here in Atlantis of another curse, one on all the mer people in existence. I wondered if you knew whether it was true or not."

"I haven't cursed your people, if that's what you're asking."

Justin shook his head. *"They believe it's your mother who cursed them."*

"Ah." Caspian nodded thoughtfully.

"Well? Did she?"

"Yes, in a way."

"What do you mean? Either she cursed us or she didn't."

"She did something which resulted in a rather unfortunate side-effect for the mer people, one which could be called a curse."

"Why?"

"It's a long story and not important. Don't you think you have enough to worry about with Medina's curse? Perhaps you should concentrate on that one."

"But – "

Caspian shot him a sharp glare. Justin knew better than to prod him for more information.

"Medina's curse is the one you need to undo. Don't waste your time trying to untangle my mother's mess."

Caspian vanished with those final words of wisdom, leaving Justin to consider his options. In the end, all he could do was take Caspian's advice and concentrate on one curse at a time.

* * * *

Justin spent a lot of time over the next few days with King Nereus. He could not seem to think of the merman as his father, but he was starting to spot a few similarities between himself and his sire. The king was opinionated and an expert at getting is own way. Justin could tell he also inherited his temper from his father.

There was one thing he most assuredly got from his mother, and that was his visions. He hadn't yet brought up the subject of those with the king, and in the end, the matter was taken out of his hands.

His vision clouded while the king was in the middle of explaining about the policy for clans who wished to join the residents of Atlantis.

Lucas swam before him, his movements graceful and smooth. Justin recognized Atlantis now he had seen so much of the city, but he couldn't quite figure out where they were. Many of the buildings appeared much the same.

This time the vision seemed to be clearer and he could tell they weren't alone in the room. Other mermen and mermaids were scattered around, though none appeared to be close enough to Lucas to cause him any harm.

Lucas smiled at Justin, just as he had in his previous vision. His face was filled with joy one moment before it contorted in an expression of agony.

Justin couldn't stop his own sound of pain as he watched his lover take his last breath. He reached out to hold him, but Lucas was yanked away, as if caught in a strong current, before he could grab his arm.

Again, Justin's vision took a while to come back. He was sure now it was much longer than it used to be. When his sight did finally return, he saw the king watching him expectantly.

"*I see you inherited your mother's gift,*" King Nereus commented. "*Why didn't you tell me?*"

Justin shrugged. "*It hadn't really come up in the conversation.*"

His father nodded. "*You aren't a true Oracle,*" he remarked. "*That is, you have your sight. Have you always had visions?*"

"*Since I hit puberty,*" Justin confirmed. "*I don't get them very often, though they've been more frequent during the last few months. I only see my own future and the lives of those connected to me.*"

"*Your powers are probably growing since you came here.*"

"*That's what the Oracles told me.*"

"*You've been to see the Oracles?*"

"Yes. I thought you'd have known since nothing tends to happen in Atlantis without you knowing about it."

King Nereus chuckled. "There are many things that happen here without my knowledge. I just have the ability to find out about them if I wish to. I do try to stay out of the minds of my people as much as possible. I certainly wouldn't appreciate it if anyone was poking around in my head without my permission. I also tend to discover that when I do read the minds of my people I seldom like what I see."

"Sounds like an occupational hazard," Justin said.

"As you will come to learn when you take my place as king of the sunken city."

"If," Justin reminded him firmly.

"Does anyone else know about your visions?" King Nereus asked. "Besides the Oracles, I mean."

"Lucas knows."

"I can't say I'm surprised to hear that. I must ask you not to tell anyone else about this gift."

"Why not?" Justin asked. Following his conversations with the Oracles, he already suspected the reasons, but he wanted to hear the king's views on it.

"Oracles are forbidden from going to land or having sexual relations. This is a law I cannot change and unless you intend to live a life of celibacy, it would be best if no one knows of your visions."

"You broke that law when you slept with my mother," Justin pointed out.

"I did, but I shouldn't have done so. That law is there for a reason. It cannot be changed for you."

"I thought the law was to prevent Oracles giving birth to children who would inherit their powers?"

"It is."

"I'm a gay man."

"Gay?"

"I only have sex with other men. Children would be an impossibility."

"Nevertheless, I will not be changing the law pertaining to the Oracles for you. I would ask that you take every precaution to ensure no one else knows of your powers."

Justin noticed the king hadn't mentioned the law forbidding homosexual relations. Maybe there was hope that one might be less rigidly adhered to. He didn't feel now was the right time to bring up the subject and decided to stick to the matter at hand. *"I can't control when I have visions. They come when they come. I didn't intend to have one in front of you just now. There's no way I can avoid having a vision in front of someone else and if I do, they'll spread the word anyway."*

The king considered him thoughtfully as they contemplated the problem. *"I would suggest you train with the Oracles to see if you can find a way to control the visions, or at least recognize the signs that you're about to have one and can take the appropriate precautions to ensure you maintain your secret."*

"I'll do that," Justin agreed. *"Can I ask you something else about the visions?"*

"Of course. What is it?"

"How did my mother handle them? The bad ones especially. I see my own future, but I never see enough to steer myself onto another course."

"That should change now you're here," the king replied. *"The stronger your powers get, the more you'll see. As for the bad ones, your mother did what she could to prevent them from coming to pass. It was not always possible, but she gave those who needed it all the information she had. Often she was successful in altering the course of fate. I know she was saddened when she failed in this regard, but she tried her best and never gave up."*

Justin felt sick to his stomach at the thought of failing to alter Lucas' future. He had hoped maybe knowing the future would mean he could stop it from happening.

"What was the vision you saw?" King Nereus asked.

"I saw death," he replied quietly.

"Your own?"

"No." Justin shook his head. *"Would you excuse me please? I'd like to consult the Oracles about my visions."*

King Nereus nodded and waved him away. *"We'll talk another time about this matter, but remember what I've told you. The law cannot be changed."*

* * * *

The Oracles were expecting him, as Justin expected them to be. They gestured to their servants to leave the room as soon as he had arrived.

"How can you tell if they've all gone?" he asked.

Kai laughed. *"I can see if they are still here."*

"How does that work exactly?" Justin asked. *"If you see the present, then why can't you see what is happening around you?"*

"The present is not just what is happening in this room, it's what's happening anywhere in the world. While I could, if I wished, see the world around me continually, it would be too draining on my powers to do so. A quick flash to check if the servants have left the room doesn't take much strength, and is, like today, sometimes necessary."

"Besides," Delwyn added, *"we'd trust you to tell us if someone was lingering back to listen."*

Justin supposed they had a point. *"Do you know why I'm here?"* he asked.

"King Nereus knows you're an Oracle," Kai confirmed. *"It was only a matter of time before this happened."*

"He's told me to keep it a secret, but since I have no control over the visions, this might be difficult."

"Then we will train you to recognize the signs," Ula suggested. *"If you know when a vision is about to occur,*

you can make sure you are not with anyone other than those who are aware of what you are."

"Thank you," Justin replied. *"Though I have no idea what these signs are. They come so quickly. I get no warning at all."*

"That's because you're resisting and suppressing your gift. The power builds up inside of you until it has to come forth. If you learn how to nurture your gift and trigger visions yourself, this won't happen as suddenly. When you trigger your own visions you'll also begin to recognize the signs to watch out for."

"I'm not sure I want to have any more visions than I already do."

"If you remain in the sunken city then you have no choice. Your powers, like ours, are most potent here in the city created by the Atlantean gods."

Justin could see he had no choice in the matter. *"Okay, what do I have to do to trigger a vision?"*

Ula guided him toward one of the soft sponges and gestured for him to take a seat. *"Now, the easiest way to trigger a vision is to ask yourself a question."*

"What sort of question?"

"Anything you like. Who will be the first person you see when leaving our temple? What you'll have for dinner tonight, or something else equally simple. Just ask the question in your own mind and see what happens."

Justin chose the first question and repeated itself over and over silently. A knot formed in his stomach and he felt the familiar tingling at the back of his eyes that signaled he was about to go temporarily blind. As usual, his vision vanished a moment later, far too late for him to do anything about it had he been in the middle of a crowded room.

He found himself outside the temple and saw a pretty young mermaid swimming past with a net full of sea fruits. She held one in her hand as she bit into it.

"You saw what you asked to?" Ula asked, once his sight had returned and the vision done.

"Yes. At least I think so. I won't know for sure if it was a true vision until I leave, but it certainly seemed to be."

"And did you recognize any of the signs that were the start of the vision?"

"Other than the tingling behind my eyes? No, and that always comes too late for me to do anything about it."

"Try again," Ula suggested. *"And this time listen to your body."*

"What am I listening for?" Justin asked. *"Wouldn't it be easier to just tell me what to look out for?"*

"No. I'm afraid the signs are different for everyone. For me it is an increased heart rate first, then my fins become overly sensitive."

Justin couldn't say he had noticed either of these things, though since he didn't tend to touch his fins a great deal, he probably wouldn't have noticed if they were over sensitive when he was about to have a vision.

"Try again," Ula suggested. *"Again with something simple that will come to pass today. The farther ahead you try to see, the more power it takes."*

Lucas nodded and this time chose the dinner question. He tried to concentrate on his body as well as the question. He felt a tingling running across his scalp followed by a shiver down his spine. The feeling wasn't particularly unusual — nothing he hadn't experienced a hundred times before. Yet maybe that was one of the signs. He thought about the question of dinner again and the shiver in his spine became more intense the longer he concentrated on it. He was certain he had never felt anything quite like this before.

"It's because you're concentrating on it," Ula told him, without Justin having spoken a word. *"Focus on your body and the vision will wait."*

The tingling over his scalp also intensified and he pulled his hair from the band he had taken to wearing to keep it out of his eyes while under the water. He ran his fingers over his head, but it made no difference to the feeling.

"*Hold it back,*" Ula advised. "*You control the visions. They don't control you. Don't lose your focus.*"

Justin tried to do as she instructed, even as he wondered whether this would, in fact, draw more attention to him when a vision was about to occur.

"*That's it,*" Ula encouraged. "*Now think about your question and let the vision happen.*"

The instant Justin shifted his focus from the shivers running over his scalp and down his spine, the tingling at the back of his eyes began and the vision started. He saw himself sitting in the king's private chambers, eating a simple meal of fruits. Justin felt disappointed because he had hoped to spend the evening with Lucas, but since his lover had been keeping Justin at a distance, he wasn't entirely surprised to discover he wasn't going to eating with him tonight.

The vision cleared and Justin faced Ula.

"*You'll need to practice every day,*" she advised. "*You can come here and do so if you wish.*"

"*I don't know how this will help keep my secret,*" Justin said. "*Won't people notice there's something wrong with me?*"

"*Not if you leave the presence of others as soon as you start to recognize the signs that you're about to have a vision. Just excuse yourself from their presence whilst concentrating on your body. Then, once you're alone, let the vision happen. Although the feelings you just experienced were powerfully intense, it is only because you were holding the vision back for so long. Most times it'll be unnecessary to hold them back for such a length of time.*"

"Then why make me hold it back so long this time?" Justin asked.

"So that you could be sure that it was a sign of a vision and not simply a regular reaction for you. For a long time Delwyn thought the sick sensation he felt was his sign for an imminent vision, when it fact the nausea was just nerves. That passed with time. Now that you know what to look for, you'll be better prepared."

"Thanks. I guess it's going to take some practice."

"Yes, it will. Let's have something to eat to restore your strength, then we'll see if you can do another."

Justin agreed and Ula called for the servants to bring them snacks. He liked the Oracles and he supposed it would be useful to know how to recognize when he was about to have a vision, yet he could not help but feel that if he returned to England, his powers would not be so strong and all this training would be unnecessary after all.

They were still in the middle of eating, while telling Justin more stories of his mother, when the next vision hit him. Even with the training he had just undergone, it still took him totally by surprise.

The vision was the same one he had seen already, of Lucas' death. He felt sick to his stomach as he saw the merman's dead eyes staring sightlessly ahead of him. He didn't know if the vision happening now, so close to the last time, was a sign he was honing his powers or a warning Lucas' death drew closer.

When the vision came to an end, his sight took longer to return again. When it did, he saw Ula's face bore an expression of horror.

"What is it?" he asked.

"I saw what you saw," she replied. *"At least I think I did. Lucas dying, here in Atlantis."*

"Yes," Justin confirmed. *"If I don't find a way to break Medina's curse, then that's going to happen."*

"*Maybe you should leave,*" Kai suggested.

"*It won't work. We thought that on our journey here, but the moment we made the decision to turn back, the vision changed and I saw his death back in England.*"

"*There is no escaping fate,*" Ula confirmed quietly. "*Your best hope is to set it on another course.*"

"*By breaking the curse, I hope to do just that.*"

Ula nodded. "*I will see if I can see anything else of Lucas' fate.*"

"*A date and time would be useful.*"

"*It would, but as you have already discovered, dates are seldom used here. We don't mark time by human calendars. We only observe the seasons and the winter and summer solstices. No matter how many times you and I see Lucas' fate, we will never be able to see the exact time of its occurrence.*"

Justin had already figured this out. He didn't like the fact, but he could do nothing about it. And it wasn't like he had seen a date and time, or even a firm location, for the vision of Lucas dying in England.

All Justin knew was he had to stop this event coming to pass. Each time he saw Lucas dead his heart broke a little more. He ached to run to his merman and take him into his arms, the law be damned.

"*Why don't you?*" Kai asked. "*You have private chambers where you can at least spend time together.*"

"*I really need to work on shielding my thoughts better,*" Justin grumbled. "*To answer your question, I don't want to live my life in a closet, hiding my love for him as though it were something to be ashamed of.*"

"*Surely it is better to have him in your life in whatever capacity you can?*" Delwyn asked. "*As Oracles, we can never have what you have. You don't know how lucky you are. We'd give anything to have a lover in our lives, even if we can never be with them in the most intimate of ways.*"

"How do you get through the mating season without going to land?" Justin asked.

"With great difficulty," Kai muttered. *"I meditate and Delwyn loses himself in visions of the past. It does a little to ease the ache of need, but it never goes away completely."*

Justin knew he wouldn't trade places with the Oracles for anything. He renewed his resolve to concentrate on his training. Failure could mean his own imprisonment and separation from Lucas forever, regardless of whether he saved his life or not. On the other hand, if he were to lose Lucas, life as an Oracle might be preferable to life completely alone.

Chapter Twenty

Justin thought he knew the merman swimming toward him, though he could not immediately place him. It took him a minute to recognize the guard who had been dismissed from a previous Council meeting — the guard who had been goading Lucas during the meeting. Close up he recognized Otus, the merman he had seen treating Lucas so badly in Medina's vision. His initial surge of annoyance quickly escalated to the desire to punch the merman on the nose.

"How are you enjoying the sunken city?" the guard asked. *"I'm Otus, by the way, second in command over all the guards."*

Justin frowned at Otus' words. The king had gone through the detailed ranks of the various factions with him several times since his arrival in Atlantis, and he was fairly sure Otus wasn't second in command to anyone, least of all Calder. In fact, he was positive Otus wasn't anything other than a regular guard, albeit one with big ideas way above his station.

"It's pleasant enough," he replied evasively. He made to swim around the guard and go on his way, but Otus blocked his path.

"How do you like Lucas?" the guard asked. *"He's quite a good fuck, isn't he?"*

Justin looked Otus up and down, putting as much disdain into his expression as he could manage. *"Did you want something?"* he asked impatiently. *"Only I'm rather busy at the moment."*

Otus used his tail to brush against Justin, who quickly swam out of his way. *"Oh I want many things. Another chance to bend pretty little Lucas over and ram my cock up his tight arse would be high on my list."*

Justin snorted. *"Dream on."* He tried again to swim past Otus, but the merman didn't seem to be able to take a hint.

"I'll share him with you," Otus suggested. *"I fuck him first and loosen him up for you, then you can have a go at him. He's quite the little whore. Most of the gatherers have had him, you know."*

Justin had heard enough. He might not be a trained guard, but he was more than capable of taking care of himself. He used the element of surprise to disarm Otus and push him up against the wall, holding the guard's own spear to his throat. *"Hold your lying tongue,"* he snarled. *"I don't know what your game is, but I can tell you right now, you're never going to touch Lucas again. Understand?"*

"Who do you think you are to tell me what I can and can't do?" Otus replied, though his voice wasn't as sure as it had been a moment before. *"I'm second in command of the Atlantean guards."*

"I don't give a damn who you think you are," Justin sneered. *"You stay away from Lucas or I'll make sure your life isn't worth living."*

"*You have no idea who you're dealing with,*" Otus snarled. "*I have the ear of the king himself. I wonder what he would say if he knew his kin was fucking a member of his precious Council.*"

Justin gave him a nasty smile. He had never liked bullies and he was sorely tempted to tell Otus exactly who he was and watch him squirm. It took some effort, but he managed to hold his tongue long enough to send Otus on his way, minus his spear.

When Justin turned round he saw Lucas hovering behind him. "*How long have you been there?*"

"*Long enough,*" Lucas replied. "*It's not true, you know.*"

Justin didn't need to ask Lucas what he referred to. He swam up to him and gathered him into his arms. "*I know.*"

"*Stop it,*" Lucas said as he twisted out of Justin's embrace. "*We can't let anyone see us together.*"

Justin sighed with frustration. "*There's no one around to see us at all. Except Otus, if he's still lingering, and I don't give a fuck what he thinks. What is he going to say when he's clearly gay himself?*"

"*I have to think of my career,*" Lucas insisted.

"*So you keep saying,*" Justin complained. "*I'm starting to think that's all you care about.*"

Lucas pulled him aside and into an empty chamber. "*It's just difficult for me to change the way I've been brought up.*"

"*You didn't seem to have any difficulty back in England.*"

"*That was different. No one was watching me there, waiting for me to make a mistake that they can take advantage of.*"

Justin could tell Lucas was in a difficult position, but he hated hiding their relationship from everyone. "*Is that the sort of life you want? Hiding and sneaking around all the time? Always worrying in case the wrong person sees something you don't want them to? You would prefer that to coming back to England with me?"*

"I have a life here and a career I've been working toward my whole life. The king's advisers can't be homosexual. If any are, they might as well just quit before anyone finds out. Being gay in the sunken city is the worst thing you can be."

Justin thought back to what he had seen of Calder and Marin in the barracks. They seemed to be quite happy in their posts, even if they too, like the rest of the gay mermen, hid what they were from everyone else. *"You talk as if being gay is a bad thing. It's a part of who you are. You can't deny it your entire life. There are clearly other gay mermen here and they seem to manage to live with it without giving up their careers."*

"I'm not like Otus."

"I wasn't talking about him. What about Calder? He's gay, right?"

Lucas stared at him in wide-eyed surprise. *"Is he? How do you know?"*

"Just something I saw between him and another merman. But he seems like a decent enough merman, and from what I've seen, the rest of the population doesn't appear to be so bad either. The only one who's been acting like a dick is Otus."

"I'm not saying all the gay mermen are like Otus, but I don't want to give up my position. I want to follow in my father's footsteps, take his place on the Council and help make the city a better place. If the other advisers found out for sure I desired another man, I'd never be voted onto the Council. I'm still trying to repair the damage you caused when we arrived."

They were going round in circles and getting nowhere. Justin didn't know how to convince Lucas being together wouldn't necessarily mean the end of his career, not when he knew so little about Atlantean politics, and from what he had seen so far, Lucas may be entirely accurate in what he was saying.

"Maybe we should just find a way to lift the curse and go our separate ways?" he suggested. The thought of going through the rest of his life, not to mention the mating seasons, without getting off wasn't pleasant, but right now he couldn't see a future for the two of them that he could live with.

Lucas shook his head quickly. *"No! That's not what I want. You don't know what it's like to be without someone during the solstice."*

"I'm seeing a lot of cold showers in my future," Justin said. *"But right now, I'm not seeing you in it."*

He was about to leave, when he felt Lucas' hand on his arm. *"Don't go. Let's swim up to the island where we can talk without being interrupted."*

Justin suspected they might not get much talking done if they went up to land, but he told himself maybe reconnecting sexually would help. The gods knew nothing else seemed to be working.

* * * *

Lucas and Justin left Atlantis together, but only because Justin reminded his lover he had no idea where to find the island. Lucas, who had apparently forgotten this, had at first thought they should leave separately and meet up on land.

"You're just being paranoid," Justin said when Lucas commented that the perimeter guards had given them a bit of a strange look as they had left the city. *"I'm sure plenty of mermen leave the city in pairs all the time. It would be safer than heading out alone."*

"Yes, the gatherers leave in pairs all the time. How do you think they got their reputation?"

"What is the deal with the gatherers anyway? Are they really all gay?"

"I doubt it. But they are one of the few factions who have frequent cause to leave the boundaries to go work in the more fertile lands outside the city. It means they can pass the guards and the sea dragons without being questioned. And once they're out, they can go to the island and fuck each other as much as they want. Anyone else who wants to pass the boundaries gets stopped and questioned, just as we were."

"It's not like we had any trouble getting out."

"This time," Lucas warned. "But our leaving will be reported to the Council and if we are noticed to be leaving together too frequently, we could be stopped."

"It just sounds like paranoia to me."

Lucas didn't argue with him, but Justin spotted him glancing back over their shoulders several times and he kept his distance from Justin as they left the area.

When they arrived on the island it was a relatively warm winter day. Justin hadn't realized how much he had missed breathing in air and feeling the sun on his face until he stood on the beach.

He pulled Lucas into his arms, but the merman slipped from his grasp. "Not here. If someone comes to the beach, they'll see us right away. We should go inland a bit."

Justin again held his tongue. There was no point in arguing, and in truth he wasn't too keen on the idea of having sex where anyone could see them. He wasn't exactly thrilled at the prospect of that when the mating season rolled round, but he was trying to put off thinking about it too much.

He followed Lucas into the trees and they found a grassy clearing a short distance in, where they could be alone with at least a little privacy if anyone else from Atlantis had the same idea they had about visiting the island.

They sank down onto the soft grass and Justin eased Lucas onto his back. This time he didn't resist.

"I haven't been with all the gatherers," Lucas told him. "I just need you to know that."

Justin kissed him gently. "I know you haven't. Otus is a lying dick and even if what he said was true, it doesn't matter. It's not like I haven't been with other men before I met you."

Lucas frowned at him curiously. "Have you been with a lot of men?"

"Quite a few," Justin replied evasively.

"How many?" Lucas asked.

Justin chuckled. "I didn't keep count, but don't worry. You're the only one who I've stayed with this long."

"Because of the curse," Lucas reminded him. "If it weren't for Medina, you wouldn't even have come back."

Justin frowned down at his lover. "I thought we'd come here to have sex, not talk about the curse."

"We did."

"Then be quiet and let me make love to you."

Lucas smiled up at him took his hand. He sucked Justin's index finger into his mouth, then guided his hand between his legs. Lucas closed his eyes as Justin touched him, pressing his finger up against his anus. It had been a long time since they'd last been in human form and Lucas was tight. He rubbed his finger round his hole, easing the tip inside and wishing they had some lube with them. He swore if he ever got the opportunity, he would buy a boat load of the damn stuff and drag it back to Atlantis with him.

Lucas didn't seem to mind the lack of supplies, though for him this was the norm, rather than whatever the local pharmacy had in stock. He keened and moaned as Jake fingered him, stretching him thoroughly and readying him for his cock.

They were both hard and aching from the moment they took human form. Even though it wasn't the mating season, they had been apart long enough that they were eager with anticipation.

"More," Lucas moaned as Justin slipped in a second finger and Lucas pressed back against his hand. "Fill me, Justin."

Justin took away his hand and brought Lucas' legs up to rest on his shoulders. "Are you ready?"

Lucas nodded. "Do it."

Justin took his erection in hand and guided it to Lucas' anus, pushing the cockhead inside and waiting for Lucas to adjust. "That's it. Relax and let me in."

Lucas breathed deeply and Justin eased in a little more. "More," Lucas gasped. "Need more."

Justin spat on his hand and rubbed the saliva round Lucas' hole and the exposed part of his dick. When he had made them both as slippery as he could in the circumstances, he pushed in the rest of the way until his balls slapped against Lucas' buttocks.

"That's it," Lucas moaned. "Now fuck me, Justin. Let me feel your heat inside me."

Justin eased out a little and pushed his way back inside, causing Lucas to gasp out a choked cry of pleasure. "Like that?"

"More," Lucas begged. "Give me more, please. Fuck me. Please fuck me."

Justin pulled out an inch or two before thrusting forward again. Lucas moaned loudly. When he did it again, Lucas grabbed his arms in a death grip.

"More, more, more," Lucas cried out in time to each of Justin's increasingly deep thrusts.

Justin didn't know how long he would last. From the moment Lucas had clenched his buttocks around his cock, Justin had been on the verge of coming.

Lucas' dick was hard and dripped pre-cum onto his abdomen. Neither of them had a hand free to give it the attention it begged for.

Justin continued his thrusts, slowly pushing Lucas toward the brink as his lover begged him for more.

"So close," he managed to say as Lucas moaned beneath him, his words reduced to nothing more than unintelligible babble. "So close."

Lucas screamed out his pleasure as he came. Neither of them had touched his penis, but he had managed to come without any stimulation to his cock. It was enough for him to feel his lover buried in his arse.

Justin held still while Lucas rode out his orgasm. Lucas' arse clenched round his shaft and it was enough to send Justin over the edge too. He came hard, his seed filling Lucas in hot bursts.

They collapsed in each other's arms, still locked together. Justin's penis softened and he tenderly stroked Lucas' dick. He gathered up the cum from his skin and licked his fingers clean of the salty substance.

Lucas gave several small shivers as Justin brushed his fingers against his over sensitive flesh. "What are we going to do?" he asked.

"I don't know," Justin admitted. "I want to be with you properly, not just sneaking around like we are now. I never wanted a life lived in secret or fear and I hate that this is what I've been reduced to."

Lucas seemed to be on the verge of tears. "I'm scared," he whispered. "What if we can't find a way to break the curse?"

Justin held him close and rubbed his back comfortingly. "We'll find a way to appease Medina. I won't lose you to a curse."

"But you'd leave me and go back to your life on land," Lucas reminded him.

Justin kissed Lucas on the top of his head and tightened his hold on his lover. "I don't know if I can ever leave you now I've found you," he admitted. "I might hate living like this, but I think I'd hate being apart from you even more."

"I don't want you to be unhappy here."

Justin didn't know what to say to set Lucas' mind at ease. The truth was, if he had to spend his life hiding his love, he would be miserable.

* * * *

They lay on the grass, kissing and touching for a long time. The sun passed overhead and the light dimmed as dusk came. It was full dark before they stirred. Justin didn't want to go back to Atlantis and he suspected Lucas might be equally reluctant.

"We should probably return soon," Lucas commented, though he made no effort to move from where he was wrapped around Justin's body.

Justin nodded, though he too didn't bother to move.

The sound of a twig snapping made them both jump.

"What was that?" Lucas whispered.

"Maybe it was an animal," Justin suggested in a hushed tone of his own.

The sound of whispering voices made them rethink their guess. A moment later two mermen stumbled through the trees, laughing quietly together. They hadn't seen Justin and Lucas, yet.

Justin recognized Calder and Marin and breathed a little easier. After what he had seen at the barracks, he had no doubt they had come to the island with similar thoughts to those of himself and Lucas. Although he didn't know either of the guards particularly well, and had only spoken to Calder a handful of times, he trusted they would keep their secret since it was in their own interests to do so in the circumstances.

Lucas seemed to be frozen against his side. Justin could feel his heart pounding rapidly against him and he tried to soothe him as best he could without giving away their presence to the others. While he trusted them not to give them away, he wasn't entirely comfortable with being seen by anyone when it was quite obvious what they had been doing for most of the afternoon and evening.

Marin spotted them first with a surprised squeak. "Oh fuck."

Calder, who seemed to be calmer than either Marin or Lucas, took in their appearance with a quick glance. "Good evening," he greeted them pleasantly.

Lucas trembled against Justin for a moment before he jumped up and bolted in the direction of the beach.

"Lucas!" Justin shouted as he scrambled to his feet and ran after him.

He caught up with him on the beach and grabbed him by the arm. "Stop. It's okay. They won't tell anyone you were here with me."

Calder and Marin had followed them to the beach and nodded their agreement.

"It'd raise too many questions about what we're doing here," Marin pointed out.

"See," Justin said. "They're here for the same reason we are. It's okay."

"No, it's not," Lucas insisted. "We shouldn't have come here. It's too dangerous. Anyone could have spotted us leaving and followed us here. All it takes is someone like Otus to see us together and that'll be the end of my career."

"Otus is vindictive shark bait," Marin commented. "I wish he'd never come to the sunken city."

Calder patted Marin on the arm. "Yes, quite. But he's not going anywhere, so I'm afraid we have to put up with the hypocritical little troublemaker."

Lucas still edged toward the sea, but Justin kept a firm grip on his arm and prevented him from escaping into the water.

"Come and sit down," Calder suggested as he took a seat on the beach. Marin sat at his side and Justin coaxed Lucas to join them.

"You won't tell anyone what you saw?" Lucas whispered.

"Of course not," Calder replied. "As Justin pointed out, we'd come here for the same purpose as the two of you, and as you might have noticed, there aren't any mermaids here tonight – or at least not with us."

"You're together?" Lucas asked. "A couple?"

"Oh yes," Marin replied with a wriggle of his eyebrows. "And we're trusting you not to tell anyone about us either. We have just as much to lose as you."

Lucas assured them he would keep their secret and relaxed enough to curl up against Justin as they talked.

"There's nothing wrong with desiring another man," Calder told them. "It's perfectly natural. That there are those of us who need the touch of a male during the mating season should tell you that. You might have to hide your feelings here, but you aren't alone. There are many of us who are similarly inclined."

"In the gatherers," Lucas muttered.

"And elsewhere," Calder amended. "There are three of us in the guards — that I know of — and I suspect more that I don't. As the leader of the guards, the men are extra careful around me, though I suspect they are more open in front of Marin."

Marin nodded. "I know of a few others in the guards. I would also be quite surprised if there weren't at least a handful working in the palace itself. There's at least two I have my suspicions about."

Lucas stared at him in surprise, but Marin refused to elaborate.

"There's nothing wrong with being in the gatherers," Marin continued with a hint of censure in his voice. "My father was one of them. He hoped I would follow in his footsteps, but I wanted to choose my own path and join the guards, even though it meant many years of training."

"Some guards taking more years than others to complete it," Calder teased as he poked Marin lightly in the ribs.

Justin was starting to like Calder and Marin. He suspected from the easy way they were with each other, they had been in a relationship for quite a long time.

"Oh shit," Marin suddenly exclaimed.

Justin looked at him and saw he was staring over his shoulder toward the tree line. He saw immediately what had caused his expletive. Otus lingered, almost out of sight, watching them intently.

"You might as well come out into the open," Calder called to him.

Otus walked closer and sneered down at them.

"How long have you been loitering around?" Marin asked.

"Long enough to see our esteemed leader here taking it up the arse the minute you hit the beach," Otus sneered.

"Don't you have anything better to do than spy on us?" Marin asked with an air of boredom. "Or is that how you get off?"

Otus ignored him and turned to Lucas. "I'm afraid I missed seeing Lucas spreading his legs for our visitor, but I'm sure there'll be other opportunities for me to catch them, especially when I'm leader of the guards."

Marin laughed. "Leader? You? That'll be the day."

"It'll come sooner than you think," Otus warned. "How long do you think Calder will keep his post when the king finds out what the two of you have been up to here on the island?"

"Even if you tell King Nereus what you've seen, you won't be leader of the guards," Marin pointed out. "Unless you think your skills at spying on men fucking and wishing you were joining them qualifies you for the position."

"Marin, calm down," Calder warned. "He's not worth it. Just let him go. We'll do what we always do and deny the accusations and carry on as normal."

Otus kicked at the sand, spraying them in grains. "You can deny what you like, but we all know the truth. You came here tonight with one of the guards who is under your command. With, in fact, the worst recruit ever to train in the sunken city. Any other leader would have dismissed Marin from his post long ago. But now we know why you keep him on. It's so you can feel his cock in your arse whenever you want, though I'm not sure why you'd want to bother, since he doesn't exactly have a lot hanging between his legs."

Justin couldn't stop himself from focusing on Marin's groin, then over toward Otus' dick. Personally, if he had been in Otus' position, he wouldn't have been pointing out deficiencies in anyone else when he wasn't exactly generously endowed himself.

Marin, however, didn't seem to share Justin's opinion. He shot to his feet and tackled Otus to the floor.

Even with the sandy surface beneath them, they hit the ground hard. Marin, small and wiry, could certainly pack a punch and he had laid two on Otus before Calder had even got to his feet.

"Marin!" he shouted. "Leave him."

"You hit like a mermaid," Otus sneered.

Marin replied with another punch to his jaw that Justin was sure must have loosened several of Otus' teeth.

"I order you to stop!" Calder yelled. His voice rang out with the authority of someone used to giving orders. Unfortunately, neither Marin nor Otus were inclined to obey him right now.

Otus raised his knee and brought it up sharply between Marin's legs. Justin cringed in sympathy.

Calder glared at Justin and Lucas. "Well, don't just sit there, help me separate them."

Justin and Lucas stepped forward and tried to see the best way of pulling the two merman apart, preferably without catching a flying fist or leg in one of their own tender spots.

"Oh for goodness' sake," Calder shouted as Otus rolled Marin onto his back and yanked at his long hair.

Marin retaliated by biting him on the arm, hard enough to draw blood.

"I swear it's like being in charge of a bunch of children," Calder complained. "Enough!"

Both mermen ignored him as they continued to pummel each other.

Marin was running out of steam fast. He raised his hands to try to shield his face from the blows.

Justin grabbed hold of Otus' arm and tried to drag him back, but Otus was stronger than he appeared and he wrestled his arm free with ease.

"Slippery little git," Justin muttered as he tried again to stop him from hitting the smaller merman. Otus threw him off again and this time he tumbled into Lucas, who was standing close beside him as he too tried to help.

They fell backward onto the sand.

Justin struggled to his feet and moved forward again.

He was about to rejoin the fray when Calder grabbed Otus round the neck and heaved him backwards with a loud grunt.

"Help me get him to the water," Calder ordered. Justin and Lucas grabbed a limb each and they hoisted the merman above them and tossed him into the surf. "If he's got any sense, he'll stay in the sea."

"He doesn't seem to have much of that," Justin commented.

"Maybe not, but at the very least, it'll give me time to check on Marin while he's transforming back."

Thankfully, Otus seemed to have more sense than they had given him credit for and he didn't come back to the beach.

Calder hurried back to Marin, who was struggling to sit up. "What possessed you to do that?" Calder scolded him. "You know Otus is a dick."

Marin muttered something Justin didn't hear, but it caused Calder to chuckle.

"Is he all right?" Lucas asked.

"He should be," Calder replied. "Split lip, black eye, maybe a broken nose and a lot of bruises. It looks worse than it probably is, and is going to serve as a reminder to Marin to keep a hold of his temper."

"You forget the most important injury," Marin muttered as he glared down at his groin. "You aren't going to be getting anything from me for at least a week."

Calder laughed. "I'll live, and you know as well as I do that the pain will subside as soon as you get your fins back."

Marin pouted at Calder who kissed him quickly on the lips. "Ouch," Marin whined as he fingered the cut lip.

"Yeah, that's going to hurt like crazy as soon as you enter the sea," Calder warned. "Salt water and cuts are the worst combination."

Justin crouched down beside the two mermen. "There seems to be a bit of history between you two and Otus."

"Not as much as you'd think," Calder replied. "He was a fighter and leader of his clan before they came to the city. He doesn't enjoy taking orders and has his eye on my job."

"Do you think he could ever get it?" Justin asked.

"Not a chance," Calder replied. "He's a long way down the pecking order and likely to remain so, especially if he keeps getting into fights. He's got no idea how things work here. He's used to being in a society where the strongest fighter is in charge. His grasp of politics is slim at best."

"Kind of like mine," Justin admitted. "I had enough trouble with politics back home. I'm still trying to figure out Atlantis."

"You'll learn," Calder assured him. "Unlike some people."

Justin helped Calder get Marin on his feet and smiled as he saw the way the older merman cared for his younger lover. "You seem to have things figured out pretty well. A good job and a good man to share your life with."

Calder smiled down at Marin and Justin could see the love in his eyes. "Yeah, I'm a pretty lucky merman. Though you seem to be doing all right for yourself too."

Justin glanced over at Lucas, who watched them carefully. "We're still figuring things out, but I'm kind of hoping we can get there soon."

Lucas gave him a small smile and took hold of Justin's hand. He leaned in close and kissed Justin on the cheek. It was the first time he had shown him real affection in front of anyone else since they had arrived in Atlantis.

Even though he knew they still had a long way to go, Justin felt perhaps their trip to the island had been worth it, and maybe they had made a little progress in understanding where they were each coming from.

Chapter Twenty-One

As the four mermen reached the perimeter of Atlantis, a guard approached them.

"Calder, you'd better report to the palace. Otus swam there with talk about seeing you removed from your post."

Calder sighed with frustration, but as soon as they had passed the sea dragons, he shifted course for the palace. Justin, Marin and Lucas followed him, along with the guard who had met them.

"Can he really get you fired?" Justin asked.

"I hope not," Calder replied as he sped up and darted round the other mer people who were going about their daily business.

"What's happened?" the guard asked. *"And why does Marin look like he came off worst in a fight with a hammerhead?"*

"Otus," Calder said shortly. *"You go back to the barracks and tell the men I might be late for my shift."*

The guard obeyed him immediately and hurried away.

Justin and the others swam into the palace where they found one of the senior advisers waiting for them.

"Eryx," Calder greeted him with a bow. *"Have you seen Otus?"*

Eryx pointed toward the king's audience chamber. *"He asked for a private audience with King Nereus. I don't know what about since he was careful to ensure his words were for the king alone. I did, however, catch King Nereus say your name before I left the room. What's happened?"*

"Otus wants my job," Calder replied.

"We've known that from the day he arrived. Would you care to elaborate?"

"Not really." Calder tried to swim past Eryx, but the other merman held him back.

"Calder, I don't often pull rank on you, but if you don't tell me what's happening, I will."

Justin remembered Eryx was the adviser who liaised between the guards and the king. There were so many advisers he was still learning who was who.

Calder stared at Marin and although Justin could not hear what they were saying, he could tell they were communicating with each other. When they had done, Calder took Marin's hand in his. *"Otus saw Marin and myself on the island. We were having sex together."*

Eryx nodded firmly. *"I suspected as much. You know the law and the penalties for what you've just admitted to me."*

"Yes."

"You'll also know it isn't my place to judge," Eryx added. He swam back from their path and waved them into the king's audience chamber.

They swam into the room and saw Otus had apparently finished his report to the king.

The king waved them over as they approached. *"Come in then. Don't linger in archways."*

They swam toward the throne, Marin shooting daggers at Otus.

The king leaned forward as they approached. *"Come here, Marin."*

Marin swam nearer so King Nereus could look him over. He kept his gaze lowered but the king reached out with his trident and lifted his chin so he could see the whole of his face. He then turned to Otus. *"Your work?"*

Otus nodded. *"He attacked me. I was defending myself."*

Justin thought it was something of a stretch for Otus to be pleading self-defense, but unfortunately Marin had been the one to throw the first punch.

"You should remove them both from their posts," Otus continued. *"Marin for attacking me and Calder for the crime of engaging in forbidden relations. I would be happy to take over the position of leader of the guards pending your formal appointment."*

King Nereus glared at Otus. *"Don't tell me how to do my job."*

Otus bowed in response, though from where Justin was standing, it wasn't exactly respectful. He clearly didn't enjoy taking orders from anyone, not even the king.

"Tell me, Marin," King Nereus continued. *"Did you cast the first blow?"*

"Yes, Your Majesty," Marin mumbled.

The king nodded and turned to Calder. *"And how do you plead to the charge laid against you?"*

"He wouldn't dare deny it," Otus interrupted. *"I saw Marin fucking him with my own eyes."*

The king pointed his trident at Otus and Justin could see he had every intention of spearing him with it if he spoke out of line again. *"Silence."* He focused his attention back on Calder. *"Answer my question."*

Calder held his head high as he answered for everyone present to hear. *"Otus speaks the truth."*

"You know the penalty for what you have done?"

"Banishment," Calder confirmed.

The king sighed. *"Which puts me in a rather difficult position, because you're the best damn guard in the city."*

Justin studied the king and for the first time he began to see him as not just a king, but as a man—maybe even as his father. King Nereus, despite his faults, clearly cared for the men who resided in his city.

Otus swam forward a few feet and bowed his head low. *"Your Majesty, I assure you I will be able to make the Atlantean guards the most feared in all the oceans of the world."*

"Are you forgetting we are a peaceful race? I don't want my guards to be feared," King Nereus snapped. *"I want them to be respected and under Calder's command, they are."*

"I would earn their respect and I'd filter out all the other lovers of men from the ranks too. There's quite a few I've had my eye on for a while now."

Justin shook his head. Otus just wasn't getting the point.

King Nereus swam from his throne until he was face to face with the merman who dared to speak out of turn. *"Even if I were to remove Calder from his post, you would not be my first choice to take his place. In fact, you would be my last choice. As for removing all mermen who prefer the touch of men from the ranks, do you include yourself in that number?"*

Otus paled.

"Do you think I don't know that you too prefer to seek pleasure with men?" King Nereus asked. *"There is nothing that happens in the sunken city that I can't find out about. Do not presume to think you can lie to me or hide your own secrets while seeking to expose others. Now leave us and do not let me see your face in my chambers again."*

Justin couldn't quite hide his smile as Otus swam away, shooting daggers at everyone present.

King Nereus swam back to Calder. *"Tell me, Calder. Do you think Otus will tell others what he has seen?"*

"Yes, Your Majesty."

"Me too."

Justin and Lucas waited as the king circled the leader of the guards, looking him up and down carefully. *"Do you think your men will respect you when they hear what Otus has to say?"*

"I don't know," Calder replied.

"They will *respect him,"* Marin interrupted. *"Some of them already suspect the truth and like Otus said, there are more of us in the guards."*

"There are?" the king asked.

"I won't tell you who," Marin stated firmly, even though the king had not asked him for names. Justin could tell Marin had no idea the king could pluck the names from his mind if he chose to do so. *"I've not even told Calder of those who I suspect or know are like us."*

"Good lad," King Nereus told him. *"Even as the worst recruit the city has ever seen, you'd probably earn more respect from the men than Otus would."*

"Am I really that bad?" Marin asked.

"Yes," Calder replied immediately.

The king chuckled and swam back to his throne. *"You will keep your post, Calder, but if I hear of any trouble in the ranks due to the incident today, I will be forced to reconsider."*

"What of Marin?" Calder asked. *"If he's to be banished for what we've done, I'll be leaving with him."*

"No one is being banished," King Nereus assured him. *"I would recommend demoting him for fighting, but unfortunately since he is already at the lowest rank, I'll leave you to decide upon a suitable punishment in the circumstances. You may leave now."*

Calder and Marin bowed low as they swam backwards from the room.

Justin and Lucas moved to follow after them, but King Nereus called them back. *"Not you two. I have more I wish to say to the two of you."*

When the two guards had left, Justin and Lucas took their places in front of the king.

"I assume you had gone to the island with the same intentions of Calder and Marin," King Nereus guessed.

Justin waited to see what Lucas would say. He wished he had perfected private communication so he could ask him how he wanted to play this without the king hearing, but unfortunately he was still rather lacking in that particular skill.

"Yes, Your Majesty," Lucas finally replied.

Justin couldn't have been more surprised if Lucas had kissed him in front of the entire city.

"And you are aware of the punishment for engaging in homosexual relations?" King Nereus continued.

"Yes," Lucas confirmed.

"You are in a different position to Calder," King Nereus stated calmly.

"I know, Your Majesty. No lover of men has ever been allowed amongst the senior advisers on the Council."

"That's true, but not what I meant," King Nereus replied. *"I was referring to the fact you have been engaged in sexual relations with my son."*

Lucas hung his head and Justin took hold of his hand. *"There were two of us on the island,"* he told his father.

"Yes, I know that," the king replied. *"Lucas, look at me."*

Lucas stared up at the king and Justin could see the fear in his eyes.

"I knew of your desires long before I sent you to find my son. As I told Otus, there is nothing that happens in the sunken city that I cannot find out. As you already know, I can read the thoughts of anyone who has sworn allegiance to me and the city, which means I know just how many of my

mermen and mermaids are miserable here. That is not what I want."

"I never meant to fall in love with Justin," Lucas said. "It just happened."

King Nereus smiled at him kindly. *"I can understand that very well indeed, but you must see you cannot be in a relationship with my heir as well as a member of the Council."*

"Why not?" Justin asked. "You practically gave Calder and Marin your blessing."

"And I give you two my blessing too, but Lucas cannot be a member of the Council as well as your lover."

"Why not?" Justin repeated.

"Because each adviser must be, first and foremost, honest and brutal when they give their advice to the rest of the Council and myself. As your lover, Lucas' first thought would always be of protecting you."

"Then it's not about us both being men?" Justin asked.

"No. Even if you were a mermaid, Lucas could not be your consort as well as a member of the Council." He turned to Lucas. *"Which means you need to decide what you want to do."*

Lucas gazed at Justin pleadingly. He had no idea what to tell him.

King Nereus studied them thoughtfully. *"Would it make your decision easier if I changed the law banning homosexual relations?"*

"You could do that?" Lucas replied.

"Of course I can. I'm the king and in matters of the law, my word is final. It's something that has been on my mind since I realized Prince Finn was showing far more interest in the palace guards than the prettiest mermaids."

"You would change it, just for us?" Justin asked.

King Nereus shook his head. *"I will not make you exempt from the law. I could, however, have it re-written for all mer kind. The law is an old one and it has become clear over the years that it does not serve the purpose it was created for. Our numbers are still falling and the banning of sexual relations between those of the same gender has done nothing to change that. Mermaids are most fertile during the summer and winter solstices. My ancestors believed forcing all mermen and mermaids to engage in intercourse on those two nights would help increase our numbers."*

"Even knowing that there are some mermen who cannot release within the body of a female on those nights?"

"They believed the mermaids who prefer the touch of women could still conceive, which is quite correct in fact. Initially the law only forbade mermaids from taking female lovers on the nights they were most fertile, but there were many who took offense to that, when two mermen were allowed to be together. To make the law for all seemed the fairest thing to do. Later, when the number of mermen dropped considerably, the law was reinforced on the basis that each merman should do his part to preserve our people. They also hoped the mermen who needed other males would manage to perform with mermaids when the need for release was great enough. "

"It doesn't work like that," Lucas pointed out.

"And time has proved this to be the case. Which is why I feel the time might now be right to convince the Council it would be appropriate to re-write the law."

"I'll need to talk to my father," Lucas said. *"He's expecting me to take his place on the Council."*

"Then by all means, seek his advice," King Nereus told him. *"I give you my permission to tell them the truth about who Justin is, so they are fully informed before you make your decision. Though do not mention who his mother was."*

Lucas bowed out of the room. *"I'll find you later,"* he told Justin privately.

"And what of you?" King Nereus asked Justin once they were alone. *"Do you intend to make a new life here in the city?"*

"*I don't know,*" Justin admitted. "*Lucas hasn't exactly said he'll give up his career for me yet.*"

"*Oh, I'm sure he will,*" the king replied with a smile. "*He would be a fool not to. Besides, from what I've seen of him during the Council meetings, he wouldn't be happy as a senior adviser. It is his father's ambition, not his.*"

Justin grimaced as he considered he wasn't in so different a position himself.

"*You're quite right.*" King Nereus answered his unspoken thought. "*But I won't force you to stay here if you truly wish to leave.*"

"*How is it you can read my thoughts when I've not sworn allegiance to Atlantis?*" Justin asked.

"*Only because you're still projecting when you don't mean to,*" the king replied. "*Not as often as you used to, but every now and then.*"

"*I really need to work on that.*"

"*You'll learn, at least if you stay here.*"

"*I don't know if I want to stay here,*" Justin admitted. "*I miss England and my life there, and there's something else too.*"

"*What's that?*" the king asked. "*Is it something I can help with?*"

Justin shook his head. "*Not unless you know how to break a curse.*"

"*I wouldn't worry about that so-called curse. We mer people have survived many centuries since the curse began, and even if it is real, it won't affect your daily life.*"

"*That's not what I was referring to,*" Justin admitted. "*I was cursed by the Atlantean Goddess of Love and if I don't find a way to break the curse, Lucas is going to die.*"

The king considered him without judgment even though Justin knew he sounded crazy. "*Are you sure?*"

"*Yes. I need to make some sort of sacrifice to Medina, the goddess, or I'm going to lose Lucas forever. If that happens, I don't think I'd want to stay here in Atlantis at all.*"

"*Even if being here means being with your family?*" King Nereus asked.

"*I have family in England too,*" Justin reminded him. "*I'm sorry, but I can't give you my answer yet.*"

"*Very well, but don't take too long to make your decision. My patience is not unlimited and I'm under pressure from my advisers to produce an heir.*"

Justin nodded that he understood. "*One way or another, the curse will come to an end, then I'll be able to tell you whether I can stay here or not.*"

King Nereus nodded. "*You say you must make a sacrifice?*" he asked.

"*Yes, but I don't know what.*"

"*Have you considered that staying here for the rest of your life, giving up what you had on land, might be a suitable sacrifice?*"

Justin hadn't, though now he thought about it, he wondered why he had not considered the possibility. Medina had told him losing his job wasn't enough, because he could no doubt get another if he chose to, but maybe losing the entire life he had known would be sufficient.

"*I'll leave you to think it over,*" King Nereus said.

The king didn't pressurize him any further and Justin returned to the guest quarters to wait for Lucas.

* * * *

Lucas found his father at home. Halcyon had come to visit and was also there when he swam in the room.

"*Father, can I talk to you?*" Lucas asked.

"*Of course,*" Eneas replied.

"*I should be heading back home,*" Halcyon said.

"*No.*" Lucas stopped him before he could move from his seat. "*You should be here too.*"

"*What is it?*" Halcyon asked.

Lucas sank down onto a spare sponge. "*You remember when I left the sunken city to go to the queen's clan?*"

Halcyon snorted while his father nodded.

Lucas gave his brother an annoyed glare. "*As Halcyon guessed a while ago, I wasn't with the queen and her clan. I'd really been sent to land.*"

"*Banished?*" Eneas asked. "*Does this have anything to do with your, er, tendencies?*"

Lucas shook his head. "*I wasn't banished. The king sent me to find his son.*"

"*Prince Finn?*" Halcyon asked. "*Did you see him? Is he all right?*"

"*Yes, he's perfectly fine, though that isn't who I was sent to find. I was sent to find Justin. He's King Nereus' older son.*"

"*I knew there was a strong resemblance between them,*" Halcyon crowed.

"*Are you sure?*" Eneas asked. "*I don't remember the king fathering any other children before the arrival of the queen.*"

"*The king had already been promised to Queen Coral when Justin's mother became pregnant. She left the ocean and went to live on land.*"

Lucas' father frowned as he tapped his lip. "*I wonder who the mermaid was.*"

"*I don't know,*" Lucas lied. "*She died giving birth to Justin. He was raised on land without knowing either of his parents.*"

"*And why are you telling us this now?*" Halcyon asked. "*Is the king to make some kind of announcement making Justin his heir?*"

"*He wants to, but Justin hasn't decided if he wants to stay here yet. I'm telling you because the king knows Justin and I are lovers. He has told us we can continue our relationship, but I must give up any hope of a place on the Council.*"

Lucas studied his father closely to see his reaction. His face was stony and he didn't know whether this was a good thing or a bad. His father's expression gave nothing away. *"Father? Say something,"* he finally asked.

Eneas smiled a little. *"What would you like me to say?"*

"Something. Anything. Are you angry?"

"Angry? No. Disappointed maybe, but I think we all knew this day was coming. I might not have realized it as quickly as Halcyon, but after your return to the city and Justin's declaration in front of everyone about sharing your bed, I started to watch you a little more closely."

"It doesn't seem very fair that you can't be on the Council just because you want to be with a man," Halcyon commented.

"That's not the reason," Lucas explained. *"It's because I'd be a consort to Justin, the heir, and later the King of the sunken city. King Nereus does not believe I could give him impartial advice, and he's probably right."*

"Then you intend to give up your post at my side?" Eneas asked.

"I don't know," Lucas whispered. *"I've been following your footsteps for so long, I'm not sure I know of any other path."*

His father patted his hand kindly. *"Every merman must follow his own path, not that of another. If your decision is to give up your post and dreams of being on the Council, I won't stop you."*

"What if my path took me away from here?" Lucas asked.

"Would the king banish his own son?" Halcyon asked.

"I don't think so, but Justin grew up on land and he might not want to stay here, no matter what the king wants."

"It sounds to me like Justin needs to choose his own path as well," Halcyon commented.

"We both need to," Lucas admitted. *"And whatever we choose, we're bound together. If he decides to leave and resume his life on land, I'll be going with him."*

"*You could still come back and visit, though,*" Halcyon reminded him. "*And maybe we could come and see you too.*"

Lucas smiled and hugged his brother. "*You'd better,*" he warned. "*Though we haven't made our decision yet, so we may end up staying anyway.*"

"*What will you do if you give up your job?*" Eneas asked. "*I don't like the idea of you living a life of laziness just because you're lover is the heir to the throne.*"

"*I'm sure I'll find something to occupy my time,*" Lucas replied with a grin.

"*Something productive,*" Halcyon teased.

"*I happen to consider spending time with Justin very productive,*" Lucas joked. "*And I've really missed him since we came here.*"

"*Have you told him that?*" Eneas asked.

Lucas shook his head. "*Not yet, but I'm going to make sure I do.*"

With the burden of his decision off of his mind he swam back toward the palace guest quarters to track down Justin and tell him he was ready to give up everything he had worked for in order to be with him.

* * * *

Lucas swam into Justin's guest chambers and found him reclining on the sleeping sponge.

"*Did you talk to your father?*" Justin asked.

"*Yes, and he's happy with whatever I decide.*"

"*And?*"

Lucas swam over and nudged Justin aside so he could join him on the sponge. "*And I'm going to give up my post as junior adviser on the Council.*"

"*Really?*"

"Yes. Whether we spend our lives here or back in England, I intend to spend mine with you, if you'll have me. If that means giving up my job, then so be it."

"And you're okay with that?" Justin asked. "You aren't going to change your mind in a few months' time and wish you'd made a different choice?"

"Never. I can live without the job, but I can't be without you. Even without the whole issue of never having sex again if it's not with you, I don't want to lose you."

Justin kissed him and Lucas knew he had made the right decision. "What about you?" he asked. "Have you decided what you're going to do yet?"

"You mean about staying here?"

"Yes."

"I don't know," Justin admitted. "I want to be with you, but if I agree to stay here as the heir, there's no turning back and..."

"And what?" Lucas prompted.

Justin sighed. "What if I can't break the curse? I'll be stuck here in Atlantis without you and no way of escaping back to land."

"We'll find a way to break the curse," Lucas promised. He hoped he was right.

"I think maybe I'd like to stay here in Atlantis," Justin said. "King Nereus doesn't seem anything like the man I imagined. I'd like to get to know him better, and to find out more about who my mother was, not to mention the powers I inherited from her."

"Really?" Lucas looked him in the eyes, hoping he hadn't misunderstood what Justin was saying in his eagerness to get that which he most desired.

Justin grinned at him. "Yeah. I think we could do very well here and if you're giving up your career for me, the least I can do is let you keep your family. And who knows, maybe those sacrifices will be enough to please Medina."

Lucas hoped that would be the case and he hugged Justin tightly. *"If you giving up your entire life isn't enough, then what would be?"*

"That's what the king says and I think he's right. It has to be that. Now are you going to stay here tonight?"

"It's nearly morning," Lucas pointed out.

Justin snorted. *"Like anyone can tell the difference this far under the surface of the ocean."*

"It's morning," Lucas insisted.

"Then how about we spend the day in bed?" Justin suggested.

Short of going back up to land, Lucas couldn't think of anything else he would rather do and he brushed his fins against Justin's, delighting in the shivers he caused his lover.

"It's not nice to tease when we can't follow through," Justin told him.

Lucas ran his index finger down Justin's chest, stroking his nipples until they tightened under his touch. He tweaked them a little as he leaned in for a kiss. For the first time since their arrival in the sunken city, Lucas didn't worry about whether someone might swim in on them or see them doing something they shouldn't. He hoped the king did change the law so none of the other mermen and mermaids in a similar position needed to worry like he had done.

They kissed until they fell asleep, wrapped in each other's arms. Around them, the mer people of the palace began to wake, but the two of them slept on, their golden fins brushing together.

Chapter Twenty-Two

King Nereus was delighted when Justin told him he intended to stay in Atlantis as his heir. He beamed with pleasure and pulled a rather startled Justin into a tight hug.

"*What about this curse?*" he asked. "*I thought you wanted to wait until you'd figured that out.*"

Justin turned to Lucas and squeezed his hand. "*I need to make a sacrifice to break the curse. You said it yourself. What can be bigger than giving up everything in my life to stay here in Atlantis?*"

"*It's agreed then, I'll make a formal announcement today.*"

"*So soon?*" Lucas asked.

"*I've already called a meeting to announce the change in the law regarding homosexual relations. I can make this announcement at the same time.*"

"*Won't people think you're just changing the law because of us?*" Justin asked.

"*Maybe, but does it really matter?*" King Nereus replied. "*Now, regarding your mother...*"

"*No one can know she's an Oracle,*" Justin guessed.

"That's right. I will tell people she was a mermaid from a clan who sought sanctuary with us. I'll say she left with those who didn't take the oath of allegiance when she found out I was promised to another. She got word to me that she was carrying my child, but did not return here. No one will question my word, especially considering the strong resemblance between the two of us. There are already rumors circulating regarding your paternity."

"There are?" Justin asked. He hadn't heard any such rumors.

"Oh most definitely," King Nereus replied. *"I started them myself."*

"What will you tell them about why you didn't make this announcement when I first arrived?" Justin asked.

"We'll simply tell everyone the truth. You were unsure as to whether you wanted to remain here as my heir."

Justin agreed with this course of action. It would be best to stick to the truth as far as possible.

"Yes, it would," King Nereus agreed to his accidentally communicated words. *"We'll just keep the Oracle aspect out of what we tell people, in respect of both your mother and yourself. It would not be good for the general population to know you are also an Oracle, albeit one with limited powers."*

"Then you can't change the law with regard to the Oracles having relationships?" Justin asked.

"No, it would be far too dangerous. I should never have broken that law myself. Even though I'm delighted to have you here as my son, the truth is you should not have been born. The Oracles will train you with regard to controlling your visions, but they are the only ones who are to know about your powers."

Justin nodded that he understood what was being asked of him. The idea of hiding any part of himself didn't sit entirely right with him, but it seemed he would have to do so. At least he was not going to be forced to hide his love for Lucas.

* * * *

King Nereus didn't waste any time when he set his mind to doing something. The Council meeting was convened later that day and this time Justin sat at the king's right hand, rather than to the side.

"Thank you, everyone, for coming to this unexpected meeting," King Nereus said. His thanks were merely a formality, everyone knew they had no real choice in the matter.

"I've called you here in respect of two matters, firstly I would like to formally introduce you to Justin, my heir."

Justin tried not to cower under the collective gazes of the entire Council. There were several murmurs whispering through his mind, but nothing came through to him clearly to tell him what the king's advisers thought of the announcement.

"As you know," the king continued, *"Justin has been raised away from the sunken city, but he is eager to learn everything he can about our wonderful sanctuary so he can one day take over my duties as king."*

The advisers called out questions, asking where Justin had come from, where his mother was and whether any more of his clan would be coming to the city in the near future. King Nereus answered all of their questions until their minds were set at ease.

A few of the advisers seemed to think this was the end of the meeting and started to make their way toward the archways so they could carry on with their duties. The king raised his hands to halt their departures.

"I'm afraid I haven't quite finished," he said. *"I have also decided that now would be an appropriate time to look at one of our rather outdated laws, specifically, the law regarding the prohibition of homosexual relationships."*

"*Does this have anything to do with the incident yesterday?*" Eryx asked.

"*Partly, yes,*" King Nereus confirmed. "*I refuse to lose perfectly good mermen simply because of a law which does not even fulfill the purpose it was created for. Forcing my people to engage in the mating rituals with those they are not attracted to has done nothing to increase our numbers. If anything, they have continued to fall even more rapidly than before.*"

"*Are you getting rid of the mating rituals completely?*" Charax asked.

King Nereus shook his head. "*No. We will each still need to take whatever action we need to break our mating fevers. Also our mermaids are still most fertile during the solstice, and I believe we should encourage sexual relations during those times. The only thing that will be changing is that if a mermaid or merman needs to be with one of their own gender to break their fever, they will be allowed to do so without fear of banishment.*"

"*All this fuss just because a couple of the guards were caught fucking,*" one of the advisers complained. "*I see no reason why the law should be changed.*"

King Nereus glared at the merman who had spoken. "*Do you have a problem with homosexuals, Davos?*" he asked quietly.

"*I believe they should be doing their duty and getting our mermaids pregnant.*"

"*A merman who desires other men cannot get a mermaid pregnant on the night of the solstice,*" King Nereus stated.

"*And how is it you're an authority on this subject?*" Davos replied. "*Is that what the guards said?*"

King Nereus turned to Justin who gave him a small nod in answer to the unspoken question. "*No,*" he replied. "*This is what my son has told me, and I believe him, as should any merman who has ever gone through a mating season.*"

"Then your son and heir won't be producing any children," Davos said. *"And now we see the real reason why you want to change the law."*

"Yes," King Nereus said. *"My son will also be benefiting from this change in the law, as will every merman and mermaid who has had to hide their sexuality. I hope that in time word will spread to other clans about the change in our law and that this will encourage them to come here and make it their home. Far too many clans have decided against settling here because of this law. We need to encourage them to stay, not drive them away."*

"And how is your son going to carry on your line if he won't fuck a mermaid?" Davos asked. *"What happens then?"*

"My son and his partner will deal with that when the time comes," King Nereus replied. *"I imagine they will be adopting and raising one or more children who come to us without family. The sunken city already takes in many such children in need of a home. However, that is something they will be considering in the future and not right now."*

The king's word was final and he quickly halted the few complaints his announcements had produced. Only one question asked by the advisers remained unanswered. Did Justin have a partner?

Justin smiled across the room to Lucas, who sat in his usual spot beside his father. They had spoken already about how they were going to announce their relationship and had decided to do so at this meeting.

Lucas raised his hand to get the attention of the room. *"I would like to make an announcement."*

King Nereus smiled at him. *"Of course, Lucas."*

Lucas turned briefly to his father, who also gave him an encouraging smile. *"I wish to formally renounce my claim on the hereditary position of senior adviser on matters pertaining to the law."*

King Nereus nodded in acknowledgment of his announcement. *"You're sure about this?"*

Lucas swam to Justin's side. *"Yes, Your Majesty."*

Justin took hold of Lucas' hand and kissed the palm. There was no need for them to say anything else.

* * * *

After the meeting was over, Justin and Lucas swam out into the city. Lucas felt a little self-conscious, but with his hand in Justin's he found the courage he needed to face the stares of the mer people.

"It's just because they've not heard about the change in law yet," Justin assured him. *"You should be grateful Atlantis laws can be changed so quickly. If we were in England, it would take years to get the law passed."*

"No paperwork here," Lucas reminded him with a grin. *"Where are we going?"*

"I thought we could go and see Calder and Marin," Justin said. *"They won't know the law has been changed yet and they're probably still hiding their relationship as best they can."*

Lucas suspected Justin was probably right.

They swam to the barracks and found Calder in his element, shouting commands at his recruits.

"I can't see Otus," Lucas commented as they swam closer.

"Otus is doing inventory," Marin informed them as he swam up behind them. *"A job we all despise, but which he is going to be doing for the rest of the winter."*

Lucas chuckled at the thought of the merman who had planned on taking over the command of the guards being forced to do the most tedious of jobs. He looked Marin over. His face still showed signs of his fight, but

Lucas suspected he would soon be fully recovered. *"And what of your own punishment for fighting?"*

Marin pouted. *"I'm confined to the city for the next month."*

Lucas wondered how long it would take Marin to convince Calder to take him to the island. His punishment would be felt by both guards. *"Does everyone know what happened?"*

Marin nodded. *"Otus told everyone, though we knew several of the guards at least suspected we were in a relationship together."*

"Any trouble?" Justin asked.

"One or two have made a few comments to me, but they're too scared to say anything in front of Calder. I'm ignoring them the best I can."

"Good," Lucas said. *"And just so you know, King Nereus has changed the law today, so there's no need to hide your feelings anymore."*

"Really?" Marin asked. He glanced down at Lucas and Justin's joined hands. *"Ah. This is because of you two, isn't it?"*

"Partly," Justin admitted. *"My father also wants to encourage more clans to come here and thinks the law change will help with that."*

"Your father?" Marin peered closely at Justin. *"You're King Nereus' son?"*

"Yes. He's made the formal announcement making me his heir a little while ago."

Marin grinned widely. *"I can't wait to see Otus' face when he finds out."*

"Marin!" Calder yelled. *"Is there any particular reason you're gossiping instead of doing drills like everyone else?"*

Lucas and Justin both cringed at the shout. Marin didn't seem bothered at all. He swam up to Calder and kissed him soundly.

"What in the world?" Calder asked, loud enough for everyone in the yard to hear. Lucas noticed he didn't break the kiss, though.

If Marin replied, Lucas didn't hear it.

Calder finally eased Marin away from him and sent him back to his drills with a swat to his tail. He swam across to Lucas with a smile. *"Is this your influence that got the law changed?"* he asked.

Lucas shook his head. *"No, this was all King Nereus' idea. I'm not even on the Council anymore."*

"You're not?"

Otus chose that moment to come into the yard and took in the scene. Lucas made sure his words carried so Otus would hear them. *"I've given up my place on the Council so that Justin and I can be together."*

"You can't have both?" Calder asked.

Lucas shook his head. *"As heir to the sunken city, Justin needs advisers who can be totally objective. King Nereus doesn't think I'll be able to do that and be in a relationship with Justin as well. I chose Justin. How could I do otherwise when the king has altered the law to let us be together?"*

Otus swam closer. *"Does that mean there's a position open on the Council?"*

"Not yet," Lucas told him shortly. *"My father has a great many years still left in him."*

"But when he's dead, they'll need someone to advise on the law."

Lucas glared at the merman. *"I wouldn't call him bait just yet. And what does it have to do with you anyway?"*

"I was thinking I might look into taking up the post. I might even see about reinstating the law so you can't be together."

"And how do you think you'd manage that?" Calder asked with a laugh.

"I'd be the senior adviser on the law," Otus stated loftily.

"Who still has to answer to King Nereus and later to his son, Justin here. Even if you do take the place on the Council, I can promise you won't be in a position to change the law back at all. You'd be advising on the law, not changing it. Perhaps if you're planning on becoming an adviser, you should learn what the job entails before you make an even bigger fool of yourself."

Otus swam off in a huff, leaving the others to roll their eyes at his behavior.

"I don't understand him at all," Calder said. "We all know he's homosexual, so why try to make things so difficult for the rest of us?"

"Because he's jealous," Justin replied. "He wants what we have and if he can't have it, he'll do whatever he can to spoil things for everyone else, even if it means cutting off his nose to spite his face."

Calder nodded. "You're probably right. I'll be keeping a close eye on him to see he doesn't cause any more trouble."

"Me too," Justin said. "If he even looks at Lucas, I'll make his life miserable."

"I'm keeping him away from Marin too," Calder admitted. "Though in that regard, it means keeping Marin away from him as well. Unfortunately Otus knows just what to say to cause Marin to see red."

"Speaking of which," Lucas said with a nod toward Marin and Otus, who appeared to be about to start fighting again.

"Get back in formation!" Calder roared.

Lucas and Justin left the barracks and swam back to the palace. They still had to find a way to ensure Medina's curse was lifted and Lucas had a feeling time was rapidly running out.

* * * *

Justin still wasn't entirely sure how the mer people, living so far below the surface, could tell when it was night time. Lucas, who had spent all of this life underwater seemed to have some sort of internal clock.

"It's long past time to retire for the night," Lucas said as they swam back toward the palace after spending the rest of the day chatting with various groups of mer people around the city.

Justin looked up toward the surface of the ocean. *"I still can't see how you can tell what time it is."*

"I can't, but my body is telling me it's time to go to sleep."

Justin darted ahead of Lucas and let the other merman swim into his arms. He had noticed during the course of the afternoon and evening Lucas had become accustomed to being touched. *"What else is your body telling you?"* he teased.

"Nothing while I'm down here instead of on land," Lucas replied.

Justin laughed and pulled Lucas into a long slow kiss. *"Are you coming to my rooms tonight?"*

Lucas hesitated a moment before nodding.

"Are you sure?" Justin asked.

"Yes. Can we stop by my quarters first, so my parents know where I'm going to be?"

"Of course," Justin agreed and they made their way there.

* * * *

A short while later, Justin was on his sleeping sponge with Lucas curled into his side. Their fins tangled together, tickling slightly as they moved into a comfortable position.

"You're going to hog the sponge, aren't you?" Justin teased.

"Of course," Lucas replied as he played with Justin's hair. *"We'll have to get a bigger sponge if I'm going to move in with you."*

Justin could hear the question in Lucas' voice and he smiled to himself. *"You'd better be living with me. Though we may not be staying in these rooms. They are the guest quarters, after all."*

"I don't mind where we stay, as long as we're together."

Justin felt exactly the same. *"If we were back in England, I'd ask you to marry me."*

Lucas sat up and stared at Justin in surprise. *"Two men are allowed to marry?"*

"Yes, though it's only a recent development. If mermen had marriages, what would you say?"

"I'd say yes," Lucas replied immediately.

Justin tugged Lucas into a kiss, even though they weren't in a position to follow through with the promise their kisses held. He ran his hands along Lucas' arms and maneuvered the smaller merman on top of him. They stayed chest to chest and fin to fin as they tasted each other.

"I want you so badly," Lucas whispered into his mind without breaking the kiss. *"We should have gone to spend the night on the island."*

"Live and learn. Though I'm thinking I want you so much, we'd probably be better off building a house there. Days in the ocean and nights on land."

"I like that idea," Lucas said. *"But I'd never want to come down here again."*

"I can live with that," Justin quipped, even though he knew he wouldn't neglect his responsibilities. He had agreed to remain in Atlantis as heir and he intended to comply with all that entailed.

Lucas rubbed against him as they continued to touch each other. Justin's fins quivered each time Lucas' brushed against his own. Lucas' heart pounded against his chest and his own raced in a similar manner.

"Maybe we could take vows here," Lucas suggested. *"Say, in Medina's temple."*

"What are you thinking?" Justin asked.

"That maybe what we're giving up to be together will be enough to appease her. You're leaving your life in England permanently. I'm giving up my career as well. What more can she want?"

Justin didn't know whether it would be enough, but maybe Lucas was right. They didn't have anything to lose by taking vows in her temple and he had said he wanted to marry Lucas. Even if it didn't work to break the curse, they would still be making a commitment to each other.

"Let's do it tomorrow," Justin declared with enthusiasm he had never imagined he would feel over something like a wedding.

"Don't weddings take time to plan?" Lucas asked.

"In England they might, but there's no paperwork or other formalities down here. All we have to do is set the time and place and turn up."

"That's it?"

"Well, we should probably invite our families and friends," Justin said. *"That should be simple enough for those here in Atlantis."*

"What about your friends in England?"

Justin frowned. *"I wish they could be here, but they're not mer. They don't even know of our existence."*

"Are you going to miss them?"

"Yes, but not as much as I'd miss you if I returned to them."

"What about your foster parents?"

"I can summon them at their temples here and invite them."

Lucas nodded and rolled off of Justin so they were side by side again. *"I guess we should probably get some sleep then."*

Justin shifted onto his side and moved so he could spoon Lucas. *"I guess we should,"* he agreed.

Chapter Twenty-Three

King Nereus was delighted to hear of Justin's plans to marry Lucas. He too expressed his hope that their joint sacrifices would be enough to break Medina's curse and using her temple for the ceremony was certainly a great honor.

Justin's foster parents were present, as was Lucas' family. They had also invited Calder and Marin to stand as witnesses, though it was not really necessary, since the mer people didn't have weddings. Justin had also, after some internal debate about how others might view it, invited the Oracles. The three powerful beings attended together with their servants.

They gathered in Medina's public temple since it was a little larger than the private one in the palace catacombs.

They had decided against choosing someone to officiate a ceremony. Instead they intended to simply say their vows and share a kiss. They had talked long into the night about what they would say to each other and Justin was happy with what they had come up with. Lucas was a little unsure, but since this was all new to him that was understandable. Justin assured him the exact words didn't matter as long as he spoke from the heart.

They had just taken their places when the statue of Medina lit up with an unearthly glow. The goddess appeared before her monument a moment later.

Cari stepped forward to place herself between the goddess and Justin and Lucas. *"Welcome, Medina."*

Medina raised her hand. *"I'm not here to cause trouble. Justin and Lucas have chosen to commit to each other in my temple. It is my right to be here, as you know."*

"Yes, Medina," Cari agreed. *"My foster son shows you a great honor in choosing to take vows here."*

"He does," Medina said.

"Justin is sacrificing his life on land to remain here in Atlantis with Lucas, who is sacrificing his career to spend his life with Justin."

Medina nodded. *"Lucas has no real choice in the matter,"* she pointed out. *"The law forbids him to take up his post and remain in a relationship with the heir to the throne."*

"Justin has a choice, though," Cari replied. *"He has chosen to remain here and give up his life in England."*

"He has, yet what is to stop him from changing his mind a year or two down the line?" Medina asked.

"I won't," Justin insisted.

Medina stepped closer to him and placed her hand on his forehead. Even his training with the Oracles couldn't prepare him for the suddenness of his vision.

He saw Atlantis from above, a sight he had seen several times since his arrival. Then, as he watched, one temple after another seemed to glow in the same way Medina's statue had. The dirt and weeds fell away from the buildings and the stones were washed clean even though no one was present to do work. Fallen stones righted themselves as the city came back to life before his eyes.

He saw a few mer people swimming around, each appeared as astounded as himself. Then he saw them walking out of the temples. The gods and goddesses of Atlantis were waking.

"It's okay, Justin," Cari said. *"Caspian has frozen time for everyone, save the immortals, Lucas and your father. What did you see?"*

"Give me a minute or two," Justin asked. *"My sight hasn't come back yet."*

"It won't," Medina stated.

Justin reached out into the darkness, trying to find his foster mother's hand. He caught hold of it and held on tight. *"She's lying, isn't she?"*

"No," Cari replied. *"You are now a true Oracle and will only have your sight when you take human form. Had you nurtured your gift all your life, as well as your mer heritage, this would have happened long ago."*

"But if I'm blind, everyone will know I'm an Oracle and Lucas and I won't be allowed to be together."

"There's no need for everyone to know you're an Oracle," King Nereus told him. *"We'll tell everyone something else to explain your sudden blindness."*

Medina spoke from his side and Justin tried to concentrate on where her voice was coming from so he could face her. *"Your vision while underwater, is a suitable sacrifice to break the curse. A small price to pay for the life of your lover, don't you agree?"*

Justin felt Lucas' hand—he knew it was his—against his back. *"Agreed."*

"Justin, no," Lucas whispered into his mind. *"It's not worth it."*

"You are worth it," Justin replied immediately. *"We'll tell everyone about the curse and that my sight is the sacrifice made to save your life."*

"And what about when you go to land and can see perfectly well?" Lucas asked. "That's when people will know you're an Oracle."

"Can my sight be taken on land as well?" Justin asked Cari.

"No. Without that, you'll be unable to have visions at all."

"Then I'll have to pretend to be blind on land as well," Justin concluded.

"Then it is done," Medina announced. "The curse is lifted and you will never again see a vision of Lucas dying, at least not until he is a very old merman and his mortal life is coming to a natural end."

"Thank you," Justin said. Lucas' grip tightened round his body and he thought he heard the sound of a sob in his mind, but he could no longer see Lucas' expression to ascertain his mood. Justin suspected he would have to learn to read Lucas' sounds as well as he did his face.

"What did you see in your vision?" Caspian asked.

"I saw gods and goddesses waking as their temples came to life," Justin said.

"Which ones?"

"All of them, I think." Suddenly Justin heard a bunch of gasps in his mind. "What's happening?"

"Medina's temple is suddenly clean again," Lucas explained. "The fallen stones are moving into place."

Justin felt himself dragged aside and the brush of a boulder against his skin as it sailed by him. "What's happening?"

"Medina's powers are growing," Cari explained.

"By coming to my temple to take vows, you've given my powers a boost they haven't had in thousands of years," Medina announced with obvious delight. "I can feel it coursing through me as it once did when Atlantis was the greatest of all cities."

"Are the other gods waking up now?" Justin asked.

"No," Caspian said. "*It will take time for them to wake, but they are beginning to stir. It won't be long before one of them wakes – a few months, maybe a little longer.*"

"We will need to prepare our people for this," King Nereus said.

Cari sighed. "*Nothing you do will prepare your people for what is to come. I would advise leaving Atlantis, except nowhere in the ocean will be safe from the wrath of the gods.*"

"Why would they be angry with us?" King Nereus asked. "*We're a peaceful race.*"

"Not all of them will be hostile," Caspian assured him. "*Some will be here to protect you from those who would see your people driven from Atlantis. Cari and I will do what we can to help the mer.*"

"I too," Medina added. "*As a former queen of Atlantis, I do not wish to see this city fall into ruin.*"

There was little more they could say and so Caspian unfroze the rest of the wedding guests. Justin could hear more gasps as they also took in their altered surroundings.

Medina explained away the revitalized temple by saying it was her presence and Justin's sacrifice in her honor that had caused the building to return to life.

The mer people were shocked that Justin could no longer see, but they accepted the explanation of his loss of sight with no trouble at all.

They didn't bother to tell everyone about the gods waking up. There would be time for that later.

Justin couldn't see Lucas, but his lover placed his hands on Justin's shoulders so he could tell he was directly in front of him.

They spoke their vows for the whole room to hear and kissed deeply to seal them.

"I love you," Justin whispered into Lucas' mind for him alone to hear.

"I love you too," Lucas replied.

When they were done, Justin let Lucas lead him back to the palace and the small feast that had been prepared for them. He couldn't see any of the food, but he quickly discovered he liked Lucas feeding him small bites. He licked at his fingers as he took each morsel between his lips.

"Tonight we're going to the beach," Lucas told him. *"No arguments."*

"Who's arguing?" Justin teased.

Lucas' laughter echoed through his mind and even though the underwater world was dark to him Justin felt he could see the joy in his lover's face anyway.

He didn't know what would happen when the gods woke, but he knew with Lucas at his side he would not be alone in facing the days to come.

Epilogue

Justin let Lucas lead him through the waters to the island on the night of the summer solstice.

Although they had been to the island many times since they had taken their vows, this was the first time where others would be present. They had been extremely careful in recent months to avoid other mer people who were on land with their lovers. There would be no avoiding them this time.

Justin held Lucas' arm as they rose higher in the water until finally breaking through the surface. He could tell from the coolness of the air that the sun had already disappeared over the horizon. He could hear other mermen around them, calling to each other as they made their way to the island where the mermaids waited for those who wished to take their pleasure with them.

They swam for the beach and dragged themselves onto land. Justin's legs returned as his fins dried out and as soon as he was back in his human form, his sight was restored once again.

"Just remember, you're supposed to be blind," Lucas reminded him. "No one can know you're an Oracle."

"I know," Justin replied. "But just let me look at you for a minute before anyone notices what I'm doing. I've missed you."

"I've been right by your side," Lucas reminded him.

Justin snorted. "Okay, I've missed ogling my gorgeous husband."

They kissed with a passion they didn't try to dampen. Unlike when they were in Atlantis, here they could carry out the promise in their kisses.

"I'm still not sure about the idea of public sex," Justin said as Lucas tumbled him back onto the sand.

"You'll get used to it," Lucas promised. "No one will be watching your technique or anything. They'll be too busy doing the same thing."

Justin wasn't convinced, but they had little choice in the matter if they wanted to break their fevers.

"Is there anyone close by?" Justin asked loudly, hoping to convince the merman and mermaid nearby that he couldn't see them.

"Of course there is," Lucas replied as he crawled back on his knees and took Justin's penis into his mouth. With the first touch of Lucas' lips on his dick, Justin completely forgot about everyone else on the island. He closed his eyes and let Lucas work his magic.

He only opened his eyes again when he heard a familiar voice calling out an equally familiar name. A couple of dozen yards down the beach Calder was on his hands and knees with Marin kneeling behind him, driving his cock into his leader's arse with hard thrusts.

The live sex show nearly sent Justin over the edge. He had never considered himself a voyeur, but he couldn't seem to take his eyes off the other couple.

He was still watching them when Lucas nipped his ear sharply. "You're supposed to be blind," he reminded him.

Justin groaned at the reminder as he turned back to Lucas.

"Fuck me," Lucas demanded as he twisted round and stretched out on his back on the sand.

Lucas put his hands behind his knees and pulled his legs back so Justin could position himself between them. Justin was pretty sure he could do this in the dark and with his eyes shut, but the thought of taking his eyes off the merman in front of him was utterly abhorrent to him. He bowed his head and swiped his tongue over Lucas' entrance.

Lucas moaned and so Justin did it again, this time dipping his tongue inside just a little.

"Oh fuck," Lucas cried as Justin continued to run his tongue around his hole.

When he considered Lucas ready, he pushed a finger into his arse, stretching him and readying him for his cock.

Lucas pulled him into a kiss that left Justin breathless. Justin continued to finger him while they stroked their tongues against each other's. The one thing Justin missed about kissing underwater was the ability to talk to each other at the same time. Lucas was quite adept at making his thoughts known and Justin was pretty sure the way he was pushing onto his finger was his lover's way of saying he wanted more and he wanted it right now. Justin complied with a second finger and Lucas broke out of their kiss to give a wordless cry of pleasure.

They were both hard but Justin knew neither of them would be able to come until Justin was buried deep in Lucas' arse.

"Need you in me," Lucas begged. "So badly."

"I know," Justin whispered back. "Soon. I'll fill you so good."

"Now," Lucas demanded. "Want you now."

Justin replied by crooking his finger and Lucas screamed out as he bucked and writhed at his touch.

From the corner of his eye he saw a mermaid watching them as her lover led her off the beach and into the trees. Mermaid or not, she certainly seemed to be enjoying the view, at least until her merman took her out of sight.

He turned his attention back to his lover. "Maybe this public sex isn't so bad after all," he whispered into Lucas' ear. "I kind of like the idea of everyone seeing me take you. Claiming you as mine. Hearing you call out my name as I take you and knowing everyone will hear your screams."

"Do it," Lucas ordered. "Fuck me and I'll scream so loud they'll hear us at the bottom of the ocean."

Justin wasn't so sure about that, but he knew Lucas couldn't take much more of his teasing. He removed his fingers and lifted Lucas' legs onto his shoulders. He spat on his palm, still mourning the lack of lube, but resigned to making do with what they had. He coated his erection with saliva and slowly pushed his way inside Lucas' tight entrance.

Lucas moaned and panted as Justin slid his way home.

"That's it," Lucas cried. "Give me it all."

Justin inched his way inside, waiting for Lucas to relax enough to take him all. Slowly but surely he buried himself in the tight arse of his lover.

"Fuck me," Lucas pleaded. "Let me feel your heat inside me."

Justin eased out and pushed back in as Lucas closed his eyes and moaned repeatedly. His words were completely incoherent, but Justin knew exactly what his lover wanted. Slow and steady was what Lucas craved most of the time, and most especially tonight.

As Lucas clenched around Justin's penis, Justin felt his orgasm nearing. His balls drew back and he came hard, his seed filling his lover's arse. Lucas came without any stimulation to his cock, his cum spilling between them as their fevers receded for the season.

"So hot," Lucas gasped.

"You are indeed," Justin whispered back at him.

"That's not what I meant," Lucas replied between gulps of breath.

"I know," Justin teased. After learning that for Lucas the ultimate pleasure was found in feeling the heat of Justin's release inside him he had made it his mission to ensure Lucas experienced it as often as possible.

They fell onto the sand, Justin cursing it getting into all the cracks, which caused Lucas to laugh, as it always did when he complained about such things. He said it was a small price to pay if it meant they could be together. Justin agreed and tried not to let the sand bother him.

They stayed on the beach until the sun rose the next morning. They had made love several more times during the night. Justin had been pleased to see several pairs of mermen, like Calder and Marin, who were able to be with the lovers they wanted to. There were several mermaids with each other too and Justin thought that if nothing else, his coming to Atlantis had at least brought about equality for those who desired their own gender.

"We should probably be heading back to the city," Lucas said. "Your father will require your presence at the meeting this morning."

Justin nodded, though he continued to watch the sunrise.

"Come on." Lucas stood and pulled Justin to his feet.

Justin followed him into the water and took hold of Lucas' hand before they plunged below the waves, and for Justin into the total darkness that had become his everyday life. With Lucas' hand in his they swam back to the city, ready to face their next challenge.

About the Author

I live in England, in a quaint little village that time doesn't seem to have touched. No, wait a minute—that's the retirement biography. Right now I am in England in a medium-sized town that no one has ever heard of, so I won't bore you with the details. Keeping me company are numerous sexy men. I just wish that they weren't all inside my head.

L.M. loves to hear from readers. You can find her contact information, website details and author profile page at http://www.pride-publishing.com.